THE LONE WOLF

An immensely calm voice behind him said then, "Mr. Wulff. Please wait for a moment."

When he turned, Wulff saw sitting on the bed near the bodies, dangling his little legs as if in an excess of glee, a tiny man with a mustache and an empty face. Slowly, then, the sense of the situation burst upon him. The little man held a gun with an opening as large as a mouth.

"I do like your work," the little man said. "I'm really quite impressed by your work, but then I expected to be. Please drop the gun, by the way. I can pull the trigger long before you can reach yours. And they're slow action too; I wanted them to be that way."

Wulff said, "This is crazy."

Death followed Wulff everywhere. And now Death was laughing at him.

"Hang on for a wild ride through the dangerous darkness of America in the Seventies!"
—George Kelley

D1566009

THE LONE WOLF #7: PERUVIAN NIGHTMARE

THE LONE WOLF #8: LOS ANGELES HOLOCAUST

by Barry N. Malzberg

STARK HOUSE

Stark House Press • Eureka California

PERUVIAN NIGHTMARE / LOS ANGELES HOLOCAUST

Published by Stark House Press
1315 H Street
Eureka, CA 95501, USA
griffinskye3@sbcglobal.net
www.starkhousepress.com

ISBN-13: 978-1-951473-94-5

Cover design by Jeff Vorzimmer, ¡caliente!design, Austin, Texas
Text design by Mark Shepard, shepgraphics.com

First Stark House Press Edition: September 2022

Some Notes on the Lone Wolf

By Barry N. Malzberg

Don Pendleton's Executioner series started as a one-shot idea at Pinnacle Books in 1969. By 1972 George Ernsberger, my editor at Berkley, called it "the phenomenon of the age." Eventually Pendleton wrote 70 of the books himself and the series continues today ghosted by other writers. Mack Bolan's continuing *War Against the Mafia* (the working title of that first book) had sold wildly from the outset and less than three years later, when Pendleton and Scott Meredith had threatened to take the series from a grim and obdurate Pinnacle, New American Library had offered $250,000 for the next four books in the series. Pendleton stayed at Pinnacle—the publisher faced a lawsuit for misappropriated royalties and essentially had to match the NAL offer to hold on—but the level established by the properties could not fail to have inflamed every mass market paperback publisher in New York.

A few imitative series had been launched by Pinnacle itself—most notably The Butcher whose premise and protagonist were a close if even more sadomasochistic version of Pendleton's Mack Bolan. It was Bolan who had gone out alone to avenge his family incinerated in a Mafia war while Bolan was fighting Commies in Southeast Asia. Dell Books launched The Inquisitor, a series of books on the redemptive odyssey of Simon Quinn (by a then-unknown William Martin Smith, who under a somewhat different name was to become famous in the next decade), Pocket Books and Avon began series the provenance of which is at the moment unrecollected and Ernsberger at Berkley, under some pressure from his publisher, Stephen Conlan, was ready to start his own series.

What he needed in January 1973 was someone who could produce 10 books within less than a year and although my credentials as a Pendleton-imitator were certainly questionable (they were in fact nonexistent), there was no question but that Ernsberger had found one of the few writers close at hand who clearly could produce at that frenetic level. In 1972 I had written nine novels, in 1971 a dozen, in 1970 fourteen; ten books that quickly were not an overwhelming assignment. What he wanted was a series about a law enforcement guy, say maybe an ex-New York City cop, thrown off the force for one or another perceived disgrace, who would declare war upon the drug trade. The cop could be a military veteran with (like Bolan) a good command of ordnance; it wouldn't hurt if he had a black sidekick either still on or just off the force so that they could get some *Defiant Ones* byplay going in those pre-Eddie Murphy days, and the violence was to be hyped up to Executioner level as the protagonist, after an initial festive in New York, took his mission throughout the States and maybe overseas. Ten novels, $27,500 total advance with (it is this which caught my total attention) 25% of it payable upon signature of the contract. Only a brief outline would be necessary and the tenth book was due to be delivered on or before 10/1/73.

I had never read a Pendleton novel in my life.

Hey, no problem; $6750 for a five-page outline at a time when I perceived my nascent career to be in a recession-induced collapse cleaved away scruple and, for that matter, terror. I read Executioner #7, which struck me as pretty bad, mechanical, and lifeless (like most debased category fiction it depended upon the automatic responses upon the reader, did not create characters and an ambiance of its own), wrote the usual promise-them-a-partridge-in-a-pear-tree outline, signed the contracts and began the series on 1/16/73. The third of the novels was delivered on 2/14/73.

Incontestably I could have delivered the entire series by May (the early plan was for Berkley to bring out the first three novels at once, then publish one a month thereafter) but George Ernsberger asked me to stop after *Boston Avenger* and wait for further word. There was a problem, it seemed. In the first place, I had given my protagonist, Wulff Conlan, a name uncomfortably close to that of the publisher whose name at the time I had not even known, and in the second place Conlan's victims, unlike Mack Bolan's, were real people with real viewpoints who seemed to undergo real pain when they were killed which was quite frequently. Would this kind of stuff—real pain as opposed to cartoon death that is to say—go in the mass market? Berkley dithered about this while I sulked, wrote a novelization (never published) of Lindsay Anderson's *O Lucky Man!* for Warner Books, and waited around to accept an award for a science fiction novel, which award caused me much difficulty, you bet, in the years to come. (See the letter column of the 2/74 *Analog* for any further information you want on this.)

Eventually, Ernsberger called—during dinnertime, in fact, on 3/16/73—to say that I could go ahead with the series and would I please change the name of the protagonist? Grumbling, fearing that I might never get back to the center of those novels, I started again and in fact did deliver the tenth book on 10/1/73 after all. (The first three were published in that month.) As is so often the case with imitative series, sales steadily declined from volume #1 which did get close to 70,000) but held above unprofitability through all of those ten, and I was allowed two sequels in 1974 and then two more in conclusion (at a cut advance). I insisted upon killing off Wulff in #14 against the argument of Ernsberger's assistant, Dale Copps, who reminded me of Professor Moriarty.

I signed off on #14: *Philadelphia Blowup* in 1/75. That means that I am now at a greater distance from these novels than many readers of this anthology are from their birthdates ... and for that reason my opinion of the series is not necessarily any more valid than would be the opinion of Erika Cornell on her essays in ballet class in the mid-seventies.

The purpose and development of these novels would, in any case, be clear to anyone, even the author. It is evident to me now as it was then that Mack Bolan was insane and Pendleton's novels were a rationalization of vigilantism; it was my intent, then, to show what the real (as opposed to the mass market) enactment of madness and vigilantism might be if death were perceived as something beyond catharsis or an escape route for the bad guys. As the series went on and on and as I became more secure with the voicing and with my apparent ability to circumvent surface and not get fired, Wulff became crazier and crazier. By #13 he was driving crosscountry and killing anyone on suspicion of drug dealing; by #14: *Philadelphia Blowup*, he was staggering from bar to bar in the City of Brotherly Love and killing everyone because they obviously had to be drug dealers. Finally gunned down for the public safety by his one-time black sidekick, Wulff died far less bloodily than many of his victims while managing a bequest of about $50,000 to his overweight creator. The novels sold overseas intermittently—Denmark stayed around through all 14; the other Scandinavian countries bailed out earlier; the gentle Germans found it all too bloody and sadistic and after editing down the first 10 novels quit on an open-ended contract, paid off and shut it down. I haven't seen anything financially from these since 1979 but entries in various mystery reference sources and the invitation to discuss the series in this anthology suggest that it might have found a particle of an audience. (My real pride in this series, beyond its ambition and sheer, perverse looniness is that I was able to run it through the entirety of its original contract and manage four sequels as well; no Executioner imitator other than those published by Pinnacle went past four or five volumes.) The vicious Rockefeller drug laws ("drug dealers get life imprisonment") were being debated and eventually rammed through the New York State legislature at the time I was writing through the midpoint of the series. It was a propinquity of event which led to some of the more profoundly angry passages in these novels and imputed a certain timelessness as well. (The laws were horseshit and we are still living with their existence and terrible consequence.) Calling a crazy a crazy, no matter how anguished may have been the aspect of the series which was the most admired but for me the work lives in the pure rage of some of the epigraphic statements, notably Kenyatta's. Writing these brought me close to some apprehension of how Malcolm, how H. Rap Brown, how the Soledad Brothers might have felt and how right they were: The Lone Wolf was my own raised fist to a purity and a past already obliterated as they were written, rolled over by the tanks and battery of Bolan's ordnance. (Operating under Bolan's pseudonym: "U.S. Government.") Bolan killed to kill: I think Wulff killed to be free. It all works out the same, of course.

THE LONE WOLF #7: PERUVIAN NIGHTMARE

by Barry N. Malzberg

Writing as Mike Barry

"Gordon Liddy had a speech, a set routine
for these meetings . . . and after half an
hour of that stuff sensible people would
walk out of the hall thinking that marijuana
was the first step on the road to death.
    —From a reminiscence of a friend

"He was right."   —Burt Wulff

PROLOGUE

Wulff found himself in something called the Hotel Crillon in Lima. It was steel and glass, looked like a Hilton, from the windows he could see views of what appeared to be a modern city but Wulff wasn't fooled. It was banana country: there was a technological front for the tourists and one percent of the population controlled the machines and did pretty well, but one mile out of the central city it was wild country. There were beggars living in the eaves of the hotel; he had seen them. Up in the hills somewhere was Cuzco, the ancient city of the Incas filled with ruins and the artifacts of a long-vanished civilization that would probably stay around longer than the technological front, but he had no interest in seeing Cuzco either. He wanted to get the hell out of Peru—even though it had been very thoughtful of Calabrese to stash him here. He supposed that he should be appreciative.

The man who was going to be his ticket out of Peru leaned against a wall in Wulff's room and said, "I have my reasons for this, Mr. Wulff. Do not question me too closely. For sufficient reasons I want to get a few million dollars of heroin out of this country and you are the means by which I can do it." He was a small man with an expressionless face; he had done something with mustache and sideburns, Wulff thought, to look vaguely Spanish but the effect wasn't working. Actually, the man was probably German if anything. "It should be a relatively simple assignment," the man said. "We'll give it to you here and arrange passage out and when you get back to your country there will be a man for you to give it to. The fee will be one hundred thousand dollars." The man brushed some imaginary lint off a sleeve of his coat. "Payable at the other end."

"I don't think you understand the situation," Wulff said. "I'm not in your country or hotel of my own free will. There are a lot of people watching me here. I don't think that an inconspicuous drop is what you're going to get from me."

"Let that be my problem," the man said. He appeared pleased with himself. He looked as if he had the situation entirely under control. "I respect your credentials," he said. "Let me put it this way: I respect your work, your potential, what you can do."

He looked at the two bodies lying in sprawled postures on the floor, one on either side of the bed. They were breathing shallowly but at least one of them, the heavier man on the far end, would not be doing much more than breathing for a short time unless he got some help. Maybe he would not even be breathing. The man against the wall, however, looked away from the forms with disinterest and said, "I can deal with the men who are watching you. It is, after all, my hotel in which you were placed. I have certain prerogatives, certain methods of my own. The question is, will you do this job for me?"

"I don't think you understand," Wulff said. Despite the circumstances, the dialogue with the man who claimed to be the owner of the Crillon was settling down to the same kind of exchange he seemed to recall having had many times before. Order out of disorder; it was amazing how there were only a few basic combinations which time and again would reassert themselves. "I don't think you understand," he said again. "I'm not in the drug distribution business. I'm trying to blow it up."

"I know about that."

"I've even made a little progress," Wulff said.

"I'm quite familiar with your record," the man said. "Do you think that I'm a fool? I know exactly what you've been doing and why you're here. And I'm not asking you to adopt a moral position on this."

"It would be easier if I knew your name," Wulff said. "Wouldn't it?"

"That is not necessary," the little man said. One of the bodies on the floor shook in its coma, limbs flailing like an insect's, then came to rest again. The form gulped and groaned. The respiration of the other one seemed to have become uneven. "I'm afraid that we cannot extend our conversation, Mr. Wulff," the little man said. "We are going to have to call some people and get these from the room. Also I do not have the time for an extended dialogue." He moved away from the wall, came toward Wulff, stopped a few feet in front of him and looked at Wulff flat on, his face shrouded, the eyes strangely penetrating. "I can get you out of Peru," he said. "I can get you back to your country to continue, as it were, your excellent work. I may be the only alternative you have at this time, and after you make the transfer of the goods you are perfectly free to go on and do what you will. It's merely a business proposition, Mr. Wulff."

"What makes you think I'll do your job for you? If you send me out of the country with that quantity of stash on me how do you know I won't—"

"I'll take my chances, Mr. Wulff," the man said solemnly. "I am perfectly willing to take my chances; I've been doing so for a long time. Life is a gamble or haven't you noticed? Your job will be to take delivery of the narcotics, convey them to a destination of which you will be advised and go on about your own distinguished work. There will be no follow-up, of course."

"You must think I'm desperate," Wulff said.

"You are desperate," the man said. "You have been desperate for a long time and now your desperation has peaked. You'll never get out of Peru alive unless you accept my help, don't you understand that? Which would you rather be, Mr. Wulff, alive and able to continue on your so-called mission or dead as a man of integrity who refused to participate in an assignment which would enable him to continue?"

Wulff looked at the little man and the man looked back; momentarily he felt himself locked into a frieze where nothing—the country, the hotel, the two bodies on the floor—seemed to exist. There was only that intensity and an exchange; at some base level of calculation, then, Wulff felt that they probably understood one another perfectly.

"All right," he said then, "I'll run your shit. If you think you can trust me you're crazy but I'll take your shit out of the country for you if you can get me out of here."

The little man smiled but the smile was not an unbending; it was in fact a tightening, an increased intensity passing from his face to limbs. "That's quite reasonable," he said, "that's a very reasonable attitude. I think that we can cooperate remarkably on that basis."

"I hate your fucking country," Wulff said with a flare of rage.

The little man nodded. "What makes you think it's my country, Mr. Wulff?" he said.

And then he picked up the telephone.

I

The man whom Calabrese knew as Walker said to the old man, "That was stupid. That was very stupid. You had him right in front of you and a gun in your fucking hand. Why didn't you kill him?"

Calabrese let that one go by. He looked at Walker trying to hold onto that feeling of fondness for the man that was the only thing holding him back from killing him on the spot. That would have proven if nothing else that Calabrese had lost none of his willingness to kill. There were certain people, however, whom he indulged with the impression that they could talk to him this way. If they wanted. It made for a certain safety valve effect, besides which there were worse people around than this Walker. He owed the man these little prerogatives. For the moment. Just for the moment.

"No, it wasn't stupid," Calabrese said. "It would have been a weak man's decision to kill him here in my house."

"Out of the house, then."

"Or to have taken him somewhere to do the job. Why tie it to me in any way? Send him out of the country," Calabrese said and, taking the pack of cigarettes from his pocket, he split one and tossed it into the ashtray—only his third of the afternoon. That wasn't bad, it showed that he was in control. "And take care of him very quietly. Why poison Lake Michigan?" he said lightly.

"I don't believe that," Walker said. His speech was easy but his position—a stance in front of Calabrese's desk, where he tried to find a relaxed position by leaning back on his heels—belied that easiness. In fact, Calabrese decided looking at the man whimsically, he was as fearful as any of the others.

Well, good. That was good. He would not want Walker to regard him without fear; that would have created problems too. This way he could have the fondness. "All right," he said mildly, "don't believe it."

"You had something else in mind, Calabrese," Walker said and went to the window, looked out at the lake, its dull vapors miles out, then came back again. "I think you like knowing he's alive," Walker said in a different tone as if having made a decision to plunge ahead. "Having him in your hands, getting him someplace where you know you can kill him anytime . . . But there's just the chance that he might be able to come back to you. Letting that little chance stay around, that's your style. It excites you."

Calabrese said nothing, holding his position. He lifted his eyebrows in what was meant only to be mild inquiry, but it seemed to shake the man, and rapidly Walker became a mass of small, uncoordinated motions. "I don't want to talk about it any more," Walker said. His eyes seemed retracted, his face smaller. "I'd better get back," he said. "I've got nothing else to say here. We've got nothing left to conduct now, you know that. I just wished you had gotten rid of the fucker, that's all, but it's your decision and I don't give a shit, all right?"

Walker got his hand on the door, touching it, his fingers clawing for the wooden surfaces when Calabrese said, "Wait." Calabrese raised a hand and Walker locked himself into position against the door, not moving, a strange alertness coming and going from him as he reached for a gun that was not there and then took his hand off his pocket. No one saw Calabrese with a gun. The man named Walker tried a smile which fell off his face like a teardrop under Calabrese's gaze. "Well, all right," he said, mumbling, "well, *all right.*"

Walker was a lieutenant on the Chicago force. Calabrese knew everything about the man: home, mortgage payments, wife's age, two sick kiddies, badge number, and so on but if it suited Walker to think that Calabrese knew nothing of him and that their relationship was protected, so be it. Calabrese would not break the pact. He would not even call Walker by his true name. "That's interesting, Walker," he said then, "that you would say that it *excites* me, letting him off the hook as I did, or at least giving him a long line." He paused, looked at Walker ingenuously. Walker's hand came off the door as if it were hot. "Just what do you mean?" Calabrese said.

"I didn't mean a thing," Walker said. "Not a fucking thing. I don't even want to talk about it," he said, turning back toward the view of the window. Then, as if he were displacing some substantial weight, he faced Calabrese again and said, "All right. I do think it's your style."

"Go on."

"You let that crazy fucker get away. You were the first man in maybe four months, since this whole crazy thing started to get a clear shot at him and you let him slip away anyway."

"Not too far," Calabrese said, "not too goddamned far at all."

"You know why I think you did it?" Walker said and now he was not guarding himself. Calabrese could see that he was really caught up. Well, so be it. "You did it because knowing he's around, having him in the picture, having everyone know that you could have killed him but you didn't . . . that's kind of a check on people, isn't it?"

"I don't know what you're talking about."

"It makes people think. That's a hell of a way to operate, Calabrese, but that was really what it was all along, wasn't it now?"

"You're not talking like an officer of the law."

"I'm no more a fucking officer of the law in this room than you're an officer of the law. We have mutual interests, remember?" Walker put a knuckle into his mouth, bit it, brought it away with a drop of blood. "This guy is a killer. Maybe if this killer is walking around somewhere, free and clear, people will figure that you worked out an agreement with him, right? That you have him under supervision. He might even be working for you now. It makes for a tight organization."

"I don't work in drugs," Calabrese said softly. "I don't believe in it. I stay clear of that shit."

"Maybe you do," Walker said, "and maybe you don't. Our arrangements have nothing to do with drug shit but if there's a percentage in it, Calabrese, you figure you might as well go for it as anything else. The organization is what matters to you, holding onto it."

"You're a cop," Calabrese said, "but that doesn't give you the right to talk to me that way."

Walker exhaled, bent over slightly as if Calabrese had punched him and all the effect went out of his voice. "I was just speculating," he said. "It was just **a** line of thought, that's all."

He went over to the door again. "I'm disgusted with the thing," he said. "You want to play games, Calabrese, that's your affair. But the games are starting to get dangerous. Having that guy still around was a big mistake, letting him get away was a worse one."

"You've made a worse one," Calabrese said.

Walker stood at the door. Calabrese could see him struggling with the impulse to turn, fighting it, trying not to, but fear or attention won out; he slowly wheeled around and Calabrese looked at his eyes, those eyes slowly shifting from dullness to apperception. "Is that a threat?" he said. He tried to keep his voice down but it shook. "Is that a fucking threat, Calabrese?"

"I never threaten," Calabrese said. "Making threats isn't the way I do things." He held himself behind the desk in rigid posture but a sudden thrust of tension lashed out at him. Son of a bitch, I'm getting old, Calabrese thought. Was Walker telling the truth? Was he losing his grip on matters after all? Impossible. He broke another cigarette. "Threats are for weak men," Calabrese said. "You're a cop, you ought to know how and with whom you're dealing by now."

"I don't know anything."

"Why do you think I told you about this, Walker?"

"You didn't have to tell me," the man said sullenly. "The word on this was around. Everybody knew that the guy was in Chicago."

"You didn't answer my question. I don't care what's around. Why do you think I told you?"

"I don't know," Walker said. He tried to hold himself level at the door but something in his shoulders quivered. It was like a claw had gripped him at a place in his body. Calabrese smiled. With all of them there was always that point of breakage—some sooner, some later . . . but the difference between men was always only at the point that they would break; each of them would do so in the same way. "I don't know why you did anything," the man said. "I've got to get going. I just dropped by."

"I told you because I thought you'd be interested," Calabrese said. "I like you and I value your opinion. But I didn't expect to be called stupid. Friends don't call each other stupid, Peter."

At the use of his real first name the man shook again. He turned and faced Calabrese slowly. "Don't you ever," he started, "don't you ever—" and then he saw what Calabrese was doing and he became very quiet.

Calabrese, moving from the desk, had the pistol in his hand. It had been a while since he had last had a gun in hand but there were things you never forgot. The metal curved warmly into his hand as he held it on the man called Walker. He said nothing.

"You wouldn't do it," Walker said. "This is crazy. You just wouldn't do it."

"Why not?"

"Because you're a careful man. You run a tight shop: you're a professional and you're not going to start pulling triggers without a reason. I'm too useful to you to kill, Calabrese."

"You don't believe a word of that."

"Yes I do."

"Maybe I'm not so careful. Maybe I'm not so bright as you think I am. I let him go, remember. That wasn't so smart according to you, even if I know exactly where I stashed him and my men are with him all the time. But you thought that that was stupid. So I can be stupid twice, eh?" He looked at the pistol, turned it so that it caught a fragment of light coming in from the window, bounced that light off Walker's eyes. "I'm an old man," Calabrese said. "I think about dying all the time now; there's very little else to occupy me. Maybe I want to take risks, maybe I'm bored with the careful life. The careful life gets you mostly as dead in a hundred years from now as the risky one. Maybe I'm looking for a little bit of a challenge, something to keep my mind off the fact that age is going to kill me; I want to control my life myself."

"That doesn't mean shit to me," Walker said but his hand did not come off the doorknob. "I really don't care what you do or how long you live."

"You're a cheap informant, Peter," Calabrese said. "Mostly that information of yours stinks. I think that you're three quarters of a cop at heart anyway, maybe even a double agent."

"That's bullshit. It's just not so."

"But mostly," Calabrese went on in a slow, patient tone, "I've been getting bored with you recently. You're not doing me any good alive, anyway. Maybe it would be interesting to see you dead."

Walker shook his head again. "I'm leaving."

"You want to leave. You keep on saying that. But you're not moving, are you, because you know that I'd probably shoot you."

"This Wulff has gotten to you. Maybe it's contagious, whatever he's got. Whatever the hell it is I don't want any part of it."

"Don't you?" Calabrese asked softly. "Don't you want to cut in on it?"

"No," Walker said, "no," and as if fighting himself up and over some level of attention, gasped, inhaled irregularly and then fell against the door, struggling with the doorknob. His motions were irregular, he did not seem quite able to coordinate but finally, in a spasm, he did. He seized the glistening knob and turned it, opening a thin sliver of light into the empty hallway.

Calabrese smiled in a private way.

He shot the man in the back of the neck.

Walker staggered in reverse—two steps, three—in a posture of astonishment, reaching a hand toward the wounded area as if he were dabbing tentatively at a sneeze, as if the wound were in the front rather than the back. He half-turned, showing Calabrese profile, his eyes rolling and then tried to say something, something which no doubt was profound and would have addressed the heart of the issue in a basic way (Calabrese had always wished that he could speak to a dead man) but the sounds only came out like those of a frog. Sounding like a frog seemed to amaze Walker. He reached his other hand toward the area, gripped the back of his neck as if trying to seat his head into place. He twisted. He turned, looked at Calabrese fully, trying to hold his head on his shoulders.

Calabrese shot him in the forehead.

Walker squeaked. He leaped, danced two dance steps and then, like a man making himself a careful bed in the woods, knelt, patted the floor twice and then lay in the spot that he had made. Lying on the rug he kicked once as if descending into sleep, then lay quiet. Blood moved cautiously away from him in bright, red rivulets.

Calabrese, sighing, put the gun away, looked at the corpse for a moment and picked up the intercom. Killing a cop, even this cop, was supposed to be a bad business—even for Calabrese—but he figured that this was not the major problem; he could always get around it. What he could not get around so easily was the loss of control which the murder had betrayed. But then you could not, he supposed, have everything. Better to discharge one's feelings than to bottle them up; that was the secret to a long, healthy life. "Get a couple of people," he said into the intercom. "I've got a goddamned accident on the rug here and I'd like to have it cleaned up."

"Yes," the voice said and clicked off. The person on the other end had heard this before but not for a while. Probably, Calabrese thought, they'll be thinking that it's like old times around here. It isn't, not quite—but there were certain purgative effects in blood. They could not be discarded. Always, no matter how far you got away from it, you might have to come back to the blood eventually just to retrace your origins. It was what made you strong.

Calabrese leaned back, broke another cigarette, looked impassively at the man on the floor. Was Walker right, he wondered. It was important in his position to hear all angles and discard none of them; a lot of people in similar positions had gotten into trouble eventually because they had not kept open minds. Calabrese did not consider himself to be in that class; nevertheless Walker might have brought something to his attention that he had not acknowledged. Maybe if he had shot Wulff he could have saved himself some difficulties. He did not think so, he thought he had the man under the tightest wraps possible and he believed that he could get rid of him with a simple phone call anyway . . . but still, you did not know. You simply did not know.

Wulff was an unknown element in the tight equation of the operation. Surely Walker had had a point. It had been stupid to leave the man alive. Hadn't it? Calabrese leaned back in the chair, realized that he was humming unconsciously in a cracked old man's quaver. Getting old. He cut it out.

On the other hand, he thought, sooner or later, at some stage of this game, a man *had* to allow a variable into the equation of himself. He had to do it if only to convince himself that he was still alive. It had been too easy for Calabrese for too long; he still had to know if he could meet a challenge if one erupted.

Bullshit. Walker was *right.* He had had no business letting the fool walk away from him, under any kind of custody. Instead of leaving Walker for dead on this carpet he should have made it Wulff. All that he had done with this poor bastard of a rogue cop on the floor was to transfer the desire, the change of heart. *Admit it. Admit it, Calabrese.*

He heard sounds in the hallway; two men came through the door without knocking on it. Calabrese looked at them with rage. "What the fuck are you doing here?" he said.

Looking between the corpse and Calabrese one of them said, "You called—"

"I called, I didn't call," Calabrese said. "Get the fuck out of here. Get the fuck out of here right now."

The door closed, the two men were gone. Scared shitless. Yes, he could still scare the shit out of them. He could do it to anyone. He was in command here and it was time to deal with Wulff. He had been a fool to let it go to this point.

Calabrese picked up the phone and looking at the corpse in a detached way got an outside line, got the operator, and asked to put through a person-to-person call, international, to Lima, Peru.

II

Half an hour before his interview with the hotel owner, three days after he had been dumped in the hotel, Wulff had walked into his room on the sixteenth floor of the Crillon, fresh from the coffee shop where he had spent an hour looking at tourists and wondering which of them was keeping him under observation that shift. He hated them. He hated the tourists. He hated the Crillon and Peru; it was better, maybe, than the alternative Calabrese had offered him, which was death, but not by so much that you wouldn't think of it long and hard if you were offered the time to make a careful choice. Dead city, dead country: dead hotel, steel and glass smacked into the middle of it, the tourists curiously internationalized, no one set of characteristics which would define most of them as being from a particular place, all of it blending into the heat, the dust, the very odor of the Incan ruins which Wulff felt that he could smell lofting from Cuzco miles to the north. Something was very wrong in this country; it was even rottener than Havana but it was not a definable rottenness either, nothing that you could quite nail down. It had to do with the fact that this hotel did not belong with the landscape, that the landscape itself was shockingly out of order—old and new jammed up against one another, the ruins behind all of it. He did not want to think of it. The more he thought of it the worse it looked.

It stunk but that was only the beginning of the trouble here. He was an insect in screens; he could not get out. He could wander out of the hotel, he could test all of the spaces of the hotel itself but the observation was so close that he felt he could almost see Calabrese himself here, let alone his men. They had him under the closest guard; there had to be ten or fifteen of them working in shifts, tracking him. Sooner or later the word would come from Calabrese to dispose of him and what could he do then? He might be able to take one or more of them face to face, but it would come in a different way. And then too the madness and cunning of Calabrese was that Wulff would never know when the time was coming. They could get him anytime or they could leave him to swelter in these spaces for months.

That was the hell of it, not being able to face the situation directly. But it was also, he supposed, what made Calabrese just about the best at what he was doing.

So it was that half an hour before his interview with the hotel owner and three days after he had been dumped in the hotel, Wulff had walked into his room on the sixteenth floor of the Crillon and found a man with a gun sitting in the chair nearer the door, looking at him with the kind of low-key interest which Wulff had not seen since he left the States.

"Just hold it right there," the man with the gun said as if he were an usher working a motion-picture line. "Don't move please and we'll be perfect." He looked as if he had been waiting for a long time, but as if the waiting had meant no more to him than the confrontation did now. Peyote? Wulff thought. As far as he knew, they worked peyote down here like it was chewing gum. But that was no drug-glaze in the man's eyes.

"Check him out," the man said to someone.

Wulff's gaze swung. He saw another man come from the bathroom, walk toward him briskly, giving little nods and waves as if he were a politician walking the last mile. Maybe he was. Maybe he, Wulff, was trapped into some kind of insane campaign and these two were simply using him to impress one another. The chemistry of the looks between them said something—that they were slightly nervous but each was drawing force from the presence of the other. Good psychology; that was why you worked in pairs, even for the easiest kind of jobs. It took an unusual man like Wulff to carry off things alone.

The second man looked just as short and efficient as the first. Definitely he was an American; they both were. Wulff could not tell the identities of the tourists in this international city, this city which with too much history had simply decided to take on no more, but he could tell these. These were Chicago—Midwest. Calabrese's men? Well, Wulff thought, that was it then. If so, it was a relief. At last, no matter what happened, he was facing the end of waiting.

He held himself still, said nothing. It had been coming, now it was almost over. Still, the presence of the men was a shock. Anything, no matter how long-anticipated, was always a shock when it came. Like death. He had to applaud Calabrese's methods though. The man was a master. He knew just what the hell he was doing.

The second man came around him cautiously, sniffing at him like a dog, seemingly drawing strength from these breaths, then extended his hands. Very delicately he frisked Wulff. The frisk was not completely professional, but then it did not really have to be. Wulff was carrying nothing. They sure as hell had stripped him before he got out of Chicago and only a fool would have tried to arm himself in this kind of situation. It would have been death city: roaming through Lima, looking for a replacement tool. What he had done in those three days had been simply to track what they had in mind for him, establish some kind of routine which they could not break.

Now they had come into his room. What did that prove? It proved, among many other things, that he was in a situation where he could not protect himself.

The frisker shook his head and backed away quickly then, seeming grateful to get away. He was still breathing in shallow, rapid gulps. Interesting. "He's clean," the man said. "He's got nothing."

"That's good," the first man said. "That's very good; I appreciate that." He stood, moved over to the bed, sat on the bed convulsively. Then he faced Wulff still holding the gun in that loose but alert way. "Tell me all about yourself," he said.

"Soon," Wulff said. That kind of shit did not throw him off balance; it was standard interrogation technique. If you had ever been in or around the force you saw it pulled all the time; the man would either attempt to kill him or he would not attempt to do it. This kind of dialogue meant nothing, was just an attempt to fill space . . . and it was the interrogator's decision to wait this out, not his so he did not have to say a thing. Instead, he looked through the windows past the partially drawn shades to see the outline of the Andes, the sun glinting off them in a peculiarly off-angle way. Picturesque country. Very picturesque indeed, Peru: it was probably all of the corpses piled here through the centuries that gave the land its tint of energy, its terrible lushness. The Crillon obliterated scenery rather than worked with it, but that was modern-day technology for you. Not that he could object. Hotels like the Crillon were for people who did not want to see the country they were seeing but wanted to carry their own impressions around with them. Screw it. It was rotten anyway, all of it.

"I've got nothing to say," he said after a while and held his position.

The second man coughed into his hand, reached into his coat almost absently and took out a gun of his own which he pointed at Wulff. "I think you'd better talk," he said. "Come on."

Like the other, the tone here was flat, uninflected. Calabrese's men. They had to be; it was the flatlands he heard. But then, Wulff thought, his mind suddenly scrambling away from what he heard, it just did not make any sense. It did not fall into place at all: Calabrese could have had him killed in Chicago. What kind of man would exile him these thousands of miles just to shoot him in a hotel room? It was too expensive and Calabrese, like any administrator, knew how to control funds. He might be perverse but never profligate . . . unless there had been a change in the situation back there and Calabrese had decided it was time to pull the plug. That was a possibility.

"I don't want to talk," Wulff said. "I've got nothing to say to you."

"You've said that already," the first man said without humor. He turned the gun on himself like a man investigating suicide, leaned forward, looked into the tube of the barrel as if it were a vagina. As he peered into the empty space, one eye concealed, a horrid optical illusion made it seem to Wulff as though the man were winking at him.

"You know," the man said, still looking into the barrel, "I'm tired of you Wulff. I've heard a lot about you—your reputation has gotten around and I'm getting sick of the whole deal. It's always the same fucking stuff except that you were starting to get really dangerous up there. You thought you were making a difference." He withdrew the gun, turned it on Wulff and then, as if changing his mind shook his head and gestured toward the other one. "You take him," he said.

"Me? I don't want to fucking take him. You're the one doesn't like him. You have the pleasure."

"Fuck you," the man said. "I told you to take him and you'd better do it right now. You hear me?"

The second man heard. Sighing he stood, drew his gun and leveled it at Wulff. His gestures were not quite as professional as the other man's but he seemed to know what he was doing. The hand in the action of drawing was almost detached from wrist and shoulder as though someone else were really doing this. The implication seemed to be: *Don't bother me; take it up with the other one.* "All right," he said, "but you're the one has the quarrel with him; you ought to do it. I don't give a shit either way."

Wulff watched what happened then in a state of careful detachment, a detachment which could not have lasted more than seconds but was sufficient in his extension of concentration to seem much longer—it was as if he were putting a tentacle into the room. One's concentration under stress was always sufficient to the situation if you knew what the hell you were doing.

The second man, then, extended his gun still in that absentminded, sleepy way, the gun coming out of his hand like a deformed finger. Then as his forehead furrowed into concentration, as his eyes, concentrating on the gun in his hand as if he were seeing it for the first time, narrowed with purpose it became clear to Wulff that the man was about to administer a killing shot. One's death always afflicts a man with unreality—there was that moment of failing comprehension, of nonacceptance. But it was not going to happen to Wulff, because they had killed him in a different way, but just as thoroughly, months ago. His death was as real to him as a lover's body.

He knew what was happening. It was no bluff, they were not faking. It was real and it was happening in this world.

The gun came forward.

What he did then he was able to do with no thought at all. Thought had nothing to do with it. The distance between himself and the man on the bed was not great: either through lapsed calculation or by design Wulff had been left in reach of this one. If the man had had any sense at all he would have used the gun as a lever to prod himself away, but it had just not occurred to him that Wulff could close the distance. And without even thinking about it Wulff had. Unconscious. Everything was unconscious.

Wulff kicked out with his left leg. This slightly unbalanced him but nothing crucial to his maneuver; with one low diving kick, pivoting to hold himself he knocked the gun with his heel cleanly out of the man's hand, seeing it as if in a glaze spin across the room. It hit the wall broadside, thumped on it, then clanged to the bare portion of the floor and bounced to the rug. The man who had been about to shoot him reacted with disbelief to this, put his hands to knees in reflex, making a motion as if to rise. Then as if the implications of the situation had come to him for the first time he looked at the other man. "Shoot!" he screamed. "Shoot the son of a bitch!"

His voice was high, the voice of someone much younger and in a situation altogether different. Wulff was caught by it but the other man was not. He showed no inclination whatsoever to fire, seemed to be deaf as a matter of fact; he held his gun on Wulff in a relaxed way, not nearly achieving that funnel of concentration which, at least for the other man, was the killing point. *They did not find death easy to administer.* "Shoot him!" the man without the gun was still shouting, "you've got to shoot him now!" But the man on the bed shifted in a sudden glaze of inattention, moved away, holding himself up on the bed like a girl frightened by a mouse, all of his limbs like tentacles retracting. He said nothing. *It's yours to handle* read the message. "You dirty bastard," the unarmed man said as if with a sense of discovery. "You yellow bastard, what have you done to me?"

No. These men were no team. They were not working together, in fact, so much as at fundamental cross-purposes. God knows what had thrown them together or for what end . . . but even as he was assimilating this at some base level Wulff was already moving. He moved on the second man, the one with the gun, hit him backhanded across the cheek and sent him sprawling across the bed. Then, instead of closing that gap which would have been perilous—the man raising the gun now, willing himself to fire—Wulff reached forward and seized the man by his shoulders. He yanked him off the bed.

For a moment he held the heavy, sweating bulk of this one against him, sadness and fright leaking out of the pores with an animal's panic and Wulff breathed it deeply, inhaled that panic, felt the fear and enjoyed it for what it was. Then with an explosive thrust he half-lifted the man, grunting, and threw him at the other one who was on the bed.

There was a crack as if a baseball had been hit: skull against skull. The two of them screamed as if powered by electricity, the notes of the screams evenly spaced.

Then the impact became flesh against flesh, modulated to a damp collision as the two of them were spilled to the floor, bouncing. In that tangle it was hard to differentiate them for the instant but Wulff did not follow the arc of the motion. Instead he was already diving toward that section of the floor near the wall where the gun he had kicked out had landed. He stretched forward desperately, feeling the metal slide into his palm with the shock of wire, that cold—so helpful—curling his palm and fingers up into the gun and then he had it . . . had turned, and now was lying on his back facing the two on the bed. They were struggling like some grotesque creature trying to raise itself from a swamp but from that tangle a shot came. It was the one with the gun looking for him, placing the fire through the arms and legs of the other. The shot went wrong, hit the wall and buried itself deep within and Wulff aimed the gun. He shot at the tangle without differentiating his target.

There was a scream. The struggle on the bed accelerated as if not one but both of them forming that grotesquerie had been wounded and Wulff watched the broken thing suddenly tear into halves: the man hit falling away from the creature. Then Wulff got a second shot into the other. This one fell back on the bed with a scream and the forms interlocked again. It was a parody of intercourse. They began to heave rhythmically, crying.

Blood puddled from them. It dribbled out of both, meshed, mingled with itself, the two strains of blood coming out against the denser white of the sheets and Wulff looked at this for only an instant, then turned his attention toward the door of his room, already heading in that direction. He had seen death before; it held no interest for him. The important thing was what was going to happen next. What was going to come through that door or, if nothing came, what was he going to do here with two corpses in a room which was being clocked at every level of the hotel?

He did not know. He simply did not know what he was going to do with these two now, or what the others would do for him; he did not even know where to begin. But one thing was clear. He had to get out. He had to get out of this room and take his chances, if he could, on the outside.

Death followed him everywhere. Sometimes he had created it; other times death itself had been imposed upon him. But one way or the other it was his certain legacy. Having come to avenge death, he could only create an ever-widening pool.

And in death the two forms were no longer threatening. Lashed to one another they seemed faintly comic. In fact, collapsed as they were into their postures, there was a clownish aspect to these two who had been so menacing before, gutted as they were now like burnt-out cars, the wiring of the bodies itself now unspliced, hanging loose in the flowers of blood. He could see little ropes of exposed muscle tissue.

He went toward the door holding the gun, cursing. He had created death again, and death was laughing at him. It delighted in the trouble it had brought. What the hell was he going to do with these two now? And what were the others going to do to him?

It *had* to have been Calabrese's work. Who else's could it have been? And yet Wulff found that he could not believe this. The old man simply was not that stupid. He was not. He would not set up something as crude as this, nor would he have taken two inept men who were not a team, one of whom hated him. You did not, above all, put haters on the job. Calabrese knew this. He knew all of the angles of a job like this.

And the old man had at least taste.

Wulff opened the door to move into that aseptic hallway, poised sixteen stories above the unimaginable streets, and an immensely calm voice behind him said then, "No, Mr. Wulff. Not just yet. Please wait for a moment."

He thought for an instant that one of the corpses had spoken and that it would have been peculiar, although not catastrophic; he just would have taken another shot. But, when he turned, Wulff saw sitting on the bed near the bodies, dangling his little legs as if in an excess of glee, a tiny man with a mustache and an empty face. Slowly, then, the sense of the situation burst upon him.

The little man held a gun with an opening as large as a mouth.

"I do like your work," the little man said. "I'm really quite impressed by your work, but then I expected to be. Please drop the gun, by the way. I can pull the trigger long before you can reach yours. And they're slow action too; I wanted them to be that way."

Wulff said, "This is crazy."

"It may well be. But you're a professional and you can accommodate yourself to craziness just as well as the next professional. Consider the lessons of the last quarter-century or so, Mr. Wulff: the human psyche, let alone a superior one like yours, can tolerate anything. Now why don't you just drop that gun casually and face me?"

"Why should I?"

"Oh come on," the man on the bed said, his limbs quivering with delight. "I'm not going to shoot you; believe me that's the furthest thing from mind. It would be disastrous for me to do anything like that; I'd be losing an excellent man and, whatever else my biography may reveal, I'm not self-destructive. Not in the least. Not even a tiny bit."

Slowly, then, Wulff let the gun fall from his hand.

There was nothing else to do. The voice was too self-assured, the little man too much in control of himself. The delight was that of a cobra, a gathering rather than loosening of the situation. It was possible to Wulff that he was yielding only to the assurance in this man and not to the reality of the threat, but he could not risk it. And even so, even if he yielded too easily, what did it matter? Weariness assaulted him.

It was happening more and more often now, that weariness. Maybe it had started in San Francisco, stemming from when he had been in bed with the girl and she had sapped out of him some vital impetus, uncovered within him the knowledge that he was not so much dead as sleeping and that the stakes on life could be high once again if only he let them. Maybe it was not the girl's fault and he was only thinking of Boston, seeing the bodies go up in flame—another thirty or forty dead and for what? For what? The poison would just be pumped into a different place. From San Francisco to Boston to Havana to Las Vegas back to Chicago and now to the Andes that weariness had pursued him, and now once again it struck. There were too many of them; there was only one of him. He had fought and would continue to fight, but would it make any difference? Did any of it? All that he could do was to struggle. If ever he became too temptingly dangerous as he had to Calabrese, then he was pure target.

It was just too much.

The gun, along with part of his resolve, hit the floor. He turned then, looking at the little man on the bed. His small bald skull was gleaming, the eyes reflecting amiability, and underneath it was a pain which Wulff could see as well but never touched, his tiny mouth creased into a deep, greeting smile. He might have been someone's grandfather appearing at a wedding after a separation of decades, the difficult reunion accomplished through great effort, collisions, concern, trains ripping through the night. Now, panting from his efforts, at the wedding at last, he bestowed upon assembled relatives that smile of great kindness.

The little man waved his gun at Wulff as if Wulff were the orchestra, the gun the baton, and then put it inside his jacket with a flourish. He raised his hands. "I see no need to hold a gun on you now, Mr. Wulff," he said. "I merely had to assure myself, you see, that you would not do anything rash until I had a chance to talk to you. I know that you're a sensible man and I merely wanted the opportunity now to talk sense."

He turned, looked at the corpses huddled against one another next to him, his mouth still kindly but the eyes showing a pleasure, even an ecstasy, which that mouth would never admit. Wulff felt the coldness begin to spread within him: he knew the little man now, he knew the syndrome; this was another one who got his kicks from death. "Our interests, you see," the little man was saying, "are almost entirely the same—not only in this but in most instances."

"Are you sure of that?"

"I'm really quite positive. I merely had to assure myself that this reputation of yours was deserved. There is so much deceit in the world—so much misdirection—huge corporations which have no purpose in life other than to spread lies. As individuals become dedicated to the lies, it is more and more difficult to ferret out the truth. I am devoted to the empirical method and I'm happy to say that you have confirmed my hopes in every way. You really do excellent work." The old man patted the corpses, his hand smoothing the dead forehead of one of them as if he were coaxing splinters from a plank of wood. "Really excellent work," he repeated.

Wulff held his ground. When there was nothing to say, you simply left it that way as long as you could; sooner or later the situation would finally come around. In the meantime silence was the answer. He estimated his distance from the little man, and then with an imperceptible shake of the head that he knew could not be caught decided against jumping him. No. No, it would not pay. He had an excellent chance of disarming this man—a better chance, once that was done, of killing him—but then what? For what?

He would still be in a room, with three corpses instead of two, in a hotel in a city he hated; his prospects would be worse than ever. Much worse. He did not know this assailant at all but one thing was clear: he was not Calabrese's man. He was no one's man. And that meant that their interests, after all, might be in common.

The little old man curled on the bed like a fish, held that fixated smile on Wulff as if he had measured his prey's own line of calculation and had found it good. "You understand, of course," he said as if they already knew each other quite well (and in a sense they did, so well that conversation could be shifted from one point to the other with a shared line of association), "that I had to do this. You understand that it had to be done. To perform this test upon you . . ." he glanced at the two bodies, " . . . to find out if you were wholly as good as your advance notices indicated," he said. "They were excellent notices."

"And what if they hadn't been?" Wulff demanded. "What if it had turned out that the notices were bad copy and that I wasn't nearly the man you thought that I was? Tell me, what then?"

He looked into the little man's eyes and found himself drawn into a sense of such profound corruption that for the moment he almost gasped. Then he managed to right himself: he had seen this in the interrogation rooms before when the suspect would open up under pressure and all of the corruption would pour out; this was merely another interrogation room—you had to maintain your sense of perspective. Everything repeated itself. Everything, truly, was the same.

"I was coming unarmed against two men with guns who knew how to use them," he said. "Suppose that I hadn't performed up to snuff while you were skulking in the bathroom, watching the excitement. Would you have saved me? Or would you have sat back rubbing yourself?"

The little man took no notice of this. If it was insult Wulff's attitude seemed to be implying, he simply did not acknowledge the language. Indeed, he seemed to have moved from the issue, his mind scuttling into more complex, useful channels. "Why I would have let them kill you for sure," he said absently. After a pause he added, "And I would have given them a bonus and arranged for a very prompt and discreet disposition of the few remains. It's not that I'm a hard man you see," he said as he paused again, looked at his fingertips, brought them together, and stared at the ceiling meditatively, "but on the other hand business is always business."

He stood. "I think that we should go somewhere else," he said. "We can talk quietly for a while, Mr. Wulff, and perhaps find more advantageous quarters. I'm really quite pleased with what you've done and I want you to see how I'm going to show appreciation."

"No," Wulff said, "we'll talk right here. Right in this room."

"I'd much rather not."

"I don't give a shit what you'd much not rather. There are a lot of people hanging around here who would be very interested in seeing the two of us together. So if you have anything to say you'll say it right here."

The little man stayed rooted in place, his face bright with approval. "You're an interesting and determined man," he said, "but even though that's admirable I'm sure you don't have to worry about the, ah, security problem. The people you say are watching you are doing so on my sufferance, my grounds. I'm sure that we can talk privately and there's no reason," his eyes shifted distastefully, "to dishonor the dead with talk of more death."

"No."

"No?"

"No," Wulff said, "right here. You're not Calabrese. Do it on my ground."

"Calabrese," the man said. "Ah yes, Calabrese, of course. He means nothing to me."

"He means nothing to me too, but he's godamned responsible for a lot of things."

"Don't worry about your Calabrese," the little man said abstractedly. "You're in the right hands now. I'm sure that I can do much better for you than your faithless Calabrese ever could."

Wulff looked at him and then he believed. The little man was no longer everyone's grandfather: no, he was something else, something which had spawned no children from whom would come issue of themselves. Instead he sat there on the bed, a cold, abstract, self-contained mass so gathered unto himself that he would be incapable—this was quite clear—of giving himself to anything. He was to himself sufficient; he had come from nothing, nothing would succeed him. That did not make him bad, not at all. It was merely the way that it was.

"It's my hotel," the little man said softly, "and I'm sure we could guarantee your security."

"I don't believe you," Wulff said, although he did already, "and I don't give a shit about your security. We're going to stay right here. With the bodies in my room. If you have something to say, say it in front of death. Death sure as hell won't repeat it."

"Dead men tell no tales, you mean. But these are not men anymore, Mr. Wulff. They are merely blobs of flesh, the vestiges of what were men. I know a good deal about death and I assure you that I know the difference."

"Here," Wulff said, "right here."

"All right," the little man said. He shrugged, gestured, took out his gun again and looked at it bleakly. "How would you like to get out of

Peru, Mr. Wulff?" he said.

"I'd love to get out of Peru."

"Then listen," the little man said.

He began to lay it out.

III

Williams knew that somehow Wulff was in Peru now. He didn't know how the fuck he had gotten into Peru or what the hell was going to happen now, but at least he had that much nailed. He had it nailed tight.

A cop got around. A cop with connections got around more, and a cop with connections who didn't give a damn and was willing to use them for all they were worth got around the most of all. Williams did not give a shit anymore. He knew Walker in Chicago through some files that he had dug up downtown. Walker—a cover name—was rotten; he was working clear through the remainder of the organization out there. Everyone knew that. Everyone knew too that everyone else knew it, which was why Walker wasn't touched. He was a sieve. But Williams didn't care. He called the man almost as soon as he got out of the hospital and got the word direct. Somehow Calabrese had scooped Wulff up and dumped him in Lima. How he had done it and why; exactly what Wulff had had in mind Williams didn't know. Nevertheless, there it was. The guy was in Peru.

"What the fuck is Wulff doing in Peru?" he said to his wife. He had just gotten out of the hospital.

"I don't know," she said. Williams had lain in the hospital for weeks, half of them on the critical list with a deep knife wound just missing the heart. He had picked up the wound checking out a methadone center in Harlem and since then he had not been the same. She was worried about him, but the doctors had said that showing worry was the wrong thing. She would have to stand by him and let him make his own decisions. The department had already indicated that if he wanted to declare permanent disability and get out on half-pay pension they wouldn't resist it. That was probably the right thing, the thing he should do. But he did not seem to be working in that direction either. She did not know what direction he was working in.

"Please David," she said. He was lying on the bed, his hand still on the telephone, the hand gleaming with sweat, palpitating the phone. "Calm down," she said, "it isn't worth it."

"Peru," Williams said again. "What the fuck did Calabrese stash him down there for?"

"I don't know. I don't know Calabrese and I don't know anything about Peru." She was trying to humor him but maybe it was coming off as if she were talking down to him. "I know St. Albans and Bermuda and that's about it," she said. She was a nice girl. Williams had always liked her, even before and after he loved her. Wulff had liked her too. They had liked each other. What the fuck was he doing in Peru?

"Peyote," Williams said, "and cocaine and hashish and maybe a little bit of elegant pot but none of the really hard stuff. It doesn't figure. That's no place for him." He took his hand off the phone. "He's in bad trouble," he said, "that's for sure—if Calabrese's stashed him down there."

"It isn't your affair," his wife said. "David, it has nothing to do with you; you've got to get well—"

"I'll never get well," Williams said matter of factly. He rubbed a hand over his stomach, nearly unconsciously. "Never well that way again. I got to *find* that bugger," he said, "I got to make real contact with him; I got to tell him he was right from the start and I was wrong. That he saw it right and I was missing the boat. You can't beat the fucking system. There's no fucking system to beat. It's all horseshit. He was right and I was wrong. I got to tell him that. I got to tell him that I'll help him any way I can."

She had heard all of this in the hospital, over a period of weeks. Almost the same words every time. "David," she said, "please, David."

"No," he said, but not in response to her, "it won't work. Can't you see? It just won't work anymore; they'll knife you up in the gut for even trying. I just want to tell him that. Want to tell it to the man. Want to tell it to him loud and clear, want to apologize to him too, for sending him out to Vegas in the first place for that Bill Stoneman valise. All my fucking fault. I could have helped him, we could have worked together but instead I had to be Mr. Inside, let him play Mr. Outside. Stupid, that was stupid. How'd he get to Peru?"

"Enough David," his wife said. "I'm going to shut the lights out." They were in their bedroom in St. Albans, split-level, seven-and-a-half percent FHA mortgage, he sitting in a posture of attention facing the windows looking out toward the tiny backyard, she lying flat out. "Please," she said, "worry about it later."

"I always worried about every fucking thing later," Williams said. "It wasn't my revolution, it was the darkies down the street that were stirring things up. No, I was the white man's nigger. Fucking Wulff. How I wish I could tell him he was right."

"I'm shutting off the light," she said and did so. They lay in the darkness quietly for a moment. She put out a hand, lay it on his arm. He let the hand stay poised there but did not respond. "David?" she said after a while, "David, if you want to get out of the department then you should. You should, I'll never stop you. I can't stop you from that, David, but you can't go on hating yourself this way; you should just feel lucky that you're alive. It could have been much, worse. Oh David—"

"Don't you understand?" Williams said with sudden urgency, tossing her arm away and sitting bolt upright in the bed, sending little splinters and intimations of pain through the place in his gut where the wound had been. "Don't you see that? It's hopeless."

"What's hopeless?"

"He'll never get out of fucking Peru," Williams said.

IV

Wulff had been a New York City cop, had been one for ten years. Two years of it counted in the pension plan toward active duty retirement benefits because he had been probably the only man in the force in greater New York who had enlisted for combat in that crazy war when things were really going good. Just to see what the hell was going on; you couldn't believe a thing in the press anyway. It was always important to see what was going on, to have a firsthand look at a situation; because only in that way could you have true knowledge and if Wulff had no other outstanding qualities, he liked to think that he had a basic and real curiosity. Anyway, that was the way he had thought in his early twenties.

Ten years in the police force and Vietnam: well, they were almost the same thing. He had seen every aspect of that war from helicopter duty over the jungles dropping defoliants to getting a firsthand look at how the service clubs in Saigon operated. He had gotten a look at the New York war too, doing everything from patrol duty at the outset to three years on the narco squad when he had come back, more or less intact, from Vietnam. The narco squad assignment had been set up for him as a kind of gift, or that was the rationalization of the department anyway—a payoff for him having been so nice as to have represented the department in the war. It looked good in the public relations files, a New York cop who had served over there. They could mention that members of the department had been in the war. The idea of the narco squad had been to keep him as happy as the public relations people.

Their mistake.

But then, the personnel policies and procedures of the department had always been ignorant; consider the million dollars of heroin which had passed out of the evidence room before the property clerk's virtual line of sight back in the late sixties, the early seventies. Police work was civil service first and foremost, and the idea in civil service was to fuck up quietly, never make waves. In line with that the narco squad was the best place to be. It was easy work, setting up fake raids with the informants, palming a little stash for oneself and generally signing out early. Almost everybody on the squad was picking up a little something on the side for himself.

Up in the higher echelons, then, they had conceived of this as a nice bonus for Wulff, advancing his career, giving him a little source of extra income: had it been personnel's fault that Wulff had hated it? Personnel was certainly not to blame, they were just trying to make things pleasant. But the narco squad had probably been the worst place for a man like him, fresh from Vietnam and full of rage. To Wulff the flow of drugs out of Saigon, the flow into the narco squad seemed to be opposing sides of the same great balance wheel. It was literally the same . . . and he had had enough of Vietnam.

Well, personnel department had fucked it up but that was personnel for you. The Police Benevolent Association wasn't such a hot union either. More or less they worked with personnel; certainly it was not in the union's interest to take a stand on the narco squad. Not when it was almost every cop's golden assignment. (The vice squad was everybody's favorite, but by the end of the sixties the commissioner had just about given up on it, what with Supreme Court decisions on entrapment and the amateurs coming out of the woodwork from anywhere to compete with the professionals.)

Wulff had come out of Vietnam angry all right. It seemed to him that the army was not the problem; they were simply trying to do a job out there. The war was neither moral nor immoral, just a neutral entity which could have gone any way at all . . . but the way in which the war had been conducted was some summation of everything that was insane in American life. They wouldn't have it one way and they wouldn't have it the other. Look, but do not touch. Stop, but do not listen. Go, but not too fast. So they tried to cover everything there, have a war but not fight one, fight a war but not too damned hard, tell the truth but work it through lies. And because they would not go in and fight with the nuclear weaponry that was the only way to end an otherwise unbeatable guerilla situation, they tried to adopt the methods of the enemy on their own grounds. That was stupid. And hopeless.

You couldn't go mano a mano guerilla against an enemy that had been fighting this way for a hundred years on a landscape whose terrain was familiar only to them. Not unless you wanted to get your ass whipped time and again, which is precisely what happened. Any fool could see that. But the bastards back at the Pentagon or even higher would not have it one way or the other: a directive into the field would start them into heavy weaponry and then the directive would be cancelled. Our men were supposed to fall back, operate only defensively, and the guerillas would lash out at them mercilessly. So headquarters would insist that it could not take these losses (as if the clerks and colonels at headquarters were getting killed) and that an assault would have to be made. Our men would trudge out again to meet the enemy and be smashed from behind . . . and in this way the war had been literally passed away, pissed away, in all of the burning and empty fields of Vietnam.

But all the time that the officials were fucking around this way, trying to sustain a full-scale war without public knowledge or support, trying to fight a limited war that could only be lost . . . all of this time the army was being ground away in that country. Men were dying, fifty thousand of them, some by fire, others through the treachery or incompetence of their own troops, many by disease, some at the hands of the enemy himself (but everything in Vietnam was the enemy, there was literally nothing that could not turn on you). And they were dying through the needle also, the cheap, good shit funneled through Saigon and into the countryside, part of every good soldier's carrying kit, and the shit proved to be for many of the men in this impossible and unwinnable war literally the only way out. What else was there? Women were outnumbered fifty-to-one in Vietnam; even the cheapest whores had to beat them off in Saigon, in the countryside. But there was no competition for the shit. That there was plenty of.

It must have been then that Wulff had conceived his true horror of and loathing for drugs. He saw what the big H was doing to the army—it was breaking it up as the Russians or Germans or Japanese had never been able to. Or maybe that revulsion had started earlier, when he had been on patrol car duty in Harlem in the early years, whizzing around those extinguished streets, the landscape falling apart like ash after a paper fire . . . and he had seen, driving around, what drugs were doing, had done to the city. The city was dead. Harlem was a monument to and a map of drugs, a gigantic network of veins through which the drugs were being funneled in and out all the time, just like Vietnam. And just as in Vietnam, people were dying, turning in their death-struggles on the lovely, burning city . . . and then, cementing that insight, he had seen Vietnam.

Whether it had started there and he had merely looked at Harlem through a rookie's what's-in-it-for me eyes, whether the hatred for drugs, distributors, the high men, the low men, the entire insane network through which they worked themselves into the diseased limbs of the nation had started there and had merely been implemented in Vietnam (men in their teens, deep into shit, could look eighty; they went staggering out, turned their rifles on themselves, were quite glad to die) did not matter. The important thing was that Wulff came out of Vietnam a very angry man.

So they took his anger to be the expected combat fatigue of a man both crazy and patriotic enough (but they were the same) to leave a good civil service position to enlist in that deadly war, a war that only career men or luckless draftees or unskilled enlistees would get into. These well-wishers thought that they would give him a good start back in civilian life.

They sent him to the narcotics squad with their blessings; told him he would like it.

Maybe in their minds, Wulff thought, it was the best gift to give a crazy man; it would soothe him down with stash. But after three years of it out there Wulff could not take it any more; he could not even maintain the appearance. He hadn't, really, been able to take it from the beginning, so that was no surprise. But somewhere around the time of the incident that ended his hitch he had found that it was getting to him in a very personal and ugly way; he had come to the feeling that the narco squad not only was doing nothing to shut off the drug trade in the city but, in fact, was working with the pushers, the distributors, the users themselves to keep it going.

They were all part of the system. The narco squad was merely working for the network in its own way, keeping up a front of enforcement, an appearance of normalization so that the trade itself could roll on undeterred. The narco squad was just the way the force had of cutting into the trade and taking out its own pound of flesh, that was all. Part of that might have had to do with the fact that the squad and the informants had an entirely too unhealthy closeness. The informants, people on the bottom of the pile, used the squad to raise monies to finance them a fix or two ahead, maybe even a few weeks ahead if they could make a sufficient score. And as far as the squad was concerned, if pressure stepped up they could always bust a willing informant or two for the sake of pleasing the press; but these busts were always dropped for lack of evidence and the informants drifted back into circulation, always there in the future if needed. It was a comfortable arrangement. You could get it to the point where you could make a bust by the telephone—get in touch with your informant, that is, and have him meet you at some mutually agreeable place.

It sickened Wulff.

He could live with it, he guessed, up to a point. But then like Vietnam itself, which had simmered away so long before public revulsion burst the boil of the war, Wulff had found at a given point that he was fed up, literally fed up with all of this shit.

He should have taken it to the lieutenant which would have been normal procedure (and probably one that could have been manipulated into leave with full pay; the departmental doctors were wonderful, they would certify everything), but instead he had done something really stupid: he had busted an informant for possession.

Well it was raw, it was just too raw—even looking back on it he would not regret it. This fucking clown in Harlem with the bright little eyes was giving him false leads and laughing while Wulff estimated that there were a couple of hundred dollars' worth of shit in his pocket just sitting there beyond being grabbed while the clown giggled away. He blew his cool. He took the man in.

He took him into the station house, he pressed charges, he even threatened to take it outside to the press and blow everything up in the department's faces. His conduct was that of an angry but righteous man. The informant system stunk, he had said. He was doing this not only for himself but for the good of the department. If they did not have the strength to straighten themselves out, he would do the straightening for them.

They had taken that under advisement. They had shared, at least they said they had shared, Wulff's real sense of concern over the system which, indeed, even the precinct commander nominally in charge said probably could use some overhaul. When the stash mysteriously disappeared even before a formal arraignment could be made, they had given the informant a dismissal. Also, Wulff was taken off the narco squad immediately. It was agreed at the higher levels that he seemed to be in need of a change of assignment and was not functioning at maximum efficacy for the department in his present duties. Above all, they wanted him to be happy.

They had put him back on patrol duty, sitting side-saddle with a rookie cop named David Williams. Williams was a twenty-four-year-old black who had a split-level in St. Albans, Queens, and was a great fan of the system, he said, because the system was what was making everything possible for him; it was his shield. The rottener the system got, Williams announced, the better he liked it because that proved that it was working—and the inequities were all in his behalf. He had been very serious about this; he had said that he and Wulff could have some good discussions about all this shit later. Wulff hadn't minded the idea too much; even though Williams for his money was a fool for belief in the system on any level, he was still an engaging kid. He had the kind of ingenuousness which Wulff recollected he might himself have had a long time ago. Altogether it was a good thing to be back on the streets, doing honest work again, and in the car Williams had been all business, quiet and glad to do the driving, quite cool and correct even though it was awkward for the junior man to be the driver. But still that had been the word from headquarters—Wulff in the junior spot. He guessed that they had wanted to humiliate him; but it had all backfired, because Wulff did not give a damn. The less responsibility they gave him now the better he liked it.

They hadn't known what the hell to do with him; that was the basis for putting him side-saddle in the patrol car. They were thrashing it out at the intermediate levels, trying to keep it away from the top which they probably would. They probably would figure out what to do with him, too. He had at least that much confidence in the internal workings of the department; they could deal with their own. Unless he dealt with them first and quit. He would give that some real thought.

Or he would have given it some real thought, anyway, if things had not moved so fast. He really might have made some kind of adjustment there. Any man who could make it to field sergeant in Vietnam without becoming too embittered to do civilian work had potential for adjustment. But on that very first night of patrol, Wulff ran into something that he couldn't handle.

Someone phoned in a report that a girl had O.D.'d on the upper floor of a tenement on West 93rd Street near the river, and the call had come into them, the nearest car to the call. That was routine procedure after all. They had driven to the address and Wulff as the side-saddle man had been the one to go upstairs and do the checking out, Williams sitting cool behind the wheel. That was procedure. He didn't argue with that at all.

But when he went up the stairs of the tenement, prowling his way through the dust and fumes past all the closed, bolted doors of the dwelling he found that the girl on the floor was named Marie Calvante and she was very dead of an obvious heroin overdose. She was a very pretty middle-class Italian girl out of Rego Park and by some coincidence she was, or at least had been until she ran into a little difficulty, Wulff's fiancee. They were going to get married soon. Plans had been made. Somewhere along the way he had had the bad luck to pick himself up a fiancee.

They had been going out together for a year. They even had the house picked out. All in all, it was quite an unfortunate thing to find this very girl, this Marie Calvante, O.D.'d out in a tenement. If Wulff had been able to think straight he certainly would have appreciated the coincidental aspects of this. Small world and all that. As it is, however, he had not been able to do much thinking at all.

He kept a lid on himself though. When Williams, sitting in the car for a while, wondering where the hell Wulff was, finally came out to join him, Wulff had kept himself from showing much to the rookie at all. Instead he had very neatly taken off his badge, put it next to the corpse and then had left the two of them, Williams and the girl, that way to settle for themselves what was going to happen next and he had walked straight out of the tenement and out of the force. Maybe it hadn't been right to take no part in the funeral arrangements, but he had learned from Vietnam that a corpse was a corpse, just dead meat, it didn't matter what the hell happened to it from then on; certainly the corpse didn't care. Arrangements were for other people and he had a better idea of what he wanted to do.

So she had wound up O.D.'d out on West 93rd Street. To Wulff it was a simple proposition: turning in the informant, telling the lieutenant what he could do with his fucking narco squad, making a lot of, maybe important people, unhappy; and they had decided that it made sense to make Wulff equally unhappy as a kind of advance payment on the trouble they would make for him. If you looked at it objectively, it made perfect sense. Certainly they were being objective; from their point of view it was altogether a good move. Feelings, people—they just didn't matter when you got into that kind of calculation.

A lot of important people denied that they had anything to do with it, though. Wulff picked up that information later on. When he had walked out of the department, dumped his badge on the body, bothered to inform no one but Williams later what he had done, and made his decision to singlehandedly destroy the international drug trade, he got himself moving in circles where people were in a position to deny any involvement with the O.D.'d girl. And they did. All of them did. But by then it was too late for everyone.

He went out to destroy the international drug trade. It was crazy, maybe, but so was the drug business itself. Madness versus madness. He started to roll out his swathe of death and destruction then, roaming across the continent, moving from New York to San

Francisco, back to Boston and then to Las Vegas, on a hijacked liner to Havana, then to Chicago, and at most of these stopover points he found himself sooner or later facing a person of some importance, usually in the process of being killed. And one by one they swore that they knew nothing of Marie Calvante, much less of West 93rd Street. The word had gotten around on the organization circuit that Wulff was out for vengeance, and each of them explained that whatever else they had done none of them had any knowledge whatsoever of the girl. It looked, in short, like a setup of some kind. Either that or it was a coincidence which had sprung Wulff loose finally.

But he would have done it anyway. That he guessed was the point. He had been aching since Vietnam to take on those bastards; but only a marginal man, a man half-dead and without hope, could try anything so desperate and the murder of the girl, then, had only triggered him off. Anyway, he did not care to believe what they told him about organization non-involvement. Why should he? Why should he believe anything? All of these people were liars anyway. All of them.

But even if it was the truth, what the hell did it matter? For a little while, particularly in San Francisco early on, he had had the satisfaction of knowing that he was at least getting a job done. It might be a brief life on which he was embarked but it was an effective one—a hell of a lot more effective by any standards than the narco squad. Maybe he had taken out five hundred by now including the heads of the northeast and western sectors. The Bay area, the New England area would not be the same again for a long time, if ever; the organization was wrecked. So he plugged ahead. He kept on killing. He got a helicopter pilot somewhere along the line too; that one had really hurt, but the man in the last analysis had proved to be a traitor. What else was there to do?

He didn't like it for the most part; only a lunatic would get pleasure from killing, and despite the word that was being passed around about him Wulff was not at all crazy . . . but he couldn't say that he disliked killing, either. That would have been a misrepresentation too. It was just a job. He had little feeling. He had no feeling. He was dead altogether, or so he wanted to believe; the important part of him had died back in New York. Along the way, in San Francisco, there had been a girl and he had had sex with her and it had not been bad but it really didn't change the equation. Did it? He would not accept that. The equation was cold and hard. It had been laid to rest in a stinking, single room occupancy tenement.

Until he had hit Chicago.

He had hit Chicago carrying out of Havana a million dollars' worth of smack which he had chased from the police stash room in New York City where it had been taken out by a corrupt cop named Stoneman clear across the continent and onto a hijacked plane. And he had hit Chicago still holding on, a million dollars clear, and there he had run into a man who lived on an estate overlooking Lake Michigan named Calabrese.

Calabrese had been something else again.

Calabrese sat or stood on top of the network; he was so far above it in his estate that he did not even acknowledge its existence let alone his connection to it. He was a man who had fought all of his wars forty years ago, had won them all, now was rewriting history so that the losers never existed at all. Calabrese was a cunning old man with a deadly and precise way of handling things and he had almost killed Wulff twice. The second time, holding the gun on Wulff, he had told him that he was going to pass up the opportunity, at least this time. Killing Wulff was no challenge, Calabrese said. The idea was to keep him alive, provide Calabrese with some excitement, send Wulff under heavy guard to someplace far out of the country where Calabrese could titillate himself with the simultaneous knowledge that Wulff was still alive, still a danger . . . but totally controlled by Calabrese.

Out of the country, then, but where? Wulff had wondered when they piled him aboard a private plane at O'Hare. Majorca was a possibility, Istanbul another, or possibly postwar Saigon. Those as far as he knew were the three great throbbing hearts of that monster, the trade. They were the hearts which initiated the flow of the blood and where the poppies were tilled out to begin their billion dollar journey. But it had not been any one of those places which, in a way, was a damned shame, because Istanbul and Majorca were interesting and he would not have minded seeing Saigon again.

Instead it had been Peru.

Wulff had not even known the destination until the plane had touched down, until the men guarding had begun to talk with one another. What the hell was Calabrese sending him to Peru for? But later on in the hotel, when he had been checked in and left alone, Wulff thought it through and decided that like everything else in Calabrese's life it made sense. Peru was one of a number of the South American countries which would likely be accessible to Calabrese. Hell, half a million dollars could buy you a government, but of almost all those countries this was one of the most tightly held, the country where the concentration of power was the greatest. And also, past the urban sprawl of the few great cities where the tourists prowled, this country was wild, unsettled, just as it had been thousands of years ago. It was as unimaginable as the great forests of Brazil.

Anything could go on here.

The men had taken him to the Crillon, had put him into a room, had told him that he would be under watch at all times and that it would be inadvisable for him to think of escape but that on the other hand he could within those clearly-defined limits come and go as he pleased. At Calabrese's pleasure. His accommodations would be taken care of, the hotel would be paid off. Calabrese and the owner of the hotel seemed to have a comfortable working arrangement. At least this was the word that he got but the man telling Wulff this sounded vaguely confused, as if conveying orders which he did not understand or could be physically dangerous to him. On the other hand the message had gotten across fairly well that although Calabrese was a long distance away he was still very much there in person.

Fucking Peru. For three days he did nothing. Even if he had wanted to chance some activity, Calabrese be damned, there was something about the climate here, the very aspect of the country, that got to him. It was dead, dead: dry, hot, a faint odor of bones and death in the air. Too much history, too much present suffering. Wulff tried not to think about it.

They had never really discussed his police work. He seemed to remember that pretty clearly. They might have mentioned it now and then, she knew he was a cop, knew he was a narco, knew what the job was doing to him. But life was full of other things; there was never enough time to do and talk about all that they had to share . . . and life and times on the narco squad had been pretty well at the bottom of the list.

Only once. Only once had she really had to come to terms with it, had he had to come to terms as well with what it could do to her. He seemed to recall this much fairly well. This was when the shakeups were just starting, the word was just beginning to drift down from the Commissioner's office that pressure all up and down the line was coming on the squad and that they had better pay attention to what some of the assistant DA's were saying. Later on, of course, this had ended with revelations that something over eighty percent of the squad was directly or indirectly involved in traffic themselves through actual handling or through payoffs and with the breakup of the squad. That had been wonderful. But this was a long time before that when the first rumblings were coming through and when Wulff had found that the few real busts he was getting were going into the precinct in the morning and coming out on bond in the afternoon, usually forfeiting bond and leaving the state. That had been pretty much par for the course, you expected this all the time but Wulff on an informant had busted a medium-grade seller in Harlem who was holding three or four kilos secreted through his pockets at the time of the bust, and, in the midst of the shakeups and the lectures from the Commissioner, he had been pretty surprised when this bust too had been released on five hundred dollars bond within twenty-four hours (he had spent a full day on the papers) and the lieutenant, when he had complained about it had told him to get lost, there were elements to this Wulff could never understand, he had nothing to do with the legalistics and why didn't Wulff hit the streets anyway?

It had occurred to him then that he was probably in over his head, that even the easy and necessary cynicism which he had cultivated about narco was not sufficiently protective . . . no, if even in the face of the pressure coming through from headquarters they could pull a stunt like this, then what he had thought he understood about narco he did not. He understood nothing. All of his assumptions would have to be renegotiated and painfully; the squad appeared to be corrupt not because it was line of least resistance—shit, that part was human nature—but as a matter of conscious, persistent choice, like New York City itself it would stubbornly seize upon the worst alternatives available in any situation, those that would make the most gain for the least amount of people . . . no, he could not think about it. He did not want to pursue it any further. Yet it sickened him. It occurred to him then for the first time that the sickness might go beyond narco which he had known stunk almost from the beginning, it might go to the heart of the PD itself. It was the PD and its system which were rotten, narco being only a logical extension of this . . . and if that were true then there was nothing to do but to consider not only getting off the squad but out of PD itself.

That hurt. That would really hurt. Wulff liked being a cop. He still had a modicum of hope then.

He had talked about it with her, the only time, he seems to remember, that they had discussed his job. It must have been his apartment at night; they were spending almost all of their time together in his apartment around then but Marie with a kind of propriety and determination which he could not quite understand had never stayed all night with him . . . she was not going to wake up in his bed until it was her bed too she had said once with a smile and he had known enough not to push her further. But that had given them hours and hours together, sometimes it had been three or four in the morning when he had driven her to the little studio apartment in Queens which was nominally her own, and those hours were too important to waste in talking about anything as wasteful as narco. Except that this one time the need had overflowed within him and he had found himself ranting to her while she lay on the couch, a blanket drawn up just past her shoulders and had listened to him her eyes wide and luminous, her face impassive except for small convulsions of feeling when she could see his pain.

"Then you've got to get out," she had said finally. "You've got to."

"I guess maybe I do. Off the squad? Or out of the department?"

"You say that the department is rotten, that the squad is just one part of it. So that means the force itself, doesn't it?"

He shook his head. She was very desirable and very receptive and he supposed that in some basic way she understood more about him than he did about himself but there seemed no way to communicate what he had to. "You see," he said finally, "I wanted to be a cop. I thought that it would stink; I was never naive that way but I still thought that you could do a job. Because it's a dirty, necessary job. But they won't let you."

"Won't let you do a job?" she said, "then if that's so, if you really feel it's that way, then you've got to get out."

He paused for a while, thought about this. He did not want to answer this too quickly. "I could," he said, "and do what?"

"That's ridiculous, Burt. There are hundreds of things you can do. You're a capable man."

"Oh I guess there are things I could do," he said vaguely and let that hang in the air, leaning over, she seemed to stab at it with a hand, cup it like a butterfly, then sat up on the couch dislodging the blanket suddenly, disturbingly.

"You mean you don't want to leave," she said, "that's what you mean."

"Oh, in a way."

"You like the job."

"No I don't."

"I'm sorry," she said. "I put that wrong, didn't I? Of course you don't like the job; you hate it, what it's doing to you all of the time. But you love what it could be. That's the most important thing in the world to you, what it could be."

"I'm not a reformer," he said after a while, "I'm not a moralist, I don't believe that you can change anything really except in the long run but—"

"But you are," she said with a smile, "and you do, you do believe that it can be changed, you *are* a reformer. A moralist." She pulled the blanket up around her again, then, shaking her head as if coming to a decision let it drop. He looked at her.

"Come here," she said.

He stood, came over to her. He felt as if he were shuffling, as if his stride suddenly were that of a very weary, beaten old man although this could not possibly be so; he was thirty years old at this time, make it thirty-one, an age when the first signs of physical limits might be sensed but then only intermittently and in illness or at the long end of the day; actually you retained almost everything that you had been and added to that knowledge and a sense of pace. Athletes had their best years in the early thirties . . . he had no reason to feel so old. But he did, he felt old, he felt in stride all the intimations of his decline.

She gathered him to her and held him for a while. He let her breast rest on, then in his mouth, moving slowly against her, without passion for a time. "Poor Burt," she said, "poor Burt."

He said nothing. It felt good, finally, not to have to say anything, not to have to defend himself, to struggle. He felt the beginnings of passion, instead, as he moved against her.

"Poor Burt," she said again, "poor, poor Burt, you want to clean up the world. You want to clean it up all yourself my baby and it cannot be done, it simply can't be done . . . but you know that too, don't you?"

"Yes," he said against her, "I know that too."

And then for a long, long time there was nothing else to say; nothing else necessary. They told it all to one another first subtly, then vigorously, and finally with cries.

That had been the only time he had discussed business with her.

Thinking could only drive you straight up a wall in a situation like this. It was no habit to get into.

He did nothing; he stayed in his room, wandered through the slick, empty corridors of the hotel, tried to consider his situation. It did not look promising. True the observation here was loose, they were not on top of him, they were watching him from distances; but on the other hand he would have to be crazy to think that Calabrese's men were going to let him get far. He could take the tourist route of course, maybe they wouldn't object to that—go out and inspect the Incan ruins, what the brochures called the mysterious destroyed civilization whose artifacts would probably outlast anything in modern-day Lima. That was what the brochures said anyway. What a great prospect: to start off by trying to break the international drug trade and to end up

wandering around Incan ruins with a bunch of tourists, waiting for a
Chicago hood to decide exactly when he would be disposed of and in
what manner. That would be one wonderful outcome.

Wulff stayed around the hotel. The hell with it. He wanted nothing
to do with this, it was not his country. All of these South American
countries were the same all right: the technology superimposed on the
poverty led to repression and revolution by turns, but nothing really
changed. It would always be the same. The Incans knew that; maybe
that was why they had given up on the whole thing.

He tried to work out his moves, tried to think of what options were
open to him, but he could not avoid the knowledge, finally faced up to
it, that his options were closed off. This was how it all ended; they had
him in a box. He tried to be resigned. Hell, he had certainly done more
to hurt them than any ten men had ever done; but it was not
comforting. Wulff came to a realization. He had liked his work. On its
level it had been satisfying. He hated to give it up.

Then on the third day, toward the end, he walked into his hotel room
and there were the two assassins.

Things moved pretty well after that.

VI

Dillon was frantic by now. The order had come in by telex from
Calabrese that morning, and even in code it had been quite direct.
Dispose of the problem. Dillon knew exactly who the problem was; he
had been watching the problem for three days. Five of them in the
hotel had been working on the problem fulltime. The fact that he was
the one asked by Calabrese to do the disposition was a definite step
up—it boded all kinds of things. But he could not find Wulff.

Wulff was not in the hotel. He was not in his room, he was nowhere
in the lounges, the surrounding area. A quick check of the travel logs
indicated that he had not arranged to go anywhere, either. Where the
hell could the man be? It was impossible that he could have given all
five of them the slip. He was supposed to be kept under observation at
all times. Nevertheless, he had gotten away. What the hell did that
mean and where did it leave Dillon? What was he going to say to
Calabrese when the second inquiry came in? He could hardly lie about
it. Calabrese would want proof. The old man was no fool.

There were five of them in the hotel. Two of them had been the
escort down from Chicago: stupid thugs, both of them, but the orders
were to get along so Dillon had simply had nothing to do with them

one way or the other. The other three, including himself, were Calabrese's international detail, and Miller and White were good men. He had no quarrel with them; they had done a lot of jobs of this sort in a lot of places for Calabrese. But Miller and White were unaccountably missing now. They simply were not around, and Dillon had the feeling that he did not want to take up the issue of their disappearance with the Chicago thugs who were very much around, hanging sullenly around the coffee shop. If the thugs had been supposed to know that kind of thing then they would have gotten the kill order, not Dillon. Besides, asking them what the hell was going on, sharing his troubles with them, would have been a clear pipeline back to Calabrese. He had a strong feeling that the more that was kept from Calabrese at this point, the better off he would be. He didn't want to get into that. But Wulff was not turning up, either, and Miller and White's room was empty, their beds still made up from the night before. So they hadn't even slept in. What the hell was going on? Dillon saw no way around it. He had to talk to Stavros.

He didn't want to. He didn't want to mess with Stavros at all; there was nothing about the man he liked or trusted. He was pretty sure that Stavros was a cover name, too; he really didn't know a damned thing about the man. But Stavros was the owner/manager, or at least nominally the owner/manager, fronting for some other people, probably, and had a working relationship with Calabrese, which meant that half the responsibility for Wulff's disappearance could be put on him. It was Stavros's fault; it was his hotel, it was at least partially his problem that Wulff was unlocatable. Wasn't it? Hesitating at the door of the man's suite, though, Dillon felt a quivering reluctance which was very much unlike him. He had tried to keep his contacts with the man to a minimum. Finish up this job and get the hell out of Peru; get your ticket punched and go onto the next country. Stavros was not worth worrying about in the context of a mere passage through. But now he had to deal with him. He did not want to. The man was treacherous, that was all, and probably half-crazy. Still, you had to go ahead. You had to keep on going. You had to do your work.

He knocked at the door of Stavros's suite and then he knocked again. Something within grunted. Dillon patted his gun, held onto it in his pocket for comfort and then pushed open the door and went through. Stavros was sitting there behind his desk, holding a gun on him. The little old man's face was curiously intent and he seemed energized. "Drop your gun, please," Stavros said.

"What the hell is this?"

"Just drop your gun if you will," Stavros said. His face was friendly, his eyes quite warm. That was what frightened him most about the little man; his expressions were almost always totally out of accord with what he had on his mind. It wasn't American. It wasn't an American kind of thing to be. "I said, drop it," Stavros said.

Dillon carefully pulled the gun from his pocket. He tried to get his finger on the trigger, tried then to move it subtly up but Stavros, without moving, got off a shot. The shot hit Dillon's gun, spanged it into the wall. Dillon looked at the small threads of blood on his hand. "What the hell is this?" he said again.

"It would have been very unwise for you to have shot," Stavros said. "You are a fool. All of you people are fools."

"What is this?"

"You ask questions," Stavros said, "but you really don't want answers. All you want is blood. Sit please." He gestured with his gun toward a couch at the side of the room. Confused, backpedalling, Dillon sat on the couch. He felt disoriented. He worked for Calabrese. He was one of Calabrese's best men. Things like this could not happen to him.

"You're looking for Wulff," Stavros said.

Dillon said nothing. He looked out the windows, seeing the mountains in the distance. The mountains were deadly, oxygen-thin. He had never been there. At this moment, however, he wished that he had gone. That was it. He should have pursued Wulff into the mountains.

"I am terminating my association with you people," Stavros said softly. "I am a man who prefers to come right to the point and I wish you to understand that we have no more business to conduct." Quite neatly he moved away from the desk, leaned over and spat, came back again, the gun steady. Wheels on his chair. "You people disgust me," he said. "You have no sense of dignity, of personal worth. You have used my hotel as a charnel house. This will cease."

"I don't know what you're talking about," Dillon said.

"Of course you do not know what I'm talking about. You do not speak the language." Stavros inspected the gun, leveled it again on Dillon. "Your Mr. Wulff is an interesting man," he said. "He is certainly a far better specimen than any of you. I wish that you were on his level."

"Calabrese will kill you," Dillon said suddenly, on instinct. "You can't get away with this."

"You are functioning in your American's context again. Culpability and retribution. I assure you I am quite uninterested in what your Mr. Calabrese does. Your Mr. Calabrese disgusts me. Although," Stravos said softly, "he has done me something of a service."

Dillon had an insight, or thought he did. "You're working with Wulff," he said. "You've gotten together with him on some deal and you think that you can get around Calabrese."

Stavros raised his eyebrows. "What's that?" he said.

"You can't get around Calabrese," Dillon said, "no one can get around him. You're making a very bad mistake if you think that you can. Anything you do to me you do to him. You'll pay for this."

Stavros leaned back with a little sigh. "You are so stupid," he said. "All of you Americans are so stupid; you think that you are rational men and that the world works in terms of your crazy visions, but you are wrong. You are wrong about everything. Do you think that I care about your Calabrese?"

"You should," Dillon said. Looking down the line at Stavros it occurred to him for the first time that he was going to die. He had ducked this knowledge for a long time. Other men died, he had administered death to them often enough to be very familiar with all of its ramifications . . . but death was not for him. He was in a special, privileged category and he was going to live until the age of eighty and die in a richly appointed, quiet way. Except that he was not. He was forty-seven years old and this little old man was going to kill him right now. "You should care about Calabrese," he said.

"Why?" Stavros said, "why should I care about your Calabrese? Why should I care about any aspect of your American system. This is my hotel, this is my country, at least I should say that it is my adopted country, which is almost the same thing at this stage of the game, and all of you mean very little to me." He directed the gun toward Dillon again. "Your Mr. Wulff is a very sensible man," he said. "I find that we have an almost mutual accord on many things."

"You won't do it," Dillon said, "you won't do it, this is crazy, you can't do it," and Stavros shot him in the lower spine. The bullet came out of the gun off-angle, the shot taken almost absent-mindedly, the little man ducking down to the surfaces of the desk as if he were reaching for a cigarette, and Dillon in disbelief had half-pivoted his way out of the chair when the unexpected bullet hit him in the lower back. He tried to rise but found that he could not; the bottom part of him was disconnected. And then as he fell back in the chair, appalled, he felt the pain beginning to rip at him.

"Stupid," Stavros said, "all of you are so stupid," and then he shot Dillon again, this shot coming into the lower neck, near the jugular, just above the Adam's apple. Dillon had one moment to understand what was happening to him, the impossibility of it suddenly colliding with the actuality, and as he fell back in the chair his limbs, restored and inflamed by death, yanked once, twice, twitched like a beetle's. Then he fell back flatly, sliding all the way down, feeling nothing, not even the surfaces of the floor as they enveloped him. *This can't be happening* he thought again, the brain still intact, whimpering out its protests, but then he heard the sound of Stavros's laughter and he guessed that it was. He guessed that it was.

Calabrese had laughed during some of the kills, too. Dillon had heard him.

VII

The shit was in Cuzco. The little man had not been much more specific than that, only telling Wulff that he should take bus transportation up there; someone would meet him at the bus and give him further instructions. It was impossible to make the transfer at the Crillon, the little man had pointed out, because the observation from Calabrese's men was entirely too close. It would be better if Wulff went to the source and got a plane out from there. "We'll make arrangements to get you out," the little man had said, "but the first thing is to get you out of this hotel."

"It won't work," Wulff had pointed out, "this place is crawling with Calabrese's agents. They'll never let me get out of here."

"Oh yes they will," the little man had said. "It isn't crawling with agents, as you put it. There are exactly five men we have to contend with, no more, and I know who each of them is. I assure you, I can handle that part of it. The problem is to make the transfer, but that can be taken care of. We'll make the transfer in the mountains and you'll take the bus back here and we'll get you airport connections. Simple and routine," he said. "It's going to be a simple and routine operation, and at the end of it we'll all feel much better about many things."

"It's impossible," Wulff had said, "it's impossible. Calabrese is no fool, we're not going to get anywhere with this," which had really been a strange position in which to find himself, a strange way of putting things, because here was a man who, for whatever motives, was working to get him out of this trap and Wulff was in the odd position of defending Calabrese, who had entrapped him. Nevertheless there was a basis to it; he thought that he understood Calabrese and his methods. He was relatively comprehensible; he just happened to be better than most of the others. But Calabrese's thinking was only a heightening of conventional methods whereas this owner, this man here, was something entirely different. He was simply like no one else; the channels through which his mind plowed were not those with which Wulff or Calabrese or any American, he suspected, were familiar. "All right," Wulff said then, understanding this phenomenon, understanding, too, that the kind of corruption with which he was familiar was only a part of a vast spectrum of evil, a dot on the radius, so to speak. "All right, I'll go to Cuzco. I'll do what you say but I don't like it."

"What an American statement," the little man said then without humor. "Really, Mr. Wulff, it is admirable in all ways, the manner through which you people are capable of disassociating yourselves from all the consequences of your actions. But I'm sure," he said, "I'm sure that this will work out to our mutual benefit. In fact, I'm absolutely confident that we are embarking upon something which will be of enormous profit. I will have a difficult situation—a difficult transfer, I should say—worked out for me by one of the true geniuses in the drug field, and you will gain your freedom to continue your very useful efforts in the abolition of the international drug trade." He shrugged. "Who is not to say that we do not both win?"

"Could you at least tell me your name?" Wulff said, "and where I'm supposed to transport this stuff after it's passed on to me?"

"You can call me Stavros," the little man had said. "It is as good a name as any; in my time I have used several. Names at best are abstractions, labels of the unknown."

"You don't look like a Greek."

"Stavros is not necessarily a Greek name, and then on the other hand, appearances can be deceiving. As far as where the disposition of your package will be made, you will be informed of your destination in Cuzco. It is best, perhaps, not to complicate matters. One thing at a time and it is now important for you to get to Cuzco. After we get you there we can worry, so to speak, about the next stop."

"If I get there," Wulff had said.

"Oh you'll get there," the little man said. "You'll get there, I have every confidence in you, Mr. Wulff. I wish that I had as much confidence in myself as I do in you, or, for that matter, as you do in you."

And then Wulff had left the room, considering the interview over. If there was one thing you learned from your years in the department it was a sense of timing of the pace of a conversation—and now one day later he was on a bus in the Andes crawling the final mile to the lost city of the Incas where someone, he was told, would meet the bus, take him to the next stop. It all seemed overly elaborate and a bit childish, but then they did things differently down here. He had learned that from Havana, and Cuba was just a trace of South America.

He was crammed in with a bunch of tourists, perhaps thirty of them, all of whom were beginning to gasp already from the thin air of the high mountains. The cabin of the bus was supposed to be pressurized in some way but it simply wasn't working; the air was thin and moist, stroking his lungs unevenly. Even though he was in much better shape than the rest of them, Wulff was beginning to feel it, a slow dilation and constriction in the arteries, a light-headedness, a feeling that rising rapidly from his seat would not be the proper thing to do. The guidebooks (he had done a little guidebook reading in the hotel) all said that it was advisable to spend a full day your first day in Cuzco just lying in bed, reading, resting and acclimating yourself to the atmosphere. But that was a joke; at fifty or sixty dollars-per, almost none of these people planned to be flat on their backs. Acclimatization was out of the question for him; unless his deliverers had other plans, he wanted to take the stuff and head right out. A seven-hour ride in, a seven-hour ride back—how much damage could it do him? Behind him, one of the women was throwing up.

Wulff held onto his own gorge, looked out the window, and saw a sequence of staggering views of bare mountain ranges. There were several thin, precipitous drops, and an impression from certain angles as the bus staggered up the last hills that there was a sheer drop of several miles into the canyons below. Abruptly, as he felt the nausea begin to come at him heavily in waves, he turned from the window, closed his eyes, and rested his head against the backrest. The bus driver, gasping like the rest of them, was trying to give some travelog on the lost city of the Incas—the fabulous rumors of hidden gold, the royal hunt of the sun, that somewhere within those ruins and artifacts still lay the wealth of an ancient civilization more ponderous than any on earth today. But he could barely get the words out and seemed no more interested than the rest of the tourists. Wulff kept his eyes shut, trying to blank his mind. The bus squawled to a sudden halt.

For a moment he thought that they had reached the depot, the station, whatever the hell their destination was, but opening his eyes slowly Wulff saw that it was nothing of the sort. Something was very wrong outside the bus, someone was banging frantically at the door, and even as this registered on him he heard the sound of shattering glass. Then the bus driver, momentarily arched behind his seat, mesmerized with terror—perhaps only attention—was trying desperately to get out of the seat, trying to reach the door, bellowing, the passengers already screaming. And then there was a short dull explosion, a forty-five caliber kind of sound. When Wulff had oriented himself to the sense of it, the bus driver was already taking the hit, grasping at his belly, mumbling something midway between a prayer and a shout as he collapsed to the floor. The passengers were still screaming but their sounds were curiously insubstantial in the thin, dead air, some of the passengers already gasping in silence. And then a man, short-bearded and with glaring eyes, came through the door of the bus, clawing and gripping his way in, his arms bloodstreaked to the elbows from the small and many punctures that the glass had made in them.

Wulff saw what was happening then, was once again able to slow down the action into some kind of perspective; reaching into his jacket for the gun that Stavros had given him he thought for one instant that he would not make it, the gun catching on his clothing, straining against the fabric, threads of cloth holding on tight. With a desperate wrench he was able to bring out the gun then, bring it to bear on the bearded man just as the bearded man had spotted Wulff. His eyes had swept down the line of the bus, moving up and down the rows like a conductor trying to spot an empty seat and starting at the back like a professional then moving forward he caught Wulff; Wulff could see the recognition beginning to flare into those eyes and then the man's point forty-five was coming forward. Wulff was still fighting to get a grip on the trigger of his pistol. He had never tried it out, taken it on faith from Stavros that it was loaded and worked. No more than one clip in the gun Stavros had said with a wink; if he needed to make more than six shots to get through all this he was going to be dead anyway, so why waste the ammunition?

His first shot went wild, the bearded man in reflex getting to the floor even as the shot spanged off. It hit one of the mirrors at the front of the bus, bounced, glanced off the dead driver who was now lying lengthwise in the small entering corridor. The bearded man screamed, less from fright, Wulff knew, than from simple rage and the need to spin it off for further concentration; then he had his gun up and Wulff could feel everything slow down. Momentarily he was in a long, narrow, grayly-illuminated tube, just he and the bearded man, the bearded man readying his shot and then the shot came off, but Wulff knew even as he heard the sound that it was also too high and it went somewhere into metal above him, ripping open beams, letting a little sunlight through. Both of them were reacting to the climate, it must be something about the thin atmosphere that blocked true concentration; or then again maybe bullets followed a different course in thinner air. That was something to think about. He would have to discuss it with a physicist, the differing effects of atmospheric content upon the pathway of bullets; it was certainly an effect that he had not been prepared for . . . And, bringing the gun into his hand, Wulff aimed the shot low, trying for the man's knees, and landed a shot dead into the man's stomach.

Blood erupted, like long-hidden gold coming to light for the scavengers. Blood boiled out of the man's stomach, geysered lightly into the air, then falling back, it covered the man like a blanket, a clear opaque panel of blood locking him in from waist to face—another aspect of the thin atmosphere, Wulff thought wryly. That must be it, the pressures under which the blood was driven took it much further under low air-pressure . . . But on the other hand, if that were so, if the pumping action of the heart enabled the blood to move more rapidly and higher, then why did one become lightheaded in thin air? Why was circulation reduced? Well, this was something to think about; all of this was something interesting to think about he supposed; he could call not only a physicist but a doctor into this hypothetical conference of his on varying phenomena in the mountains and at sea level . . . but no time for it now.

The passengers were still screaming thinly, those of them that could get breath; they sounded vaguely like seals croaking to themselves in a captive pool. Wulff, rising from his seat, had an impression of their staring eyes, their desperate attention, as he worked his way toward the front of the bus, almost stumbling over the corpse of the driver, then clearing himself and moving to the well. The driver was quite dead. His face, looking out leanly from the mess his body had become, was curiously detached, his tongue lay against his teeth; he seemed on the verge, in fact of making some kind of comment which would be summary, which would clear up all the mysteries of his death—pure illusion, of course, for the driver said nothing. Nor did the bearded assassin, still pooling richly in the aisle somewhat further on, the blood running freely in the little corridor of the aisle. Some of the passengers had lifted their feet instinctively, avoiding the rush of blood. One fat man toward the back had his camera out and in a curiously abstracted way was taking pictures, lashing images into his camera, his hands quivering behind the lens. *Each to his own,* Wulff thought. *Each to his own.*

He felt impelled to make an announcement. Foolish impulse perhaps, but then again this was his responsibility; it was his presence on the bus, not the driver's, not any of theirs, which had made their entrance into the lost city of the Incas so spectacular. "I'm sorry," he said, "I'm truly sorry," and then abandoned that line; that was absolutely foolish, death was nothing to apologize for, it was just a constant like sex or life itself and the sooner that most of these people got used to it the better off they would be. He backed down the stairs into the well. There were little pieces of glass all around, splinters of glass seemed to be beating around the air like flies but he avoided them. He got one foot on the ground, the other still in the well, feeling the ground rock beneath him. Unsteady terrain.

"I think it would be best if you walked in," Wulff said. Turning, he could see, just beyond an outcropping of rock, what appeared to be a depot. The assassin had probably been waiting there, had lost patience—who was to blame him?—had come out of the depot, fearful that he would somehow miss the entrance of the bus, and coming just up the line, had met them there. One thing was clear to Wulff, it was a suicide attack. The assassin would have had forty witnesses; he hardly could have proposed to kill everyone on the bus. That would not have been his intention at all.

Well, Calabrese certainly got men to work for him. You could say that he commanded a certain amount of loyalty.

"It's a short walk, a very short walk; nothing to it folks," Wulff said, taking on the aspect of a guide shuffling along a group of tourists to exhibit B. Putting his pistol away he headed toward the depot. He had absolutely no idea who would be waiting for him there, or if the men Stavros had promised would meet him would even show up. Or if there were any police.

Come to think of it, he thought grimly but kept on plowing through the terrain, really gasping now, the bearded assassin might himself have been one of the men whom Stavros had promised. Why not? Like Calabrese it would have been foolish of Stavros to send him out of town to do what he could have easily done face to face . . . but when you were dealing with solid figures, really great leaders and individualists like Stavros or Calabrese, there was no saying, absolutely no saying at all, how they might see a situation. They just did not function like ordinary men.

VIII

Stavros thought he had it figured out. Killing the man Dillon had shaken him (killing was nothing but if it were all the same he just did not want to get involved with Calabrese; it would be best not to stir that man's wrath if he could help it, but then again he had had no alternative to killing Dillon) but only for a little while. Now he felt more positive than ever that he had handled this situation right, that he was making the best use of it. He had not expected anything like Wulff coming into the Crillon, had not even known that he was there until he had seen him, as a matter of fact. But once he was confronted by the man's presence, how could he let him go without trying to make arrangements with him? He simply could not.

The stuff had to get out of Peru, that was all there was to it. Stavros had known that for a long time; it was just entirely too difficult a situation to bluff through. You could go on and on with something like this for a long time—set it up and keep it going so that you even thought you had some kind of autonomy—but sooner or later someone like Calabrese would pick up the word. It would leak through; there was too much at stake not to have a leak somewhere. And once Calabrese or someone like that got word of what was going on here, what Stavros had, what Stavros planned to do, it would be all over. He could fight off one of them, or even ten, but he could not possibly fend off the resource of the full organization to the north . . . and whatever internal problems that organization was having they were not fools; if they knew what Stavros was up to they would mass together in any way to take it away from him because the alternative was too dangerous.

So he knew he had done the right thing. The shit had to get out. Putting it into Wulff's hands was insanely dangerous for many reasons; the primary insanity might be that Wulff was absolutely committed to its destruction . . . and there was a very slight likelihood, if any, that the goods would arrive intact at the delivery point to the north. It would be a miracle if they did.

But that was not the point. Stavros had gone through hours of agony about that one, seeing a shipment like this irrevocably lost. But in the last analysis he had to go along with it and, in fact, even be grateful. Because saving the shipment was not the primary thing. It would be a bonus if it could be done, unquestionably, and it would be nice to be able to hold onto it for its profit potential and for the leverage it would give him. But the main thing was to get it out of Peru. It was a survival matter. If they found it here, not only would it be destroyed but he would be destroyed also. They would see it and trace it back and comprehend quickly enough what he had had in mind to do, and they would deal with him mercilessly. From his point of view he could hardly blame them. It was business. It was purely a business proposition. There would be no feeling as they killed him, they would kill him simply because it would obviously be too dangerous to let him

live . . . but nothing personal. Nothing was really personal in the
organizational politics of these people. It was like the practices of
another part of his life, a part which he refused even to think about
now in which there also had been nothing personal, in which what
had been done had been done by men who did it not for the joy but
only the sense of it . . . and took no responsibility. There *was* no
responsibility. It simply originated in circumstances.

All right. Get it out then. Get it out any way he could. He did not trust
Wulff ever to turn the shipment over, but if he knew one thing it was
where interests could lie, where the checks and balances of
relationships truly rested, and Wulff and he were in perfect
accordance on this one point: Wulff needed to get out of the country,
the drugs needed to get out of the country; if each was the only way
that the other could, then they would. Then they certainly would.

Stavros sweated it out, then. If things were going according to the
schedule he had prepared, Wulff was at that moment in Cuzco,
arranging the transfer. At this moment, as Stavros sat in his office and
ran the progression of scenes through his mind, he was heading under
escort for the helicopter which would take him the first leg of the way.
But what if he were not? What if Calabrese had informants deep, deep
within his organization and had anticipated all of this, was already
working on a counter-thrust? What if—Stavros jumped as he had the
thought—what if Wulff had been intercepted and shot down?

No. He would not think of it. Life was real, rational, earnest and he
was cleverer than Calabrese. He had planned for all of this; unlike
Calabrese he had never been so stupid as to present the enemy on his
very ground the means of his salvation as Calabrese had done. He
must have faith that now as before he was superior to Calabrese and
that when their two intelligences meshed lock-to-lock through the
agencies of other men he, Stavros, would be the superior. His instincts
told him this was so. And he knew many things that Calabrese did
not.

He waited and he waited and toward nightfall he received a clear
psychic flash that he had won. Somehow Wulff had gotten through. He
had gotten into Cuzco, Calabrese's men having been either unalerted
to his coming or unsuccessful in their attempts to block him. He had
gotten into Cuzco, had taken over the shipment and now was on the
next level of operations. As the impact of this hit him Stavros almost
gasped, his body becoming a fist as it cramped over, then he relaxed
and smiled. He believed profoundly in his psychic input; it had saved
him all his life, it would not fail him now. If the inference was that
Wulff had made it, then he could accept this. He could accept the

inference. He was halfway out of it and toward survival.

He celebrated. He sat alone in his working suite and poured himself a victory drink of scotch, three fingers, taken neat. They made him feel good, and another three fingers made him feel even better. The sons of bitches thought that they could overcome Stavros but he had showed them. He had showed them! Then he remembered that the sons of bitches had thought nothing, probably, because they did not even know of the trade that Stavros was trying to set up, which was the reason they had not tried to overcome him, and this made him intensely solemn. He took another three shots of scotch to quench the solemnity.

And so he made it through the evening, made it through the evening in his own unique and individual way, just, he thought, as Wulff had to, as all of them had to . . . until one of his lieutenants got him on the phone and said that he had something to tell Stavros and said it was important and Stavros said okay, tell him, and the lieutenant came in and in a very grave and distracted way told Stavros that the helicopter in Cuzco had gone down somewhere in the mountains. Natives had seen the pieces. The pieces were unmistakable. They had brought the reports right into the Crillon and the associate knew it and now Stavros knew it too.

IX

The first thing that got you, Wulff thought, was the incredible height, the sense of distance in the terrain; unlike America where everything was impacted, driven in upon itself, here in the lost city of the Incas there was a sense of distance unknown to the north, a scale of landscape entirely different from that on which all the assumptions of America had been based . . . that life was controllable because compressed. Doubtless that was why the pioneers had cut away at the awesome continent above, closed it in with walls and cities, to restrict the unimaginable emptiness. But Peru, outside of the cities which were American imports, was a different culture; here it was not life but death, or at least acceptance of it, which was celebrated, and in these ranges one could see the outlines of one's death coming upon one as clearly and closely as if it were perceived in sleep. And this was perhaps, or perhaps not, the key to Peru; to the lost city of the Incas it was dreamlike. The conquistadors might have had that feeling of unreality as they closed ground upon the ancient civilization, a feeling of consequences simultaneously heightened and reduced because what was happening here was not happening in the ordered sense of Western civilization. Death was a constant here but not disproportionate; it co-existed with life, that was all. Life and death, two sides of the same great balance wheel and little discrimination to be made between the two.

Perhaps this was why no one at the depot had paid any attention to him as he came in except for the two men who were evidently waiting for him. Two men had died just beyond that turn in the road, one by Wulff's hand, but it made no difference; death being the omnipresent quality it was, it could hardly bestir any excitement. The two men recognized him immediately and came toward him; they reached toward him with a shared intensity as if they were wired through the same electrical socket, were being powered by the same impulse, but at the last instant each of them withdrew and Wulff saw that they were not going to touch him. He looked from one face to the next, trying for some kind of differentiation, but there was none. They looked the same—their heavy, blunt faces, their compressed aspect, the black, expressionless clothing they wore which might have been business suits if they were wearing ties, the pointed shoes and in their lapels some kind of obscure emblem which he could not fathom. More than anything else, they looked like paired miniatures of Stavros.

"What is it?" he said, "where are we supposed to go?" They looked at him without curiosity, miniature men, miniaturized eyes; in a moment he realized that they were not going to answer him and that language had not been one of the factors keyed into them, at least in this instance. Truly, there was nothing to say; he should have understood that. Much of life here was sub-verbal.

They motioned, both of them in the same gesture, and Wulff followed, trudging from the bus depot. As he came out of the enclosure, the dry hot air of the mountains hitting him fully again and filling his lungs with emptiness, he thought that something was going to happen this time to yank the situation around; for there, up the hill, were the passengers from the bus trudging slowly downward, some of them looking at him, a few waving langorously (actually they were waving frantically but in the climate could not generate much energy; Wulff knew that) and Wulff had a vivid image of flight, pursuit, entrapment, and a long, ringing collision with stone as he fell down the faces of the mountains . . . but nothing whatsoever happened. Most of what went on occurred within the spaces of his own mind, and in truth, at least here, people were simply not that interested in him. He followed the wide, flat backs of the two men, carefully putting one foot in front of the other, concentrating upon the activity of walking in the way that a child might—one step, two step, pause, hesitate, one step, two step, reaching out for the oxygen and the will to power himself between strides.

A few yards down from the depot there was an old car, a 1951 Oldsmobile he thought it might be, already idling. One of the men gestured for him to get into the rear seat and Wulff did, a faint, ominous sweetness coming up from the cushions and the floor like cyanide although it could only have been age. The man to his side slammed the door on him, got into the passenger seat while the other walked slowly around, got into the driver's seat and then sat there breathing for a few moments while his respiration slowed to normal. They acted as if they had all the time in the world. Perhaps that was exactly the point; they did have all the time in the world. American versus warm-climate concepts of time. The car began to move. Hydramatic transmission, rough on the shifts, two-speed as all of them had been until 1955 when Oldsmobile along with the other GM cars had introduced the three-speed, the what-did-you-call-it, the turbo-hydromatic automatic transmission. First shift point in normal driving at 12 miles an hour, second shift point at 27. That was a hell of a good transmission except that they had a way of going bad at forty thousand miles or so; Olds couldn't get the bands right. Of course the two-speed was nothing to rave about; generally speaking you could expect to drop two transmissions on an Oldsmobile Futuramic 88 within three years of delivery and each replacement was a cool two hundred dollars. Why was he thinking of all this? Why did it all come back to him, why was his mind racing through ancient Oldsmobile specifications when he was supposed to be picking a million dollar load of shit out of the Andes, running it back in exchange for his freedom to some unknown destination up north. Who the hell knew? He guessed that it probably had to do with the atmosphere here; he was still lightheaded. Then again, that was no excuse.

"Where is it?" Wulff said, the car rolling, "where are we going to go?" In front of him the two heads bobbed, unspeaking. "I said," Wulff said, "where are we supposed to go for the shit?"

There was a longer, thicker pause here and he realized that they were not going to say anything. Probably they did not speak English, although that in itself was no excuse for ducking the inquiry; they could have nodded, demonstrated to him with their hands, at least, that they would be delighted to converse with him but did not know what he was saying. Bastards.

The car, maddeningly, was still climbing: there had been a rise behind the depot which Wulff had not seen approaching and they were still ascending, going into the mountains. The road was barely one lane wide so that an opposing car could have mashed them to shreds if the driver of the Futuramic did not back off, and the driver showed no such disposition. The car was, in fact—thin air, age and all— managing fifty miles an hour on the ascent and picking up speed all the time. Wulff felt himself thrust into the slick, dark cushions behind, felt his own perspiration penetrating his shoulder blades. "Where are we going?" he said again. You never knew. If he kept it up they might come out with something to say after all.

But they did not. They seemed stolid, immovable, part of the machinery in front, as inarticulate as the landscape itself, just as menacing. Well, perhaps Stavros selected his men for their lack of articulation, gave them strict orders to say nothing. Why take it so personally? Why take it personally at all? "You know," Wulff said, "it's all a little too much for me. I mean I'm entitled to feel that it's all going by a little too rapidly. Don't you think so? I mean, don't you think that that's a good point, that there's too much happening here and I don't even know what the hell is going on?" He sounded plaintive, petulant. Well, so be it. Self-pity was not quite the proper emotion for the circumstance but at this time it made more sense than almost any attitude. He had been bucked from Calabrese to Stavros to these men with inconvenience and murder in between and there was still the feeling of pervasive unreality; matters were entirely out of his hands, there seemed no way that he could connect with them.

"All right," he said, "all right then, the hell with it." He settled lower into the back seat sulkily, shrugging his shoulders, closed his eyes. If they didn't want to tell him anything that was their business. See if he would care. If he fucked up their job, if everything fell through simply because they refused to address him as a human being and tell him what the hell was going on here, it wouldn't be his fault. *Let it be on their heads.* Let everything be on them; it was no longer his responsibility. As close as he could get to responsibility in his position, he was absolutely out of it now. In the normal course of events, he would have been dead, anyway. *So fuck it.*

Dazzling views of the ruined city assaulted him. Cuzco was in a plain, a shallow bowl of land nestled in the mountain ranges, as it were, protected on all sides by the mountainous territory. Doubtless the Incas had cleaved it out of rock themselves, some advantage taken of their natural terrain, but so much of this had doubtless been done by men, scrappling away at rock. He smelled something sweet in the car, something that was not upholstery or transmission fluid and looked up to see that one of the men had lit a joint, marijuana he supposed, and was inhaling it meditatively, holding it like a cigarette, taking huge irregular puffs now and then and flicking ashes from the end of it indiscriminately. He certainly was not conserving the joint the way that any American teenager would learn to within five minutes of his initiation. Any American would say it was a waste of grass. But then again, maybe the stuff was more plentiful here. Probably it was.

He was relieved to see that the driver at least did not take any part of the joint. That was good; driving and pot did not mix. Not that he was any too sure that it was pot; there could have been cocaine, hashish, peyote rolled up in that joint. Although they were usually pipe drugs, there was no accounting for foreign customs.

The car came to an abrupt halt, spinning against a rock facing to the right of it, the driver yammering. Wulff had to hold on desperately to the back seat to avoid pitching through the windshield. The man with the joint screamed and cursed, threw the remains out the window violently even as the car was braking. Then, the first of them to recover, Wulff saw that the road had been blocked by something that looked, at least at first glance, like a truck; seen secondarily it was a van of some sort from which men with guns were already spilling. They were waving their hands at the car, whose driver was now paled and slumped almost wholly behind the wheel. Abruptly there was a *spang!* something growing in the windshield. The joint-smoker screamed and himself tried to huddle down in the seat, but a second *spang!* caught him in the forehead and he fell into his blood.

Wulff was already free of the door and rolling, his body being battered by the stones. Oh shit. Shit on it anyway.

X

Calabrese knew that he had trouble early on, even before he got word of Dillon. Any fool could tell just from the sense of the situation that there was plenty of trouble, but he believed in functioning step by step. That was surely the only way to go in this business, and maybe Dillon would eventually get through to him. And, when Dillon hadn't reported back hours after he should have, well, maybe there was trouble in the international phone lines or Dillon was having difficulty in finding a phone. It was best to look at matters in that way. You simply could not get far looking too much ahead in this business. Past the end of the immediate problem, that was about it.

But by ten that evening he had known Dillon had blown it. It was a matter of instinct, that was all; you didn't need much objective material in this business to see what was going on. Those who needed it were only to be pitied. People who needed the facts laid out in front of them were stacked at the bottom of the river. A suggestion here, a possibility there, a lapsed conduct, the look in a man's eyes, the way a woman might look at that same man . . . and you knew everything. He put through an international call to the Crillon and got Stavros. Ordinarily this would have been a three-hour process but Calabrese knew a few people and he knew how to get hold of them even through the blind of pseudonyms that the phone company used. He got the call through in fifteen minutes to Stavros direct.

"Where is he?" Calabrese said without preamble. If Stavros did not recognize his voice at this point then Stavros was a fool and Calabrese would not have credited himself with such luck.

"Where is who?" Stavros said. Even through the network of the international phone lines, the ten-second delay, the flattening, mechanical interposition of wires and tapes which meant that he was not hearing Stavros' voice but only a reassembled recording of it . . . even through all of this Calabrese could sense the fear.

"You know who I fucking mean," Calabrese said. "Your house guest."

"I haven't seen him in a long time. Not all day."

"Are you sure?"

"I'm quite sure."

"I'm a little concerned," Calabrese said. "I sent some friends of mine after him. They should have located him by now."

"I wouldn't know anything about that."

"I think you know everything about that."

"Leave me alone," Stavros said after a flat little pause. "Just leave me alone. I have nothing to do with your affairs. He is merely a guest in my hotel."

"Listen to me, you fucking Nazi," Calabrese said, "I know what you're up to. I know exactly what the hell you're up to down there. You think I'm a fucking fool? I let all of that go; I didn't give a shit. After all, I'm not in the business. But you're fucking around with my life now."

There was a much longer pause and Stavros said, "I don't know what you're talking about."

"You know what I'm talking about. You fucking well know everything that I'm saying . . . you Nazi son of a bitch." Calm down, Calabrese said to himself, feeling his gorge rising in his throat. There is no need for this, no need, and you are an old man. Stavros is thirty-five hundred miles away. "I don't like it," Calabrese said, "I want you to turn him up."

"How can I turn him up if I don't know where he is?"

"I don't know. That's your problem."

"You're crazy," Stavros said. The distance was giving him courage. "You've got to be out of your mind."

"I'll show you how much out of my mind I am."

"You think that I have something to do with this man? He is not in my custody. He is merely using my hotel, that is all. My auspices, my rooms. I bear no responsibility for this at all."

"I can do anything I want to do with you," Calabrese said. "You think that you're a long way out of the picture, that you can do anything you want to do, but you can't. You're not a free man. I know everything about you. I can kill you with two phone calls, that's how far from me you are. I want you to produce him."

"Why should I produce him?" Stavros said. Slowly he was turning around. Calabrese could sense the initial, instinctive fear giving way to defiance. No, not defiance, not quite, something more terrible than that: a low-key assurance that he knew things which Calabrese did not. Calabrese did not like that. He did not like it at all. "I don't have to produce him," Stavros said, "and if you think you can kill me for failing to produce a man then you are genuinely crazy. If you do anything to me the word will get around what kind of person you are and you will never get any help in this country again. In many countries."

"Don't argue with me," Calabrese said. "Just produce him."

"I don't have to produce him. Anyway," Stavros said, almost lightly, "that is the purest kind of stupidity and foolishness. Produce him so that you can kill him, that's all. What if the job has been done for you? What if he is already dead?"

"I'm going to get you."

"I'm sick of your threats," Stavros said, "I'm sick of you Americans and your threats of murder. You hold life so cheaply that the threat of its removal means nothing to you. Or to me. I do not know where your man is and I remind you that this is my hotel. Your men are here at my sufferance. I'm going to throw them out."

"You're fucking me up."

"No I'm not. You're fucking yourself up."

"I told you. I know what you're doing down there. I let you get away with it for a long time because it didn't mean shit to me. Like I said, I'm not in the business." Calabrese reached for his pack of cigarettes, cracked two of them and threw them across the room. *Son of a bitch. The son of a bitch.* Sitting in his barred office in Peru, the Nazi, and laughing at him. "But this is too much," Calabrese said, trying to make his voice come level. "This is too fucking much. I'm going to put you out of business now."

"No. You have put yourself out of business. That's what you have done. You have delivered my salvation unto me and I am grateful."

Obviously the man had gone crazy. The distortions in the voice were not purely the product of the international lines. He had never heard Stavros sounding like this before. But there was an undertone of purpose as well, and it was this purpose which Calabrese found terrifying. "I'll show you your salvation," he said.

"You have. You already have."

"I'll show you your fucking salvation, Stavros, and I'll make you beg for release from it."

"I don't care anymore," Stavros said thinly. The connection must have been going bad; the voice was now fading. "I'm not interested in your threats or promises anymore. I'm going to attend to my own set of purposes now, and the hell with yours. This is my country and this is my hotel, Calabrese."

"That's a fucking joke. Your country? It's no more your country than mine."

"It's been mine for thirty years," Stavros said. "I'm not afraid of you anymore. I'm not afraid of anything. I don't have to be afraid," he said and broke the connection, leaving Calabrese looking at an empty phone. The first, flaming sense of disbelief modulated into a dull, gasping rage that moved through him like an electrical impulse through wire, and then Calabrese found that he was trembling all over.

He was a fool. He had been a fool. Face it: Walker, that crooked cop, that son of a bitch, had been right. He had had Wulff face-to-face in these very rooms and he had not killed him. Why had he not killed him? Was it that he was losing his grip? Did it all come down to that?

"It doesn't matter what it comes down to," Calabrese muttered to himself and he was right. It really didn't. Fuck the psychology of the thing; for whatever reason he had blown it very badly with Wulff, but that was behind him; what was ahead was the necessity now to rectify the mistake. It was a problem, one of the biggest problems he had ever had, but at least it was the kind of difficulty that could lend itself to relatively rational resolution. You moved ahead with a practical business problem like this; you brought in the artillery and you did what you could.

The only way you got into difficulty was wondering about the motives for a condition in the first place, but that had never been his

everything; doubtless the man had had no suspicion that Wulff would get into a situation like this, would have the safety of his own men to consider. *Well, consider their safety*, Wulff thought; both of them were dead in the Oldsmobile. Another high shot came out. The man inside the Buick was panicking, no question about that. As much as he had the situation in hand, he was unable to take advantage of it; three deaths to his left and right must have given him plenty to think about. In fact he might have absolutely no more taste for combat at this point, and then, confirming this line of thought, Wulff heard the engine of the Buick roar, lifter sounds, valves tapping, little golden streaks from the mufflers. The man had broken. All that he wanted to do was to get out.

The Buick reared backwards, tracking up dirt, then the old Dynaflow gearing clashed, the car bucked forward and then it was heading toward him, the driver flat out on the gas pedal, trying to run him over. Well, that was a new way of looking at the situation; the man had guts after all. But you could not both drive and shoot at the same time, not with any real accuracy whatsoever, and it was this calculation which caused Wulff to make his last effort; he allowed the car to come upon him, holding his ground tentatively at a high point, bringing his pistol high but not firing. And then as the car kept on rolling, what had occurred to Wulff must have occurred to the driver— the realization that for acceleration there must also be braking action in equal degree and that in coming off the road, roaring toward the abutment where Wulff was standing, he was taking a very real chance of losing the car and going over the cliffs. The driver, in his rage or cunning or some mad combination of the two, had lost sight of this calculation for the instant, so eager was he to ram Wulff over the abutment. But now he came back into contact and the big car slewed wildly left, the brakes screaming as the driver tried to bring it down. Wulff heard the spattering of pistol, the driver trying to struggle off a shot or two as he worked the brakes and the wheel but that was not an intelligent idea, not at all because the shots went completely wild and meanwhile, left to its own devices, the car was skittering, literally inching toward the abutment now. The shots stopped, the car began to make the croaking, screaming noises of an animal as the driver worked desperately to brake it down, concentrating on nothing else and Wulff, feeling like a matador working with an oversized, enraged and particularly clumsy bull, stepped sideways then as the car dived upon him. He moved a couple of feet out of its path and then, leveling his pistol, putting no thought into it and less calculation (because if you began to think about what should be instinctive you merely lost control altogether), he put one shot through the side window where the drivers head ought to be.

There was a spatter of glass, the old plate glass smashing and tinkling, imploding within, and for a moment Wulff did not know if he had gotten the man or not. Then the car, suddenly straightening on its skidding course, roared with power, something coming like a stone down on the accelerator; then it swayed precipitously, went out of control, headed toward an abutment and began to roll. The driver, only dimly seen from this aspect, a fish under glass in layers of water, was obviously trying desperately to regain control of the car. He was flopping within the aquarium that the interior of the Buick had become, and Wulff could hear his gulping and screaming. And then slowly, majestically, real aspects of grace in it, a grace magnified by the age of the car, the heavy, dull sheen of the metal which some prideful Peruvian had doubtless polished at one time to a second gloss that outshone the first, the glaring portholes, three of them on the side of the car catching the last of the light . . . as all of this came together the car glided toward the last possible point of stoppage, poised like a diver on the lip of the chasm . . . and then flipped soundlessly into the valley below. Hand on hip, still gripping the gun, Wulff watched it fall with a kind of wonder. The soundlessness of the movement, the scope of the disaster covered by that soundlessness, was awesome. And then the car hit—glass, fluids, metal spraying like gunshot from its surfaces as it plunged into the chasm—and as the first fires leaped from the car, Wulff heard the screaming then, fracturing the sound of metal with its long, bloody sound.

But not for too long. The screaming was cut off in mid-syllable, a lick of fire overtaking the screamer's lungs, searing them to ash in a single, terrible burst. And unable to bear it anymore Wulff turned, turned from the site where the car had hit to see the villagers staring at him—five, no seven or eight of them in a solemn row, hats in hands, a penitential posture, eyes solemn and reaching. They looked like a cluster of distant relatives arriving at a wake, unaccounted for and embarrassed but eager, eager as such relatives almost always are, to please. To please and ease. To please and ease the situation.

XII

The helicopter which was supposed to take him out with the shipment had been sabotaged and had gone down with the pilots in the mountains on their way to pick it up. Therefore he would have to get the stuff out of the mountains on foot. There was no other way. That at least Wulff was able to gather from one of the natives who was able to speak English, but the English was halting and convoluted and he was not able to get much further than that. What he gathered was that Calabrese had called in the heavy reinforcements, that Stavros's plans had fallen through and that Wulff was very much on his own. That was no surprise. Of course, it didn't help matters too much either.

The man who passed the shipment on to him and who spoke English was an old, old man with a beaten face, a face long since smashed into impermeability. These people appeared to live in a small settlement of some kind behind the tourist city of Cuzco, appeared to have blended into the landscape and were living with little more than stone-age implements. But for a product of a culture seemingly without technology of any sort the old man seemed surprisingly sophisticated and all of them, at least those that came by and who spoke to him, seemed to know a good deal. Wulff wondered about the setup—he wouldn't be surprised if they were all employees of Stavros and if this was not some kind of blind, a thriving little network tucked in behind Cuzco manned by people who appeared to be the most poverty-stricken and hopeless kind of natives—but he guessed that it did not matter. None of it mattered except getting the stuff out of here. The old man made that very clear to him, not that Wulff didn't know it well himself already.

He retched twice in the thin air, the second time, after his conversation with the old man a little blood had come out of his nostrils mingling with the sputum, and it had been at that point that the old man told him that it would be best to lie down for a while; there was certainly no getting out of Cuzco before nightfall anyway. So they had made Wulff a pallet in an empty tent thrown up against a pile of slag and he had laid in the tent for a long time, sometimes sleeping, sometimes not, coming from between the flaps a couple of times to check the terrain, seeing only the slow passage of the natives in front of him in what appeared to be a self-sufficient settlement. Two miles to the north, just below, was the tourist mill, the cable cars, the guides and the lost city of the Incas but that was merely gilt; *this*, goddammit, this right here was the lost city of the Incas and he was in the middle of it. He was a living artifact.

They had given him the shit in an innocuous-appearing burlap sack. Wulff had looked in it immediately, suspicious of course, wanting to see if Stavros was playing some kind of elaborate trick on him or, worse yet, if the people down here did not know shit from the truth; but the first look, the first careful test with a moistened finger had convinced him: Stavros knew exactly what he was doing. This was beyond a doubt the purest, the most extravagantly clean shit he had ever had contact with. It was unadulterated, in its most natural state, ready to be juiced, cut, bound, knifed; and market value was pretty much of a fiction when you got into an area of this sort but, yes, the street value here would be well into a million, maybe multiples of that. It all depended on how it was cut. *That* was what predicated market value even more than the original worth of shipment . . . how much and what kind of adulteration would be going into it. The peasants of Cuzco had done their job. They had turned out a product of inestimable worth. Now it was up to Stavros and his agents where it went from there.

If indeed this was Stavros's shipment. You simply did not know; he might be handling this for someone else. In neither case did it matter; the problem was to get the drugs out, get them out of this fucking country and back to the States. Once in the States it was a new situation altogether. The thought had occurred to Wulff that once he was back onto his own turf, if the drugs were still in his possession and he had the luck to work it through that way, it would be a new ball game entirely. What would Stavros do if he charted his own course from there? The best disposition for those drugs would be at the bottom of the El Paso. Or maybe he could play this by instinct, could use them as bait to suck out Calabrese and kill the old son of a bitch. That would be worthwhile, killing Calabrese. If he did nothing else, if he had done nothing else, that would almost justify his odyssey in itself, getting rid of that ruined, terrible, corrupt old man.

But you had to take it step by step and now he would be all kinds of a fool, a complete fool to calculate what he would do if he got the drugs out of the country. There was no saying that he would get them out of the country. Calabrese's men had almost killed him twice; now, it seemed, they had sabotaged the helicopter that would have taken him out. You could not, against an enemy like this, make any deductions on your future course whatsoever, except to accept the fact that you would have to go step by step. Obviously, the old man regretted his mistake. He regretted it severely; he wished that he had killed Wulff face-to-face. Well, perhaps he would have that chance once again. Perhaps they would have the opportunity to meet face-to-face. Wulff looked forward to that; no matter how dim the chance, it was at least a possibility and worth pursuing.

He went from retching to uneasy, clotted dreams in which Marie Calvante rose from the floor of the tenement and greeted him with open, astonished eyes, telling him once again of her love, and on the floor of that tenement he took her, bearing her back to the planks again and giving back to her what she had offered him and more as well; he passed from that dream to a muddled conception of the girl in San Francisco whom he had fucked, who had restored him at least partially to himself and the two images muddled, however dimly. The sexual content of the dreams gutted him and passed him onto another terrain completely in which he moved into asepsis, confronted by a bleak, gray panorama of the faces of all the men who had tried to kill him, from New York to Boston to San Francisco or Havana, and these dreams no less than any of the others left him quivering and spent, too much happening in too little time, a compression of incident which he could not understand, let alone handle. And then somewhere in the middle of one of those dreams, a dream in which he had confronted Albert Maraco in his Long Island home and once again on a burning staircase had killed him, in the middle of this dream he arose from it the way that a penitent after a long time, his grief done, might come from an altar, coming into all the cool, deadly spaces of the tent in which he lay and found that the old man who had talked with him was leaning over him with a mingled expression of compassion and inquiry, his eyes interested yet somehow curiously dead. There was a welter of experience behind those eyes which Wulff could hardly grasp, let alone appreciate. "Are you stronger?" the old man said and then without pausing, "I hope you are stronger, because it is time to go."

"Yes," Wulff said. He came off the pallet slowly, feeling strength reconstitute itself in all of the crevices of his body. "Yes, I'm stronger now. I think—"

"Night," the old man said, "night is always better in which to travel. Also, we have reports that your presence here is extremely dangerous."

"To whom? To me or to you?"

"To us," the old man said, "of course to us. We are not concerned with you, we are concerned with us." Some complex failure of language seemed to overtake him; he struggled for sound. "You must realize we have our own culture," he said finally, "our own—"

"Your own way of life to protect. Your own interests, your own people."

"What's that?" the old man said.

"Nothing," Wulff said, "nothing at all." He looked outside tentatively, then came back, brushed sleep and dust from him in a series of motions, then picked up the sack. It had a faint warmth. The old man looked at it implacably. "How am I supposed to get out of here?" he said.

"We will arrange an escort at least part of the way."

"But how?"

The old man shrugged. "The roads would be extremely dangerous," he said. "There is only one way in and one way out if you go by the road. You will have to go through the mountains."

"I figured as much," Wulff said, "but how am I to get through the mountain?"

"By horseback."

Wulff hefted the sack. "I should have known that too," he said, "but that's going to be a problem. You see my experience doesn't cover any time with the mounted police. Somehow I missed that one."

"What's that?" the old man said. He looked genuinely puzzled yet eager if he could to derive some information. "I do not quite understand you."

"That's all right," Wulff said, "that's perfectly all right. I don't understand any of it, either. I don't even think that I understand myself."

"That is a common problem," the old man said after a pause.

"Isn't it?" Wulff said.

XIII

Stavros said, "This is my room. This is my hotel. Get out."

The man with the gun leaned against the wall in an easy, casual posture and said, "Don't be ridiculous. I'm not going to get out and you don't control anything anymore."

"I mean it," Stavros said. He held himself in check. He held himself from doing something foolish, disastrous, stupid, something like going to the desk drawer in a lunge to try to seize his gun. This man was no fool; Stavros would never complete the action. He would get his brains blown out for his trouble. The only way around this situation was to talk his way through, but he did not know how much talking he could do at this moment. His mouth felt dry, impacted, his hands fluttering. He looked at his hands with almost clinical detachment, noting the fear that was manifested through the tremor. Odd. So it could get to him also. Philosophy and resignation be damned; he was as frightened of dying as anyone else. All right. He would remember that, he would remember that for the next time. He did not hold life so cheaply after all.

No one could hold life cheaply. No matter how painful you might have found it, no matter what the distance you cultivated, it was still the only thing you knew. The other thing, death, was an abstraction. Stavros had seen heroic men—men whom he knew to be powerful, self-contained, in control of themselves—whimpering like puppies at the moment of death because nothing in the handling of life affected the ability to manage death. It was not to be held against them. It was no disgrace.

"Put the gun away," he said to the man. One of Calabrese's operatives of course. He could be none other. But he was a different sort from the types that Calabrese had sent to the hotel in the past; this man did not have the look of being a freelancer or stringer hired out, but of direct payroll. Top troops. Top operative. He had misjudged, Stavros had, that was all. He did not think that the old man would take the trouble to move and certainly he had never pictured him moving this quickly.

"I'm not going to put the gun away," the man said. He looked at it with the absent affection with which a man might confront a friendly dog. "I'm going to kill you with it. Your trouble is that you're stupid, Stavros. We know what you've been doing here for a long time, but as long as it didn't interfere we let it go. The old man is a generous person. But now you're getting out of range."

"Don't be ridiculous."

"You wanted to turn a miserable little operation, that was your affair," the man said. "Live and let live, that's the old man's philosophy. But you didn't want that Stavros. You wouldn't let us live." He gestured with the gun. "So I'm going to kill you."

"No you won't," Stavros said with a sudden positiveness. He looked up, directly confronted the man for the first time. The man was somewhat younger than he had appeared on first impression, maybe only in his early thirties; it was merely his eyes and unshaven appearance that had given him the aspect of an older man. He was younger than Stavros had taken him to be, and that meant that he would be less certain. Always, inevitability, youth could be equated with uncertainty. That was a rule of judgment by which he would stand. "You're not going to kill me," he said, "because if you were, you already would have. You wouldn't have talked it out. You're here to bluff me, intimidate me, and it won't work."

"Yes, it will work."

"No, it won't," Stavros said. Keeping control of himself, forcing an assurance that he was trying to draw from the air and push inside himself, he opened the desk drawer, looked at the loaded pistol within. He did not reach for it at the moment, merely considered it. "Get out of here," he said, "get out of my room. Get out of my hotel."

"No," the man said but something shattered in his complexion. There was an impression of sweat on his forehead. "Don't make any moves, Stavros. Don't go inside that drawer."

"Of course I'm going to go inside that drawer. I'm going to take out my pistol and shoot you."

"No you won't."

"Yes I will. You won't shoot me. You've got your orders to bluff, to threaten, frighten . . . but you don't have a kill order. If you did you would have already. I know about death," Stavros said. "I know everything about death; I was living it before you were born." He reached toward the desk drawer. "Get out of here," he said.

The man pointed the gun at him. "You're a fool," he said, "you don't know what you're dealing with. Get your hand away from there!"

"No," Stavros said. He was very frightened but matters were in progress. He was gambling everything on his instincts but this was not the first time that he had done so. When you came right down to it, a man had only his instincts on which to draw. You could talk all you wanted to about logic, reason, causes, consequence, but that was all deceit. Typical American deceit; the pushing away of the irrational when it was the irrational on which men's lives rested. That was why America was going insane, because they had denied the irrational for too long and now it was reaching out into everything. But he, Stavros, had accepted the irrational as long as he remembered. Man was a creature of the blood, the blood was mysterious and corrupt, it moved in strange and various directions, always coming back upon itself. Could you pull a spoon of water from the sea, replace it, spoon out exactly the same water? No more than that could you pluck a motive or a reason from the stew of the unconscious. It was merely there. It was there all the time. "No," he said again, "I'm not going to stop." His hand was on the gun now. It curled into his hand in a gentle, familiar way. He had been feeling this gun all his life; it communicated little waves of pleasure into his palm. He hoisted it, looked at the man across the desk.

"See?" he said, "and now we are equal."

The man's eyes were bleak and serious. He held his own gun steadily, leveled on Stavros's forehead. "That was very foolish," he said.

"It was not foolish. Nothing is foolish. You have no orders to kill me and therefore would be in serious trouble if you did. You can take no action against me. Get out of my room."

"It would have been better the other way," the man said, the shape of his face, the arc of his mouth not changing. "We thought that we could reason with you. We thought that you could give us some information."

"I have no information to give you."

"You have a lot of information to give us," the man said. "We would like to know where Wulff went, when he will reappear, what you have assigned him to do specifically. We are much less interested in you than in Wulff, as you might suspect. You could have told us that."

"I will tell you nothing," Stavros said. Some of the fear was easing. He had been in terror at the time he had moved for the gun, he would admit that . . . it was not pleasant to face the prospect of your imminent death as you performed the only action that might possibly save your life; poised that way, on the edge between life and death there had been a sheer, knife-thrust of terror which had skewered him apart, bisecting him at the crevice between those two possibilities.

But now, holding the gun, holding the situation against himself, he had the feeling that he had passed through the crisis. This young gunman, this messenger from Calabrese would not kill him here because he would not risk the loss of his own life. Life was too precious for this young man; Stavros could play on the necessity this one had to hang on, a necessity which would go far beyond Calabrese. "I will tell you nothing," Stavros said again and clicked the chambers ominously. "Get out of here now."

The gunman shook his head. He sighed. "You understand you give me no alternative," he said. "You're calling on me to kill you."

"I'll kill you too."

"You won't be reasonable," the gunman said and sighed again. His eyes blinked, he shook his head and seemed then to leap over the void of a decision, came out on the other side, kicking for balance but finding himself. His eyes cleared as if with relief. "The trouble with all you goddamned Germans is that you're the least reasonable people who ever lived. You talk a lot about rationality but it comes down to blood-stubbornness and mysticism."

"I agree with that," Stavros said. "I agree with that. I have not been a rational man since 1945. For the last thirty years I have accepted fully the truth of what you say, that life is a mystery, a dream, a disaster, that it can be understood only in terms of its uncertainties and irrationalities. You tell me nothing," he said, "you offer me no analysis, you offer me no judgments, you offer me nothing that I have not long, long since understood," and he raised the gun then, and with a little cocking motion pulled the trigger.

The bullet hit the gunman hard in the stomach and with one groan of astonishment, he lurched toward the floor and Stavros was already falling out of the way of the expected return shot . . . but even though he had calculated everything, even taken into account the pain of what that shot might be, he had not calculated in any way whatsoever the pain of what hit him. It felt like a brick hit his forehead, tearing it open, and even as he became aware of the ringing pain, the feeling of spreading, oozing breakage above the neck, he saw the blood which sprang like a curtain in front of his eyes, a sheet of blood ripping down from his forehead and spreading its way in the ledge of consciousness. *I'm dead*, Stavros thought, *my God, he's killed me* and a far different part of him on another planet, the part of him that held the gun, tried to pull the trigger, deposit another shot, but somehow he could not connect brain and hand in the old, smooth familiar way. The command was blocked at his armpit, fibers of pain opening like a scar in that place and then, as he sat there paralyzed, the second shot caught him in the windpipe, in the bloodiest part of the neck.

Now Stavros felt himself overcome by his blood; he felt that the blood was coming not from two but from twenty parts of himself, rivers of blood roiling over him like implication and in the center of it a dim mewing, the sound of some animal in whimpering distress which he thought for a moment was the man across his desk but which became apparent to him was not; it was himself. He was crying as his life ebbed away and he was able to look at that in an almost clinical way, detached for all the hurt that seemed separate from him like an animal: he did not think that he cared for his life that much. It had not occurred to him in all those years since 1945 when he had given up upon all basic assumptions of life and had merely consented to a survival contract, which was entirely different . . . it had not occurred to him that he cared for his life that much; yet apparently he had. He did. He did not want to die. Well, be that as it may, like it or not, he was dying. Something that was not aqueous came against his forehead and he knew it was the ledge of desk as he plummeted to the floor. Lying on the floor then he smelled the odors of death and corruption coming out of him thickly, roiling further with the blood to pitch him to some level below consciousness, or perhaps it was above consciousness. Anyway it was at some point beyond the situation where he could both assess what was happening to him and at the same time not care. He did not care. He had now been dying for a long time; perhaps this was merely another level of dying for which he had been long prepared. He did not care. He did not care. The man whom he had shot was mewling in the background just as he was, but the cries were of no significance. It was merely another presence at a point from which he had ascended.

Dying Stavros heard bands: dying Stavros heard the music again and the shouting of the crowds in the great square; dying, Stavros saw 1933 again and it was good, it was everything that he remembered it as having been except that this time he saw it two ways: young as he had been, old as he was now, age and youth linking in the remembered once again. And for one perilous moment standing in that recollected square, listening to all the sounds that were coming from the speakers that ringed them, stemming out like flowers from that far place, for one perilous moment he heard the voice again and then it came crashing upon him: the blood, the chambers, the bare fields, the deaths and the deaths assaulted his second death. And so rising and falling, heaving and billowing like the sea itself Stavros died and for all the difference it made—this was his last insight—why, for all the difference it made he might as well have still been alive. What was the difference? Who cared? What sensible man, looking at the sweep of existence, could find any consequence in whether something as inconsequential as Stavros lived or died, prospered or withered away?

XIV

Two million dollars' worth of shit. Two million dollars' worth of shit. Wulff found that it was a litany, some kind of a litany anyway, riding horseback through the Andes, the sack strapped on him, he strapped to the horse, the three of them: Wulff, sack, horse, staggering their way through the thin, deadly air. Here there was an isolation so profound that the fields of Havana could not equal it; the closest might be the tablelands that five miles out cut off Las Vegas from the horizon, but there was not in Las Vegas the quality of emptiness here. It was land so barren that the living and dead could co-exist; ghosts had the same weight that people did. No wonder they had such theories of reincarnation here; the living had no more weight than the dead, the dead had the same presence as the living. There was no lost city of the Incas in these mountains, there were only the lost cities of man or men

. . . hundreds or thousands of them, some of them stalking. Wulff shuddered, a sheer superstitious awe overtaking him possibly for the first time, and huddled deeper into the saddle. Ahead of him the unspeaking man who was his guide kept on riding implacably ahead, the bobbling head of his horse casting shadows, those shadows the only break in the terrain. The man had said nothing since they had left. He would say nothing for hours more or until they reached the outskirts of Lima; always assuming of course that they *would* reach those outskirts. There was no saying. Literally nothing was sure. Wulff felt the sack cut into his ribs, grunted, loosened the strap slightly. It began to shuttle painfully against his neck, then.

Two million dollars' worth of shit. Right now, in enclosed rooms, hot dry junkies' spaces, they were shooting up; all the junkies of America were putting a prayer and voyage into their veins, carrying themselves far far out and into a sphere where consequence and calamity no longer existed. And with each of those prayers injected with the junk was an implied prayer for Wulff himself, for his burden. For more shit, cleaner shit, sharper shit, cheaper, higher, greener, whiter shit that would take them further and further into those spaces which they occupied, shit so great that they would never come down again, shit which would make the need for more of it impossible. The ultimate trip, the ultimate shit, that was what they were seeking in its various particles, and here was he, Wulff, slung across a horse, slung across his back, carrying with him a billion dreams at seven dollars a drop, moving from this one unimaginable country toward that other one in the north. If only they could see him now. The bagman to end them all. He would be a saint in every shooting gallery on the north side, south side, east and west if they only knew what he knew.

Madness: to become a bagman. But survival was the name of the game; survival and to carry on his quest. What else could he have done, Wulff thought. It was a lousy deal which Stavros had offered him, but then again it was the only deal going. The alternative was to be ground to death under Calabrese's heel in Peru. He would not have lasted long. He would not have lasted long at all in the Hotel Deal. Sooner or later, probably much sooner if he knew the man, Calabrese would have pulled the plug and then what? *Then what, Wulff?*

Better not to think about it. Better not to think about what he was doing either: plowing through the Andes, the deadly hills, the unimaginable excavations, the bag slung across his shoulder, the bag of Stavros's jewels heading for its destination in five hundred thousand veins to the north. Maybe he could pull a double-cross over the border and ditch the shipment, maybe he could not. Maybe for that matter Stavros's own planning had backfired somewhere and Stavros would not be in a position to re-appropriate the bag from him. Even so, that did not change at all the basic equation of his condition. He was running junk. Burt Wulff was running junk. *He* had become the enemy.

Well, what was there to say? What could you say about something like that except that it had happened and that the basic situation remained unchanged? Every man in his life sooner or later had to become aware of the basic ambivalences, had to realize that he contained within him a duality of purpose and that he was to a certain degree that against which he fought so bitterly. It was this in fact which might give fuel to one's determination ... knowing that one was striking against, trying to eliminate, the hated and omnipresent self. Almost all of these men with whom he had been dealing over these months were exhibit to that to greater or lesser degree: he suspected that no one could loathe these men as much as they did themselves, no man could repudiate them from the company of humanity as they had walled themselves off from all but their own kind. That duality was at the basis of all human relationships. There was a very thin line between the narco cop and the informer; scratch one and you had the other. They were working the same street for the same purposes; even the methods were the same. The only difference was the piece of paper which said that one was law and the other felon, but what did that matter? What the hell did that matter anyway when you had to realize that it was a paper discrimination and that what both of you were doing all the time was simply hustling drugs? Well, the hell with it.

The hell with it; New York was a long, long way behind him; all of the choices had been made, all of the probabilities long since acted out to this one bitter equation. He had chosen his course in a moment of grief and now he was walking down that gray, enclosed pathway; whichever way it took him there was no exit except at the very end, and he did not even see light at the end of the tunnel. Light at the end of the tunnel: that was one of the Vietnam phrases, wasn't it? They were always seeing the light at the end of the tunnel—the joint chiefs, the field commanders, the commander-in-chief himself—and meanwhile the killing went on, the drugs kept on trafficking, men died, other men replaced them and the dance continued. All of it was a game, that was all. This too. A game. The stakes changed but it was the same combination.

Wulff leaned into the saddle, put his hand on the cold mane of the horse and held on as they edged their way through a difficult rock formation, a fault line of some sort, struggling and slipping for purchase in the difficult ground.

Ahead of him suddenly something, either a horse or a man, screamed coldly in the darkness. As he reacted by grabbing onto the horse, flattening himself down against the mane, gripping the hairs which stuck to his sweating palms, there was a second scream in a different tone, then a crack of light flooding the horizon. And in that light he saw the guide's horse stumble, the form of the guide flung free. And then the light came up, there was a second crack, and Wulff was rolling on the cold deadly stones of the Andes.

XV

Where was Walker? He hadn't been able to get hold of Walker, either at home or at any of the contact points for three days, and now David Williams knew that the man was dead. That was a cop's assurance for you—you couldn't tell about life but you always knew death—and he knew that Walker was gone. And now this man Calabrese was on the phone, seeming to know everything about Williams, everything there was except for the one crucial fact which Williams could not impress upon him—that he had no idea of Wulff's whereabouts.

"I don't know," he said. "I don't know." He had no formal idea of who this so-called Calabrese was, but he could make a pretty good guess. In fact, Williams guessed that he could make a hell of a guess but he simply would not. It didn't pay. Better to let it go. He assumed that Calabrese meant Wulff no good, but even so, if he had known he might have told him. Because he wanted to dig Wulff up too, just to tell him a few things, and Calabrese sounded like exactly the man to do it. He certainly did. There was no doubt of that at all.

"I don't know," he said to the voice yet again, curling his fingers, motioning his wife to get out of the room, to leave him be. Ever since the accident he had been unable to get away from her at all, unable to shut himself off. Not that this wasn't understandable. She was terrified. Still, she had to respect his autonomy, now more than ever, if he was going to pull himself out of this. "If I knew I'd tell you," he said truthfully, "because I'm looking for him myself. But I just don't. I simply don't."

"I don't believe you," the voice said in tones of such quiet and controlled menace that, even knowing everything he did, Williams could feel himself beginning to shake, hundreds of miles from the source. It was just too much to deal with, a voice like that. It held qualities he had never before intuited in this kind of person. Was this what Wulff was dealing with? It was incredible that he had had any success against people like that. "You've had good contact with him throughout. That would continue."

"I've been sick. I've been in the hospital. I've had no contact with him at all."

"I don't believe that, either."

"He's out of the country," Williams said, surprised at himself. He had not meant to say even this much. But there was a feeling that he could not hold back, not with a voice like this. His wife was staring at him intensely now, her mouth beginning to open in an *o* of concern. The concern would begin slowly to move toward rage and then she would snatch the phone from him, hear everything. Even worse, the caller would know that he had a wife. Somehow it was important to Williams to prevent this knowledge if possible, let alone the knowledge that she was pregnant as well.

"Yes," the voice said, "we know he's out of the country. We're quite aware of that, Mr. Williams. The point is: what are you going to do about that?"

"I don't know what you're talking about again."

"The man, your friend, is out of the country. But what are your plans?"

"I have no plans," Williams said angrily. "I don't know what the hell you're talking about," and now his wife indeed was striding toward the telephone. "I can't talk," he said, "I have nothing to say."

"I would advise you when he gets in touch with you to find out his whereabouts," the voice said, "and at some subsequent time when we contact you, you can pass this information on to us. That would be extremely useful not only to you but to your highly pregnant wife," the voice said and broke the connection, dumping the line into a clear blank singing space where Williams could only gather the sound of his breath coming back at him irregularly. He put the phone hurriedly back on the receiver.

"I quit," he said to his wife. "I'm getting out of the business."

"Let's not discuss it now."

"I don't want any part of it," Williams said, "I can't put up with this; I cannot take it any more. None of this is my fault, and I refuse to be involved any more."

"Quiet," she said. "Quiet." She reached forward, touched him lightly on the shoulder. He leaned forward, partly out of the line of that touch, and said, "I nearly got my guts taken out. Wasn't that enough for them? No, it wasn't. Nothing's enough for them."

"David—"

"They want everything," he said. "Bag and baggage. The system wants your guts and the organization wants your soul and in the middle somewhere is my black ass. I thought that I could go with Wulff but that's crazy too. They're out to get him. He doesn't have a prayer."

"All right," she said. She moved away from him, her face haughty and blank now in a way he had seen it only a long time ago. She was a poised and gentle girl. "If you can't stand it then get out. I won't fight with you. But where are you going to go?"

"I don't know," he said, his hand still resting on his stomach. He could not escape the feeling somehow that it would come open at any time and that what would come out of himself would *be* himself, not only his guts but his blood and hope mingling on the floor. "There's no way out of it at all. Anywhere you turn it's the same fucking thing. Maybe we'll become a third-world couple," he said, trying to smile. "We'll plan to emigrate to the Congo or one of those exciting republics that have a full vote in the United Nations. There are about fifty of them now, aren't there? Maybe Lincoln was right in the first place; before he got around to freeing the slaves he thought that it would be a hell of a good idea to send all of them back to Africa. Go back to Africa," Williams said bitterly, "that's all; I don't give a fuck anymore. There's no way out of it."

"All right," she said.

"Do you understand? I thought that there was a way out but I was wrong. You're stuck, fucked up, trapped inside no matter what you do."

"Well, that means," she said, straightening something against the wall, "that if you can't get out, you might as well stay, right? Isn't that what you're saying. You've got no choice at all."

He thought about that for a time. He looked up at the ceiling, down at the floor, let his glance pass through the window where he could see his neighbor's hedges across the street in peaceful, vacant St. Albans. "Maybe," he said slowly, "maybe that's right."

"Maybe it is." She stood, unmoving, confronting him. "Maybe it is."

"It bears thinking," he said then. "It certainly bears thinking, doesn't it?" and he gestured toward her; she came toward him slowly, the bleakness falling away from her face in stages as she moved toward him and then she was against him, the two of them blending slowly in a way that they had not for a very long time.

"Well, I'll be damned," Williams said as he slipped inside his wife for the first time in many weeks discovering that it was the same as it always had been and that there were, at least, certain constants. "I'll be double-damned," he said, but that was not until much later.

XVI

His own horse, squalling, stumbled free when Wulff had been thrown and galloped off into a chasm; there was the sound of bone cracking as hooves hit rock and then a scream of pure terror, almost human except that Wulff knew it was no man, but his horse which had fallen into the abyss. The second, duller sound came what seemed to be minutes later at the end of a series of shrieks from the animal, the dull sound as blood and bone collided with rock, and now he heard nothing whatsoever. He lay as if embedded in rock, gripping onto the sack with both hands, stifling the sound of breathing against his palms, waiting for the assassin to reveal himself.

He had no idea how many there were. If he knew Calabrese's tactics, if he deduced the very sense of this attack there were not many at all: perhaps two, perhaps even one, no more than three in any event. But two was a fair bet, one an excellent one. One man who knew these mountains could go out himself with a good chance of success. Somewhere ahead of him in the darkness, the guide and horse were lying trapped by rock themselves; they had not fallen only because of some accident of geology, some parapet lofted against their fall so that dead horse and rider had hung on the shelf of rock rather than collapsing beneath it. Wulff was sure that guide and horse were gone; there was not even the necessity for calculation on this part. It was only him, him and one pistol taken from the man in the Buick, versus the assassin. He held to his position and waited.

The dark was total, enveloping. His guide had made a little light with a flare, casting back illumination through which Wulff had tracked, but the flare of course was gone, and that was for the best because that flare had killed the guard—would have killed Wulff if it had stayed alive. Now the darkness came like a blanket around him, swaddling, choking, taking him in all of its spaces. At the end of this darkness, hours from now, there was the dawn and with that dawn a kind of mutual discovery; but he did not think that this would go on until dawn. Whatever happened was going to happen quickly, now. For the enemy knew the darkness. All of his advantages would disappear in the light; at that point he would be on equal terms with Wulff and this would be what he wanted to avoid. The enemy was cunning, but then again he was only doing what Wulff had done, would have done in a similar situation. He was protecting his advantages.

Wulff crouched, smothered his breath against his palms. He thought
he heard something but it might only have been his blood circulating
rapidly, moving through all the spaces of his body, carrying all of its
deadly, incomprehensible messages; he put that apart from him,
attuning himself only to the external, fixating upon what was
happening. Ledged against a shelf of rock, the stone pressing against
his cheek, coldness against his knees, that coldness circulating
upward through his limbs, he felt himself to be in a position of either
vulnerability or attack; it all depended upon from what direction the
assassin was stalking him. If the man came from above Wulff was
doomed. On the other hand, if he came from the sides Wulff was in a
position, shifting his attention between those two poles, to lash back
at him. It all depended. Everything depended.

Everything depended. It was a hell of a journey from the streets of
Manhattan, haggling with informants in the bars of Lenox Avenue to
this position in the mindless and unimaginable Andes; but if only
looked at in an objective way, if only truly understood, the journey was
inevitable. If you were going to trace that vein through which the
poison was injected, move your way back to the source, then you were
going to come, would yourself have come, into a situation like this. The
drugs began in the open spaces, then moved their way through the
clotted veins into the places of compression, the cities, but it was as
logical to find yourself here in that quest as in anywhere else. This was
the reality: the mountains, the blankness, the presence of the
assassin. It could be said that of the two, Harlem was the one that was
the dream; this the reality.

Wulff crouched, held his gun closer to him. From the left there was
a subtle sound, a couple of stones clinking in the darkness, the sound
of pebbles displaced as if a form was carefully working its way toward
him. He fixated upon that sound, concentrating his attention into a
small, thin tube which moved out from himself no more than twenty
to thirty feet, a tenth of the distance of a football field, that was all.
And somewhere within that line of attention the assassin was
stalking him. He knew this. He felt that certainty beginning to flood
him. The man was closing in, using the darkness, the darkness which
manufactured haste because once it lifted advantage would be
evaporated . . . and even as he thought this, Wulff thought that he saw
a flare in that darkness, a sudden explosion of light to his left. Turning
toward it he saw a man suddenly framed within that light, a man
sparkling and dancing on the ledge. Then the man who was holding a
gun had screamed, had lurched on that precipice and was hurling

himself toward Wulff. "Bastard!" the man was screaming, "bastard, you dirty son of a bitch!" and Wulff understood, he understood everything: stalking him carefully the man had lit a flare which was supposed to be contained only to a limited area; operating on a short fuse, a short wick, the flare was supposed to kindle and die . . . but it was a dud. The equipment was a failure. The flare had worked too well and in exposing Wulff's position, now the man had exposed his own.

Wulff had his pistol out and was firing even before this set of inferences had reached consciousness. The light had come and gone, showing the man dancing on the mountaintop and Wulff fired into the center of the space where the light had been, concentrating his fire. The gun that he had appropriated from the man in the Buick was certainly a more responsive piece of equipment than what Stavros had given him. But then again it was unfamiliar—he did not know if he had been able to adjust to the different feel of it—and as if confirming this a second shot came through, this one from the assassin, splintering rock behind him. Wulff felt the rock shower into and against the orifices of the body, little shards lodging in ears and neck, pellets of the fragmentation worming their way into him and the pain was intense. It was just like flak, this secondary effect but he discarded the idea of pain, putting it into some other area of the consciousness. Instead he steadied the pistol and ripped off his own second shot, trying to put it dead into the place where he had last seen the man, lodge it into his guts. A scream came from somewhere uprange, a thin, high, bloody scream, waters warbling in the throat, and Wulff knew that he had found the assassin. He put a second shot into the same place, working to concentrate the fire, letting the line of variation stay within the narrowest possible compass. Then, as if in reward, the scream came again, and out of that scream came one final shot, going somewhere far into the air above him and Wulff was staggering forward, using his hands to guide him on that rock, guiding himself by feel, trying to close ground.

The warbling birdsong of the shot assassin was somewhere below him, he knew that much, but whether it was a lowering of ground, an incline, or whether it was a different ledge or shelf of rock, he did not know. He dropped to his knees, using hands and knees to drag himself toward that interception. Then the second shot came, the last which the assassin could manage from that posture, the bullet sending out little nervous tendrils of heat which Wulff could feel as it passed his ear and then the screaming began. Screams such as Wulff had not yet heard began to come from that point below him, the sound of some thing in terrible distress, and from the center of that scream he sensed that there was an attempt to form words but the words came blurred, almost indistinct. He had to focus his attention in order to deduce what was going on. "I'm falling," Wulff heard, "my God, you've got to help me, I'm falling, falling, falling!" and now Wulff could picture all of it, the assassin, driven back by the gun's recoil clinging frantically to some ledge, having spun back in the emptiness, his gun falling from his hand like an object chopped out by assault, the assassin now holding onto rock with both hands, babbling, babbling his life away. "Please," the voice cried again, "please help me!"

"Help you?" Wulff said. "I'll help you," and he began to move, belly to rock, low-crawl, toward the sound of the voice, spacing out in his mind the shape of the terrain, evaluating what position the assassin occupied in order that he could make that connection. The sack of drugs banged into his shoulder, the strap, caught on an outcropping of rock rubbing him painfully and he groaned; he put a hand to his shoulder to relieve the pressure of the strap. Another shot, the assassin's fourth, came out of the darkness, spanging Wulff on the shoulder, then glancing off into some crevice. *That was stupid*, Wulff thought, putting a hand to his shoulder, feeling a faint, suspicious line out of which the blood was welling against him, *that was really stupid, making a sound, giving away my position like that,* but of course this was no time to think about stupidity, not at these difficult times. Difficult, difficult, everything is problematic, he thought meditatively and used his pistol to squeeze off one more shot, very little hope in it because he could not reach the man in the darkness. But he heard a squeal, a pig-sound coming from behind layers of rock and he realized that he had.

Well, win one lose one, right? It was a percentage game, all of it, and he was bound, even in fucking Peru, to hit some luck somewhere along the way. He flattened himself against rock again and as he did so something came up from way below, some fire in the valley, or perhaps only a flash of heat lightning; he saw then the space below him, the dimensions of the drop. He was poised like a beetle against a shelf, three or four hundred feet above a sheer, clear drop, one that would take him down the length of a football field and convert him to sheer clear stone—sheer clear stone from that sheer, clear drop. But he would not fall, was not going to fall, and he hugged that rock then, grasping onto it as he had never grasped to Marie Calvante, letting the pistol dangle from his finger. He was not going to fall. He would not give them the satisfaction. You could not go through what he had merely to wind up a crushed bit of pulp at the bottom of a valley. There had to be some justice. He would accept that. He would accept the concept of justice. *You son of a bitch,* Wulff thought, hugging the rock, feeling the rock bite against his teeth, his sweat rendering that part of it against his face as slippery as the sea, *you son of a bitch, give me one clear shot at you and you're gone. That's all I ask. Is that too much* to ask? I ask one shot and then you can have me. But I won't miss it. I absolutely guarantee that I will not.

"Listen," someone said out of the darkness, "listen, this is ridiculous. I mean, we're not doing each other any good here at all. This isn't solving a fucking thing."

Keep on talking, Wulff thought. Go on talking. That conversation is the passport.

"I mean," the voice said, "here we are somewhere in a fucking mountain range, shooting at each other, right? I'm under orders to kill you and you're under orders to kill me, probably because you're supposed to kill anyone who tries to stop you from what you're doing. But I've been thinking and it's ridiculous. Isn't it? I mean we should lay off each other, try to help each other out of this fucking mess, that's what I think."

That's good, Wulff thought, *that's good, keep on talking.* Remorse would get you nowhere, not in this business; but fear was the name of the game and it was fear which was operative in that voice. It could mean anything, everything, if it could only feed upon itself, that balloon of fear. "You're there," the voice said, "I know you're out there. You're very close, you can't be more than a few feet away."

Make it ten yards, Wulff thought. The voice was somewhere to the south of him so that ten yards down, southeast make it, he might be able to deposit a blind shot with some kind of luck. Then again the speaker might be protected by a ledge of rock, it was impossible to tell. Certainly until he could tell it would be foolish to attempt anything. The thing to do was simply to wait it out. Didn't that make sense? He would simply wait the voice out. *Proper police procedure,* he thought, and it was as if a hundred supervisors in the background speaking in the voices of the academy were applauding him. *That's the stuff, Wulff. Go to it. Kill the son of a bitch. Lead him out and then get rid of him. Proper police tactics; concentrate on the assailant, let the assailant's own mood defeat him.*

"Please say something," the voice said. It sounded tentative, far more tentative than it had when it started. It had started out with the booming tones of assurance, a we-are-both-reasonable-men point of view, but now it had moderated down toward whimpering. Like Marasco. Like Marasco when he had killed him on those stairs. Put the pressure of the uncertain on them and they would always crumble. Only a very prideful man like Calabrese would not break in circumstances like these; but there was a way into them too, if only he could find it. He thought he had found it now; he hoped that he had the opportunity to put that insight into practice. "Listen," the voice said, "whether you say anything or not it's ridiculous. Can't you see the stupidity of it? We're two men a couple of thousand miles from home, struggling to get the fuck out of these mountains, and we're set at each other's throats. We've never even *seen* each other but we're supposed to kill. But it isn't the two of us, don't you understand that? It's the people who have sent us here. All we're doing is acting on orders. Can't we meet face-to-face? What the fuck are we doing in these goddamned mountains? The people who sent us here wouldn't be in the mountains."

Wulff held his position. The voice was becoming higher, less certain all of the time. If he could only wait it out, he thought that the voice might be at the point of breakage. Not that he needed breakage, that was not necessary. He had no point to prove in terms of the strengths of the individual personalities. No, it had only to do with the giving away of position and he was getting in, getting in closer all the time. "I'm right you know," the voice said, "you know I'm right. We have nothing against each other. This has nothing to do with us at all. I don't want to kill you, you don't want to kill me. If we passed each other on the street somewhere there wouldn't even be any recognition. We're just doing the job for people without the guts. Look," the voice said, "I'm going to throw my gun away now. I'm going to show you my good faith because I've got nothing to prove anymore and because I want the two of us to come out of these mountains alive. Not one, both. It doesn't have to be this way you know. We don't have to fight and kill one another. Fuck Calabrese. What did he ever do for me?"

I don't know, Wulff thought, I don't know what he ever did for you but I sure as hell know what he did for me. He made a fool of me and he sent me south, that's what he did, guaranteed himself in his own mind that he would never have to deal with me again, but I've got one reason to live if I've got no other, one real reason to live and that is simply to see him again, once more, and to prove to him that he's wrong. To show that evil, corrupt, deadly old man that he made a mistake and that you did not send a man out of your life simply by sending him out of your space, to show him that the world did not work in this fashion, that there were certain men, certain considerations which went beyond the manipulations of power. Come to me you bastard, come to me. He held out his pistol, holding it straightline and waited for the shot. He knew that it would come now. He knew that it would come.

"Be reasonable," the voice said, "be reasonable. Please talk to me. Please say something. I don't have a gun. I threw my gun away."

Good, Wulff thought, you threw your gun away and now we're going to throw you away. You are inseparable from your gun, the two of you because I know you people and who you are and how you work and the way in which you think and in the throwing away of the gun it is yourself that you've stripped. Come on, you son of a bitch. Come on now. Stand up.

"You fool," the voice said tiredly, "you damned fool, I know you're there and you haven't listened to a thing I've said, have you? It doesn't mean a fucking thing, none of it, anything I've said, anything I've meant. I'm going to stand up now. I'm going to show you myself. I'm going to give you a shot at me but I don't think that you're going to take it because, don't you understand? We're the only way that each of us has out of the mountains. We must love one another or die," the voice said, somewhat drunkenly, Wulff thought, "we must love one another or die," and then there was a sound of scrappling to the southeast, hands and knees working tentatively against rock. Then as Wulff caught his breath in his throat in the same way that he might have if an unfamiliar pretty woman was about to take off her clothes in front of him, something came against the horizon—black, black against blackness, uneven against the sky, a faint smudge against the greater dark. Wulff saw that form rearing, bearlike against the horizon, framed as if in the flash of light unseen up until now; and in one motion, bringing his gun smoothly across his chest, leveling everything into the one action, he pumped a shot high into the form, hitting it in the neck, a sound coming then from that form less solid than liquid. Aqueous, bubbling.

"Ah, God," the form said bubbling, little murmurs of water in the words, "you didn't have to do that. You son of a bitch, if you had wanted to do that you could have done it when I had a fair chance, you treacherous fucker." And then the form fell, not during but after the speech, almost as if it had been holding itself up for that one line, that one message of import and then, almost casually, fell. It bounced from one slab of rock to the next, groaning in a very informal, very human way. Then it lay there.

Wulff closed ground carefully. He felt some need to come upon the assassin, a need which he could not have labeled, could not have in any way explicated and which, yet, was absolutely profound; he felt drawn, flesh-to-flesh, to that other particle of humanity which had been out with him in this high place. (And maybe then the voice had been right in saying that they had more in common than they had apart; they had nothing against one another, but he did not, would not, have to connect that voice with the form if he were careful.) But at the same time he did not want in the lapse after victory to do something stupid like lose his grip on these rocks and fall himself. So he kept on moving instead in the low-crawl position, belly to rock, rock to belly, sliding like a fish from one place to the next, closing in upon the burbling and whistling sounds that were still to the southeast but lower down. He held his pistol straight out in front of him, the pistol digging into the stone always poised so that he could if necessary pump a shot into the assassin if the move was deception . . . but he did not think that this was necessary. It was merely technique, absent self-protection. But there was nothing wrong with technique for its own sake; you could not go wrong by doing at all times the most professional and cautious thing possible.

At length, after a long crawl which felt as if it had been for hundreds of yards but could not have been a tenth of that, he came upon the form itself. He heard fluttering, sensed motion in the darkness and then, in some occlusion of light, a light that must have come from the heat of their blended bodies, he saw the man lying in a suspension of agony, stretched across two rocks, one at his neck, the other at his knees, bleeding his life away out of a large hole in the center of his neck, the skin around it pulped. He could see everything looking into that hole; it must have been the blood itself that provided the light, an aura from which illumination cascaded. But then again, Wulff reminded himself, he was very weary and under great tension, and these hallucinations were quite common, particularly in the Andes where the peyote was so thick that it was almost part of the content of the air. He must be freaking out, he thought. As the junkies called it, this must be a pure freakout; and yet he was drawn to that hole, it was fascinating, a little vagina in the neck, protected by flaps. The man was breathing through that opening, the breath whistling faintly in that dense space. The lips were moving. "You fool," the man said, hoarsely.

There was still nothing to say. He did not know what attitude to take; it was not quite a deathwatch because this man was not yet dead; but then he owed him better than the clear, pure eyes of the morgue attendant. At length he took his gun more firmly in hand and tucked it inside his clothing. Putting death away in sight of a dead man.

"You damned fool," the man said. The words were curiously distinct. "We could have made it out together. Don't you talk? Are you a dummy?"

"No," Wulff said finally. It was strange to find speech after all this time, this tension. "No, I can talk. You can hear me."

"We could have gotten out of these mountains. The two of us. We could have saved ourselves. But all you know is killing."

"That's right. That's right."

"All you know is killing," the man said, "all that anyone in this business knows is killing, you goddamned fool. What's going to happen to me now? I'm going to die. There's an airport half a mile from here with a helicopter waiting. The two of us could have made it out."

"No," Wulff said, "it wouldn't have worked."

"It wouldn't?" the man said incuriously. He put a splayed hand to the opening in his neck, felt his wound, his eyes retracting. "Why wouldn't it have worked?"

"Because it can't be that way," Wulff said, "because they sent you to kill me and you would have waited for the opportunity and done it the first chance you had."

"No, I wouldn't."

"Yes, you would. All that matters are the positions in which you find yourself. You're wrong you know. You can't be just a man. They won't let you be. What you are is where they put you. That's all."

"You know what?" the man said with a faint grin, his eyes opening, his hand opening, coming away from his neck in an abrupt gesture, touching Wulff, then darting away, moving in the direction of the sky, "you know what? That's fucking deterministic, that's what the fuck it is," and saying nothing else he died. The ebbing of his life was quite natural and unelaborate; one moment the man was still filled with breath, gasping and thundering within him, the next the breath had gone out and there was nothing to replace it. His eyes rolled back within his head, his body convulsed faintly and then, his head rolling to one side, he was dead. Or at least he was in a posture inseparable from death, it was the same thing. Everything was the same thing, at the end of matters.

Wulff slowly stood. As he did so the darkness overwhelmed him again. There was a corpse below him, a man who had just died—one of Calabrese's best men, he had no doubt. Yet he could have been in another city, another country altogether, for all the impression that that corpse made on him from this discovered perspective. He was dead, that was all; death was a different quality. He moved away from the body, stepping out of the circle of death, and darkness came over him swiftly. He was alone again. Somewhere far down in the stones, a horse screamed again.

He held onto the sack, running his hand up and down the strap. An assassin was dead and he was alive. A little while before both of them had been alive, but now only one was. Still, it made no difference. You could hardly ponder the wonders and mystery of life and death when your own position was where he stood now.

Then Wulff remembered what the dying man had said about the airport.

And thinking of it, his attention riveted on this recollection. He thought then that he could hear the sounds.

XVII

There was a girl Calabrese called in only for special occasions like this one, a girl who was reserved for moments of crisis and doubt because she had qualities that could assign new values to all of these problems; but even with the girl it did not seem to work. Rearing above her, fucking her methodically, Calabrese thought for a moment that he would break through into a different life-frame altogether, a frame in which Wulff had been killed and he, Calabrese, no longer had reason for shame. But it was only an illusion, an illusion brought on by orgasm, and a moment after he came he was still plunging away at her in a small abscess of gloom, miming the motions of intercourse, his semen pooling in and around her vagina, moving in a stale stream to the bed. She looked up at him as if from a great distance, her eyes shrouded. She was a blonde, or at least mostly a blonde, going gray only in a few small places, with enormous breasts and the ability to take almost anything that Calabrese could throw into her. She was thirty-eight years old. He had been fucking her for fifteen years. If he was lucky he would get another fifteen out of her before it was all gone. But fucking her this time had not done what it had most of the others, and now, rolling from her, Calabrese already felt the self-revulsion building, stoking within him fires of impulse that lust before had not touched. "All right," he said. "Enough. Get out."

"Okay," she said. She was nothing if not accommodating. She had a perfect understanding of exactly what Calabrese wanted her for, and her calculations were obvious: if it suited him then it suited her. A hundred and fifty a week for a retainer, and sometimes months would pass before he needed her. At the most he might get her twelve to fifteen times a year. A hundred and fifty for that kind of action wasn't bad, the only requirement was that she be on call when he needed her—but it was a reasonable price to pay. He had no idea of her personal life. He had found her in a bar in Las Vegas, but in these fifteen years she might have gotten married, gotten married three times, even squeezed in a kid or two in the long periods when he had not seen her. Calabrese did not give a fuck. It was her life. Now, as much as he had wanted her, he wanted her out. She made no difference. It had been a bad idea to call her in the first place. Fucking her had only reminded him of how insoluble his problems were, at least by fucking. "You look terrible," she said.

"Forget it."

"You really do. You look awful." Their relationship admitted comments like this as long as they were not pushed too far on either end. As far as he was concerned she thought of him as a businessman, a successful businessman with a big estate, that was all. If she had any other ideas he didn't give a fuck what they were as long as she kept them to herself. "Okay," she said again and moved from the bed, went for her dress. Her shoes she had kept on while fucking; she knew it excited Calabrese, so that meant only one garment to put back on. She did so efficiently in a couple of motions. The woman knew her way around. "You ought to take it easy," she said, "that's all."

"I had no choice," Calabrese said suddenly. "I had to let him go."

"Oh?"

"Of course I did. If I killed him it was saying that my life was a lie, that everything I had lived was impossible. Calabrese is a big coward, they would have said."

"You're a strong man," she said. "You're no coward." She tugged her dress into place.

"I had to let him go. If I didn't let him go it would have been too easy. I had to show all of them that there was no one that I was afraid of, that I could give this man a lead and still kill him."

"You want me to go now?" she said. She raised a hand, suddenly, strangely touched his cheek in one of those gestures which had not been frequent between them. "Hey, I'd better go. You got things on your mind. It'll be better next time though, believe me."

"Don't go," Calabrese said. He was lying on the bed naked, looking up at the ceiling. Spider-lines on the ceiling, small opening cracks of corruption in the walk: strange that he had not noticed them before. The house was aging. With all the money, all the time he had put into it, yet it was falling apart. He would have to have some work done with it. "Do go," he said, "I don't give a shit."

The woman sat heavily on the edge of the bed, put a hand on his calf. "I don't know what's wrong," she said.

"Go. Stay. Just don't tell me that you don't know what's wrong."

"Is there anything you can do to help yourself?"

"Nothing."

"Is there anything I can do to help you? Just say it if—"

"Nothing," Calabrese said, still looking at the ceiling. Someday, if not worked on, those cracks were going to open up like knife-strokes and dump polluted water, filth, corruption, the bowels of the house upon him in his bed. He would definitely have to do something to prevent that. But at the moment he felt inert. He did not care. "There's nothing anyone can do to help me."

"I've never seen you like this. I've—"

"Look again."

"All right," the blonde said. "I can't get near this kind of stuff. I mean I can't even touch it; it's not my kind of thing. If there was anything I could do to help you—"

"Fucking won't help it," Calabrese said. "All you can do is fuck and that's not the solution. I'm seventy-one years old. I'm going to die soon. It's a miracle that I can fuck like this but how long can it go on? I mean even a fool has to understand that everything ends sometime. Fucking is not the answer."

"I've had enough of this," the blonde said. She said it very gently but her face was purposeful. "This isn't doing any good for either of us."

"How do you know?"

"I don't know," she said, "I don't know anything." She stood, brushed some scraps of dust from her tight blue dress. In profile her breasts were straight up even without a brassiere, enormous. You had to get on top of her in bed, Calabrese thought, to realize that they were as soft and yielding to the touch as they appeared hard to the eye. Paradox, paradox, but who gives a shit? He did not. At this moment he did not care if he ever fucked again. "I'll see you around," she said.

Calabrese half-sat on the bed. He reached toward the night table, a look of alert intelligence in his eyes, took the pack of cigarettes and carefully broke one, tossed it against the wall. "I didn't touch drugs for a long time, you know," he said. "I just didn't think it paid, you know what I mean? Who wants to get into that kind of shit, mess with that kind of poison, when there's enough around from a nice simple operation with the kind of things that maybe don't do people damage. I never really wanted to do people damage, just try to make out. But I got chased into it. The drugs I mean. I had to do it out of self-defense; if I hadn't done it I would have been knocked out of business." He broke another cigarette. "Of course a lot of other guys had that problem too," he said meditatively. "I'm not the first."

The blonde's eyes were widened, deepened; she turned on him with slow attention. "If you're talking about what I think you're talking about, forget it," she said. "I don't want to get into that kind of stuff at all, you understand? What we do, we do just as two people. I don't want to get into biography and all that stuff. I don't want to know who you are and you shouldn't know who I am. We just—"

"Cut that shit out," Calabrese said casually and ran the back of his hand against a knee, took it up his thigh, plucked some dried semen from his groin. "I don't need to hear that crap; I need it, I get it in the movies. Two ships in the night and all that kind of shit. If you don't want to listen, you don't have to listen; get the fuck out. But don't start playing Mary Sunshine now. I got driven into it out of self-defense, that's all. Even then I protected myself. I was just overseeing, really. I never messed with distribution myself. Who needs it?" he asked again. "Of course I was right about all of that."

"Drugs?" the blonde said. "I don't know anything about drugs." She was at the door now, a hand curling around the doorknob. "All I know about drugs is what I read in the papers, what I take out of the aspirin bottle."

"Self-defense," Calabrese repeated, to no one in particular, "and supervision. But then I begin to hear about this guy and before I know it, it's a storm right over my head, raining right into my territory. What the fuck could I do? He's in my lap even before I know what's going on, before I get a chance to think this thing out. Who would have believed he was that kind of guy? You hear stuff around but mostly it's all bullshit. I didn't believe a word of it, and what I believed sounded like fun. How did I know? He's killed four men on me already, *that's* what I know."

"I'm going," the blonde said, "I'm really going. I don't need to hear this anymore. I got my own troubles, honest to God." She had contracted, her skin had taken on a harder, brighter tint. "Really," she said, one hand on the door. "You tell me any more of this, I'm going to get sick."

"What you don't know won't hurt you, eh? Well life's not like that."

"My life is," she said. "That's the way my life has been for a long time and that's exactly the way it's going to be." She had the door open finally, was poised in the hall. "Listen," she said earnestly, "you're going to go on this way, you don't call me. You call me only when it can be the way it's supposed to."

"I should have killed him," Calabrese said, reached over, broke another cigarette. "I know that was my mistake, but you know the real shit part of it? You want to hear it? I know you don't, but stay ten more seconds, humor me, what the fuck do you care? I'm seventy-one, I'm going to die soon and you'll be nicely remembered. If I had it to do all over again, I mean if the fucker was standing here right now and we were replaying the scene, I'd probably let it go the same way. I wouldn't kill him. There's just something about him that's fucking unkillable."

"Goodbye," the blonde said, "goodbye," and went through the door, closed it.

Calabrese lay back on the bed, stroking, tickling, playing with his groin, plucking at the little hairs. Dead there. Absolutely nothing. Give the bitch credit: when she was finished with him he was completely fucked out. No solace down there; if there were any solace it would have to come out of his head, but things weren't happening there either. Things were happening nowhere. He was at a dead-stop.

He could call downstairs, have her intercepted, sent up again, and he could beat the shit out of her, just for kicks. That would be satisfying in a way, and Calabrese considered it. There was a lot to be said for pure, simple sadism; he liked to think that he had a higher, somewhat more refined intelligence. But as for those types who had always enjoyed it at the basic level: live and let live, that was all. But he decided to let it go. It wouldn't prove much. It wouldn't be *that* satisfying. And someday he might want to call her up again.

You weren't fucked out forever.

Calabrese thought about the blonde and then he thought about Wulff and then he thought of the phone calls he had received, all of the bad news filtering in, and something occurred to him; it wasn't all that bad after all. It wasn't as if the books were closed altogether. The last act was a long way from being played. He was going to get another shot at the bastard.

Definitely, he would get another shot at him. Everything was in flux and, if you looked at things in a certain way, the bad news was good, because it meant that Wulff was not irrevocably lost to him; the moment was a long way from being tracked back in the past. The bastard, if he got out of Peru, would be heading dead on him— Calabrese, in fact, would be stop number one—and that was good, that was really good, because he would have a chance to play the scene over again and this time it would come to a different ending. This time he would not repeat his stupidity.

This time he would kill him.

Calabrese lay back on the bed and closed his eyes, simulated sleep. In a few moments the simulation became fact; he passed from one heavy state of consciousness to the next, moved into dreams. And in those dreams thick ropes of speculation were thrown up and he clambered up them, just he, just Calabrese, struggling on the rope.

Above him was the pure, white light of the arena. Streaming through the skylight was the sun. And below him was the pit, and in the pit was Wulff himself—spread-eagled, tortured, begging for release, as Calabrese—the avenger, the athlete, the dancer, the trapeze-artist—made ready to fall upon him.

XVIII

The rest of it was easy. Wulff huddled in the ledges and rocks until dawn; at dawn the light streaked through his closed eyelids, rousing him to a corpse. Beyond the corpse, which was stiff and smelled of wood, he was able to see the outlines of what appeared to be an airport.

It was amazing how what in the darkness had appeared to be a completely isolated spot turned out to be nothing of the sort; the guide had led him toward the rim of what appeared to be half of a town carved out of the rock, midway between Cuzco and Lima. The assassin had been quite right. There was the airport from which he had come and to which he doubtless had intended to return alone. Craning around the rocks, Wulff could see it. About three miles, maybe less. He had a difficult, staggering walk to make through all of these ledges, but it should not take him more than an hour or two.

He got up stiffly, feeling the wastage spread through him, the large and small losses which the night had extracted. Somewhere far, far down on the rocks he could see the outline of a form, no two forms: larger and smaller, huddled together, and that could only be the guide and his horse, the two of them swaddled in death. But Wulff turned from them quickly because there was nothing that he could do. His own horse was a speck down on the other side, much further in its fall than these two. But then again that speck might be something else: a ruined bird, perhaps, you could not tell. He looked at the corpse of the assassin—a small, roundish man, very peaceful in death, very unremarkable; he looked something like that businessman he had murdered on Wall Street a long, long time ago.

And then, resolving to look no more, Wulff set out on his way. You had to leave the dead behind you. They could suck you in all the time, no question about it, but death was not the trip, drugs were, and that was a different trip altogether. He began to move down.

Slowly, then with increasing facility, mastering the way the rocks behaved under his hands, Wulff managed his way down the ledges, pausing now and then to catch his breath. There was a small, precise brown spot where the shot had touched him last night; just one pearl of blood had come out and then the system had shut itself down like a tap without plumbing. He was able to pick the blood away with his fingers leaving only a faint impression beneath. No trouble there. It was the third or fourth wound he had taken in his quest, but none of them serious; all of them but one in the shoulder area. A charmed life? He doubted that, he thought wryly. He doubted that very much; not when death seemed to touch almost everyone with whom he associated. And not when the quest was still in progress. Death was just taking a seat on the sidelines, that was all, a fascinated spectator; with chin in hand it was watching him struggle on, involved for the moment in his efforts. Sooner or later, however, like the old cheater he was, death would come out of the stands, pull his knife and take care of Wulff.

At best he figured he had a raincheck.

At the bottom of the valley; nothing now but flat tableland into the little airport. Wulff paused for the second time, stopping by a little gully to rub some water into his hair, clean himself off a little. The sack was intact, its contents slightly dampened by the dense night air, but nonetheless precious for all of that; forming into little blocks in the sack, it looked even prettier. He looked into the sack for a little longer than he actually needed to before he put it away. Face it: the stuff was beautiful. There was a beauty in it which could not be denied; he felt himself seized by the same emotions which must be granted the junkie before he took the needle. It had the fascination and loathsome beauty of Satan himself, this white junk; only a fool would not concede its powers. In the dreams-and-death business, it was absolutely the best that America had to offer. And considering that dreams and death were what the country was all about . . . well, you had to respect it. You simply had to respect the shit, that was all.

At length Wulff got to his feet again, tossed the sack over his shoulder and labored his way into the airport. It was a small enclosure, hardly larger than two football fields, hammered out of the native rock. There were a few discouraged Piper Cubs lined up at the sides of the slick, oily runway which circled it. A couple of the Piper Cubs were revving idly, men working on them, cursing. The dispatcher's office appeared to be closed, but then again you never could be sure with things like this; probably there was a dispatcher and he was lying on the floor drunk or coked out on peyote. It didn't matter. The airport business was probably the last refuge of the entrepreneur. He went up to one of the Piper Cubs that was being worked on. Since it didn't matter which one, he took the closest.

A bearded man was pouring gasoline into a fuel tank under the wing, humming to himself, his hands shaking as he inhaled the fumes, most of the gasoline getting into the tank, some of it dribbling out. He made a point of ignoring Wulff. But as Wulff stood there hands on hips, the sack over his shoulder, quite willing to wait the man out for hours if necessary, the man finally turned and looked at him. "Yes?" he said, "what is it?"

"You speak English?"

"No," the man said. "I speak fucking French. Can't you tell that I speak fucking French? It's my native tongue. What you're getting is an instant, unconscious translation to English, I think. Of course, I really don't know about that stuff."

"All right," Wulff said. He tried not to smile. Actually smiling would have been pointless; the man was not being funny. "I need a flight."

"Good," the man said. He was very interested in the gas can again. "Get yourself some wings and take up straight over the mountains."

"I would if I could," Wulff said, "but I don't work that way. I work in planes."

The man turned to him. "Where?" he said, his manner abruptly changed. "Where do you want to go?"

"The States."

"Not Lima?" the man said.

"No," Wulff said, "I don't want to go to Lima. I want to get all the way up north, as far north as you can take me."

"That would be a bad idea," the man said. He ducked, put the gas can down and then looked at Wulff straight on, and Wulff saw that it was no illusion, the man had changed completely. He seemed to have recognized him; now he was functioning in a different context altogether. "Ordinarily that would be a very bad idea, a Lima bypass. But not now," the man said, "right now it isn't such a bad idea." He looked at Wulff intently, then his eyes suddenly changed and he had looked away. "Stavros is dead," he said.

"Oh," Wulff said. He felt nothing at all. What was there to feel? But it was a surprise. "I didn't know that."

"We knew that somebody was coming out of the mountains today and was going to go back to him. I should have known it was you right away, but I didn't." The man shrugged. "He's dead," he said again.

"How do you know that?"

The man pointed toward the dispatcher's office. "You learn," he said, "the word gets around. You learn a few things."

"All right."

"So you want to get back to the States, eh?"

"I'd like that very much," Wulff said. "That's exactly the way I want it."

"Who's going to take care of it?"

"I don't know."

"Stavros is dead. He's not around to take care of it, then." The man looked meaningfully at the bag. "Only you are. What's in there?"

"Guess."

"I don't know if I've got enough gas even to get into the air," the man said. He looked down the line to the man at the other Piper Cub who was lying on the ground now underneath the open engine compartment. "I don't think that any of us here have enough gas."

"That's a damned shame," Wulff said, "I can sympathize with that."

"Maybe you have some gas in the bag," the man said. He had not taken his eyes off the sack. "Who knows? You might have exactly what I need in there."

"I don't run drugs," Wulff said.

"I know you don't fucking run drugs. I didn't say anything about drugs at all, did I? I just said that you might have some gas in that bag. It was what you might call a question. A speculation."

"I want to get to the States."

"We figured that," the bearded man said and paused. "That was made quite clear. Stavros is dead," he said softly. "It's every man for himself now, you understand that? Nothing's like it was. Nothing is ever going to be like it was again. Nothing is simple anymore. It's a different world. I'm no longer a working man. Nobody here is. We're on our own."

Wulff slowly took the sack down, opened it on the ground, then stepped away. "Tell me," he said, "do you see any gas in there?"

"I don't know," the bearded man said. He leaned over to take a closer look, moving his head toward the bag, suffused with alertness.

Wulff kicked him in the head. The man fell heavily to the ground, groaning beside the sack. He rolled on his back, opened his eyes. Blank, they rapidly moistened and filled with color again. Good. He had not wanted to put the man out of commission. That had not been his intention.

Wulff took the pistol from his pocket, aimed it at the bearded man. "I don't run drugs," he said again, "that's not my racket. I'm not in distribution." The other man down the line had disappeared completely behind the plane, he noticed. All through the field motion seemed to have ceased. Even the wind was drier. "You've got to get your signals unscrambled," Wulff said. "The first thing you've got to learn when you go out for business yourself is to be able to tell the difference between a live one and a dead one. I'm a dead one." He waved the pistol. "Get up," he said.

The bearded man rolled, managed to get to his knees. A fine, light trickle of blood was coming from his nose; he slapped that blood away as if it were a mosquito. "No need," he said. "There was no need to do that."

"Let me be the judge."

"You shouldn't have done that. You don't have to pull a gun on me."

"Get in the plane," Wulff said. He held the gun on the man, leaned over, picked up the sack, drew the drawstring closed. "Let's go."

"I don't think she'll fly. She needs to be checked—"

"In the plane," Wulff said. He spun the chambers, clicked the dead trigger. The bearded man turned, got a handhold on the door, arched his way in. He disappeared into the blackness; after a moment, a small ladder came out. Holding the gun in front of him Wulff came up, got into the cockpit.

"You've just filled it up," Wulff said, "you can take it pretty far on what you've got in there. If we need to refuel we can touch down somewhere."

"You're crazy," the bearded man said. "You're crazy if you think this will work."

"That's my problem."

"Stavros is dead. Stavros made things work. Without him you're not going anywhere."

"He didn't make them work that fucking well," Wulff said. "Close the door."

The bearded man leaned forward, pulled on something and the door closed. "Keep your hands on the controls and your mind on business," Wulff said. "And don't talk. I messed with one pilot up in Havana a while ago and that was enough. It's not going to happen again."

"All right," the man said, "all right." He did something with levers and the motor staggered into life. Wulff could feel the cabin shaking with the props. A miracle. A miracle if they made it north in this thing. Still, it was a miracle to be here in the first place. You kept on. You kept on going, that was all. You did so in the faith that sooner or later, at one stage of the game or the next, it made sense. If anything did. If anything did at all.

"Take it up," Wulff said.

They ascended.

THE END

THE LONE WOLF #8: LOS ANGELES HOLOCAUST

by Barry N. Malzberg

Writing as Mike Barry

PROLOGUE

Vast fucking city of the mind. Los Angeles was not a place but a mental state, the mental state of a severely deranged person. The roads ran like clotted arteries in search of a head; the smog nestled little ropes down over those arteries and drew tight. Wulff hated it. Los Angeles and New York were nominally both American cities, but New York was a great, steaming, dying beast whereas Los Angeles was merely vapor. He hated it but good. Still, it was good to be back in the States again. Not three days ago he had doubted that he would ever see his country again. It still was his country, of course. King America. Where everything began and where someday soon it would end.

Wulff found himself tenanting a residence hotel in a suburb. Everything in Los Angeles was a suburb. The residence hotel had an elegant name like the Actor's Home or the Colony Quarters, something like that; the kind of address which when put on mail would give out-of-towners the impression that the tenant was really making it out in the Golden West. In truth, the average age of the Actor's Home or Colony Quarter tenants was somewhere over fifty. A couple of them had busted out from being extras or stagehands. These were the top-flight residents of the home but the majority of them had come no closer to the movies than going to the movies themselves and they seemed to be merely a step above the derelict class. There were a sprinkling of women who were in even worse shape than the men, but the sex of the Actor's Home or Colony Quarters seemed mostly to be neuter. They were scoring a little shit in the hallways, of course, and pot blew out of the rooms like breeze at night, but Wulff was not interested in that kind of stuff. That was nickels and dimes; he had long lost any passion for complete extermination. If people wanted to blow a little pot then that was their prerogative, at least until the big squeeze could be put on. He was after much bigger game. He and a big sack of shit were waiting for a two million dollar rendezvous.

Someone was going to make contact with him at the Actor's Home for the ostensible purpose of scoring the bag. They weren't going to score the bag. They were going to lead him right up the chain to the head and eventually back to Chicago but they did not know that. Wulff had put the word out that he was in town; there had been little trouble in making contact. By this time everybody knew who he was and the fact that he had a two million dollar sack wouldn't hurt his social standing at all. And the fact that he was Calabrese's game, Calabrese's marked man, even kept him safe in this city, at least until Calabrese could get organized, get some orders through. So he hung tight in the Actor's Home, the Colony Quarters. Two days, three days; it made no difference at all. He had all the time in the world now; he could wait them out. Waiting was the least of it. It was the confrontation that made life difficult.

There was a girl stashed in San Francisco under a different name, but Wulff knew her as Tamara. He had seen her a few months back, and she had reached him in a way that no one else during his Odyssey had; maybe she was the reason that he had come back to the coast from El Paso. He could have scored New York again or Minneapolis, anything but Chicago; it made no difference. But Los Angeles sounded good. It was close enough to San Francisco to be less than a day, fast car, and the country was the same. He didn't think that he ever wanted to see San Francisco again though. Los Angeles was close enough.

He called the girl, reaching her at her parents' house where she had been stashed, and she came down to see him. Wulff really had not expected anything different. If he had thought that the girl would not be anxious to see him he never would have come here, never would have made the call. She took a bus down to the Colony Quarters, walked straight in, probably the first young, attractive girl that had been in this dump in forty years, went straight to the little room where Wulff and his sack had huddled up, and came in. He spent the next twelve hours fucking the shit out of her. Why not? He was entitled. Not that his feelings about her were really that crude, not that simple fucking would have appealed to him without a kind of emotional context at this point . . . but keep it straight. Keep it simple. He banged the hell out of Tamara, fulfilling a promise that he had made in Las Vegas, and quite reciprocally she banged the hell out of him. She was a nice girl, not without feeling and genuine emotional range, but the really nice, uncomplicating factor about her was that she liked to screw too. She saw nothing wrong with it. Besides, Wulff had saved her from nearly OD'ing out back in San Francisco. She owed him her life. Wulff had a knack for finding pretty girls who were OD'd out. Sometimes they were alive. Sometimes they were dead. This one had been alive.

On the morning after the night the girl Tamara came, Wulff awoke after an hour's doze lying naked against her, reached for her while half asleep, and felt her immediately curve like a bow into his arms, her body ripe for the springing . . . and as he leaned to take her he heard a pounding on the door and knew with a sense of regret that his Odyssey was over. Calabrese's men or the contact point? Either way the jig was up. Twelve hours, though, was not a bad Odyssey. At the pace his life had been going in recent months it was downright exceptional.

He told her to watch it and he got a gun and then throwing a robe around himself he opened the door. She leaned back in the bed, half-closing her eyes, looking at the wall, unmoving. She certainly had a lot of faith in him. Maybe he rated it.

I

The revision in the New York State narcotics law went into the books on September 1st.

For Evans, everything on his first bust after that date went like clockwork, and then abruptly all of it fell apart. Motherfuckers. All of them. Maybe he wasn't thinking of a narcotics bust here but of the country itself. You never could tell. It was easy to get confused.

Evans was supposed to score the deal at the prearranged corner, 116th Street and Lenox Avenue, while Finch, the senior man in undercover garb, covered him from across the street. The minute that Evans had paid the dealer with the marked bills Finch would move in, gun drawn, while Evans went for his own pistol. Then they would take the kid downtown. A little crowd noise might develop, but against two drawn service revolvers and identification nothing was really going to happen. Routine shit. He had gone through this ten, fifteen times before, and the only scary time was wondering if the dealer would show up to begin with or whether he, Evans, would be walking into an ambush. Once he had walked into something like that. Of course, Evans had never tried the gig in this neighborhood before. That was simple, reasonable policy: never pull the same trick twice in the same neighborhood. All of it was on the same chain. Word would get around.

Everything, to a point, went just the way it was supposed to. Finch, a young black dressed like a bum, was nodding away in his place fifteen minutes before the rendezvous. The kid himself showed, overanxious probably, five minutes early, talking to himself in a brisk distracted way . . . sampling his own goods. Evans bought three decks for a hundred apiece, cheap stuff he was sure. He was already looking forward to the lab report on this; probably it was sugar. He passed over the six marked fifties to the kid, the kid taking them with eyes half-closed, nodding away saying, "Good shit, good shit, man." He might have been nineteen years old. "You'll love this shit," the kid said dreamily and put away the fifties, heaving from a crouch to take himself out of the scene, and then Finch was sprinting across the street, reaching for his gun.

Evans at that moment moved for his own revolver and the kid, seeing the situation collapse in front of him, was already backing into the near wall, hands up, terror leaking from the open spots on his cheeks. Evans could have laughed with the ease of it: how well it was going, how much he had it all under control now and then. Just like that it broke open.

Finch was no longer running. He was being swarmed on the street. No traffic here to block his view. Three men had come from hidden doorways and had pinned Finch, and as Evans watched this Finch went down screaming, the bellow of pain quite distinct in the thick air, the sound of bone shattering as a foot went into his skull. Evans was still working with his pistol, the tube of his attention narrowed down in that way. He almost had it out and was starting to bear down on the three men for a series of shots that would get them and yet not kill Finch. But as he was concentrating something hit him on the side of the head, opening up an empty place in the skull that he had never before known to be there, and Evans fell to the ground, the vague impression that bodies were swarming over him mingling with the pain of concrete against his knees. Then the pistol was yanked from his hand, and he could see faces looming over him.

Two of them: hard, bitter, implacable, street faces these. God knows where they had come from. Like all of the street faces they simply were there, and Evans, turning instinctively, trying to pull himself into a standing position, was kicked hard in the ass, the contact striking bone, bringing undignified tears, and he went down to the street again. He was crying. No one had kicked him in the ass since the fifth grade. This could not be happening. He was a five year veteran. It could not be happening to him. Laughing; they were laughing all around, and then Evans was yanked upwards, felt himself moving through dense layers of space to confront the man who had kicked him, and as he thrashed in that grip it occurred to him that he was probably going to die. He was helpless; they had given him no lead time. The decks of heroin were pulled from his pocket by one of the men and then they were filling the air, tossed around, disappearing somewhere. The two looked the same: somewhere in their twenties, nondescript clothing, closed-in faces. Neither had a gun. They had taken him that easily. "You stupid son of a bitch," one of the men said.

Evans looked for Finch. Where the hell was Finch? The last time he had looked the man had been covered on the street and surely he must be there somewhere. Even swarmed under bodies Finch had to be there, struggling, reaching for his own revolver, trying to dig out the killing shot . . . but Evans could not see him. Nothing was on the street whatsoever, nothing in Harlem: no traffic, empty stones, the perspective seeming to have narrowed to a radius working within three feet out. There were only the two men and himself and then as Evans looked, everything swinging into slow motion, trying open-mouthed to focus the situation, the kid from whom he had scored came into view, his face still leaking that terror, his eyes perfectly blank. "Kill the son of a bitch," the kid said above Evans, "you've got to kill him now. Kill him for this."

The unreality was still probing at him, but seeing the kid caused the angles to harden once again. Evans felt that the kid must be the pivot of the situation; if he could get a grip of some sort he could swing out from there. Grab the wheel and turn. "Cut out the shit," he said weakly, "just cut it out. I'm a police officer. Now let me go before it gets much worse." He had a pregnant wife and a three-year-old girl. His wife had begged him to get out, but he was going for the good twenty.

"Fucking cop," one of the men said. He tightened his grip, banged Evans into a wall. He could feel the stones coming into him like so many fists and he would have hit ground again, but something was holding him up now, and then the two were in even tighter focus. "Fucking son of a bitch cop." He turned toward the other, the man propping up Evans, needing confirmation of some sort but there was nothing doing there at all. The other man said nothing. "You know what fucking kind of trouble you're in, cop?" he said. "Do you know now?"

He guessed he did. Oh, yes indeed, he did. Evans tried to say something, felt his throat constricting, dry, croaked, decided to say nothing. Everything had reared out of control like a crazed horse off the rein. Here had been a nice, tight, simple score and bust which had broken away from him and now it had turned into something else. He might, he thought, even have gone on to deal with that. These things, he understood, happened, but what he could not deal with was the hatred of the two men pinning him and his growing sense that what he did would have no consequence; he was going to die here and now in Harlem. It was not fair; that was about the only thought which persisted. He knew his business, he had been in narco long enough, there was nothing that was supposed to shake him at this point.

Nevertheless, here it was. Where the fuck was Finch? Where was traffic in this area, had they sealed off the streets to get him? Surely they could not have anticipated this so tightly. Everything was crazy, that was all. The kid who he had scored off had now closed the last of the ground between them. He was staring at Evans. Sweat came off his face in little chains.

The other two smiled then and stood aside as if they had been the official greeters, the kid being the celebrity, set up. "You fucking cop," the kid said, "I try to score you a little shit and you pull a badge on me. That's rotten. That's really rotten."

"You're in a lot of trouble."

"Am I?"

"A lot of trouble," Evans repeated. He tried to make the words come out evenly, aiming for some menace, but they did not. Nevertheless. Stick with it. No choice otherwise. "You're in a hell of a lot of trouble."

"You're in more, cop."

"Give up," Evans said. "It isn't worth it. If it's a first offense they'll go easy on you." He thought he had been doing well but his voice broke on the *easy*. "Easy on you," he said again, keeping his voice flat this time. Something was wrong with his breath. It leapt and stirred in his chest, out of synch with his attention. It could not be a heart attack. He was twenty-seven years old.

The kid reached out a hand, and one of the others handed him the pistol *slap!* just the way operating room nurses handed scalpels to surgeons on television. The kid pointed it at Evans. "I'm going to kill you, you bastard," he said.

"No, you're not."

"Yes, I am. You set me up. You set me up for a life bust." The kid's voice was breaking too but he made no effort to control it. Why the hell should he? He was the one with the gun. "No one does this to Willie," he said.

"Now listen here, Willie," Evans said, seizing the name for the contact. He had to establish some connection. Maybe Finch was struggling with the other two at this moment; maybe Finch was in the process of pulling free, coming to bail him out at just this moment He had never believed that he could die. "Listen, Willie, it doesn't have to be this bad. Give up. Give me the gun. Give me the gun, Willie. Using a weapon on a police officer in the performance of his duty—"

"I ain't using no fucking weapon, man. I'm going to kill you."

"Killing a cop is death, Willie," Evans said. "It's death in this state, the only capital punishment left. It's much worse than scoring shit, Willie."

"Is it?" Willie said. "Is it?"

The gun was steady in the kid's hand, and at that moment Evans knew he was going to be shot. Funny, you could live on the borderline of death for years and years. Every cop or cardiac did, thinking that it might be stalking you, too, but its presence when it came was unmistakable. It was the difference between swimming and drowning, dreaming and happening. He knew that his death was coming at him out of that hand.

"It's after September 1st, you son of a bitch," Willie said. "I'm going to go up for life, mandatory, no appeal, no parole for selling. So what the fuck's the difference between life and capital anymore? Capital's a better deal."

"Listen—"

"And besides," Willie said, looking cunning, "this way I got at least a chance; you take me in I got no chance at all. I'll be looking out bars for fifty."

"There are ways—"

"There are no ways," Willie said quite matter of factly. The two men beside him seemed to nod solemnly; he gave them a checking glance, looked back at Evans. "You see, your fucking white man's law has given me no choice," Willie said.

He pulled the trigger.

Evans saw the fire and then something strange happened as the bullet hit him; the bullet gave him an altered perspective, a feeling of vaulting insight, and suddenly he was no longer himself, he was Finch. He was Finch and he was somewhere in an alley across the street, and just as Evans had been shot, Evans/Finch had been shot, too, in the chest, a killing slug for him under the heart. Evans/Finch bellowed with the pain of it, Evans/Finch slumped and then he was only Evans again, locked into his own flesh forever. He saw the kid's face in the aftermath of the discharge streaked by terror again, looking the same as it had when he had been caught with the score, and Evans thought, my God, he really doesn't want to do this; he wasn't lying, he doesn't want it anymore than I do. We're both trapped, trapped by what they've done to us, trapped by the law. He thought he might say this to the kid, point it out to him in a casual, courteous way—hey, don't you understand; we've got nothing against each other, it's just the law that they put between—but the hell with that, the hell with casual, courteous conversation. He was falling crosswise, arching into the pavement.

Funny, Evans thought, still thinking, thinking all the way down the pipe until the end, he had expected that his body would collide with one of the other two but it did not. Instead of striking flesh he went through the point of prospective contact, sliding smoothly, and then he was on the stones, stone puncturing his throat. He must have been shot in the heart, he thought, and everything was vaulting upward.

Evans lay there, face down in a sewer. Thought slowly chased itself out of him with the pulses of blood. Then finally he heard, or thought he heard, the sound of sirens. They were coming up Lenox Avenue to save him, the governor and his legions were coming to put the shitseller into prison for life, but too late, governor old man, too late. Evan's last thought as he died, oblivious of what was around him (but he knew the men had probably run away) was that he hoped the wagon would take Finch first. Finch certainly had more of a chance than he did, that was for sure, and regardless of chances it was not fair that all efforts were not made to save Finch since Finch had just been the sidesaddle man. The bust was Evans's, the true responsibility his. Sidesaddle Finch, helping Evans on a score, Evans himself sidesaddle to the damned narcotics laws which had killed him.

Life without parole for dealing. Better to kill a cop.

Evans died.

II

A few days before, the bearded man who was piloting the hijacked copter took Wulff all the way up to El Paso in a crazy, zagging journey that had Wulff on the floor most of the way, battling the impulse to throw up, not so sick however that he was not holding the pistol steady on the bearded man. The bearded man, dodging heavy cloud cover and the fear that Calabrese's men might be up in their own craft trying to intercept, was sick almost all of the way but he was a professional; he kept the thing going. In truth, he had no choice.

"Put that fucking gun away, you clown," he had said to Wulff once over Rio, and once somewhere over Mexico he had said, "I can't ride this fucking plane with a gun in my head," but without hope, and on neither occasion did Wulff put the fucking gun away nor did he stop feeling sick. The bearded man pretty well got the idea then that Wulff would not release him from cover, and resignation added skill to his piloting. He was able to level the plane off pretty well.

They came into an abandoned military airstrip in El Paso in the dead of night. The bearded man worked the controls with one hand while he kept the other free to pray, or if not to pray, at least to make some intricate gestures of his own toward the heavens, which were, with the rotation of the copter in rough weather, sometimes one place and often the other. The copter did not hit straight, hovering to a landing the way they were supposed to do in the movies. But instead it bounced, hit again, and then began to slide down a long, thin wedge of runway, a diving, panicky slide at the end of which it collapsed in a bank of woods, nestling against a tree hundreds of yards from the impact point. Wulff, almost knocked out, was the first to recover, coming off the floor in cautious stages, holding onto the pistol, locating the sackful of shit, millions of dollars' worth that he had taken out of Peru for a dead man.

The bearded man lay on his back looking at Wulff almost without interest. All fight was gone. His eyes followed the pistol but they did so incuriously. It was all the same to him, the eyes seemed to be saying with a calm that the mouth would not have, whether Wulff killed him or not because he, the bearded man, could not be bothered with something of so little significance. After a ten-hour flight like this maybe anything would have been a relief; any change under the circumstances.

"I'm flat out of gas," the pilot said in a dull voice. "They used to have some tanks at the far end, the other side on the west, but I doubt if they even have them anymore. They closed this up two years ago when the Pentagon socked it to them. It's interesting, you know," the bearded man went on, "the war was going on for a long time and no one minded and then all of a sudden when public opinion turned against it the Pentagon couldn't raise a dime. I don't think that you could get a cent in new military appropriations nowadays if you put it up to a vote."

"I was in Vietnam," Wulff said absently.

"So was I," the bearded man said. "Two years flying stuff out of there for the Red Cross. Never in, only out, mostly sick bodies. It was a stinking mess."

"Yes, it was," Wulff said, "but it wasn't anybody's fault."

"I don't give a fuck whose fault it was. You going to let me go?"

"I don't know," Wulff said standing, supporting himself against a cabin wall. "I'm thinking about it."

"Really nice of you to think about it; I appreciate that more than I can say. Leaving me with an empty gas tank and a ruined copter in this hellhole after I got you out of Peru."

"Yeah," Wulff said, "yeah, well it's tough. Ingratitude runs rampant, you know how it is. These are difficult times for all of us."

"Sure," the bearded man said, "sure, difficult times, right down the line." His voice was emotionless. If the ten-hour flight had left Wulff momentarily without conviction it seemed to have drained the bearded man of purpose. Probably he was still disoriented from having been taken at gunpoint out of the airport down there. "You know," he said, "you're a really great man. You're everything that the press said you were. You're not only a tiger, you show a true and real kindness to your fellow man."

"I don't deal with my fellow man," Wulff said, "I don't believe in fellow men." He went over to the hatch, began to struggle with it. The bearded man watched impassively, his fingers curling. After a time Wulff was able to get the hatch open, bringing in a dank draft of air from the Texas night, the first fresh air that he had breathed since the thin fumes of Peru, which counted only in the marginally life-sustaining sense. "I deal with myself," Wulff said, "that's the beginning and the end of it."

He reached behind him, took up the sack, struggled to get it over his shoulder feeling like Santa Claus with two million dollars' worth of shit to waft down the chimney. The bag banged into his ankles knocking him off balance, he staggered, reached to support himself overhead. "It cuts both ways," he pointed out, "you don't like your position but what about mine? I've still got to make it out of Texas."

"My heart still bleeds," the bearded man said faintly.

"I'm letting you go, that's something."

"You calculate it," the pilot said, "you think about that." But Wulff had already vaulted, was into the air, hit the ground harder than he thought he would, was rolling in the mud. Three turns, the sack twisting under him, and then he was on his feet again beginning that slow, staggering walk from the dark runway to an empty, lighted space in the distance, the sack banging his rump . . . but before he had gone more than a few steps Wulff heard the sound that he must have been expecting.

Surely he knew that it was going to happen; his body, unconsciously, had already arched against it. There was the sound of metal hitting metal, then a bullet went off somewhere to his right missing him by a good distance, five yards or more he estimated. Then there was the sound of a chamber being spun clumsily, an empty click against the grain, and then the second shot came off-angle, hitting behind a little and to the left this time. The bearded man was cunning but just a shade overeager; maybe it had been overconfidence.

Well, fuck him. He had been willing to give the man a chance, small gratitude for being run out of Peru even at gunpoint, but this was ridiculous. Wulff allowed the sack to drop to the ground, turned around and ran toward the copter, that sound of the spinning chamber coming through the air again, and then the third bullet came as expected. This one was a wild shot completely, the bearded man folding in the clutch as bearded men were apt to do unless, of course, they came from Havana. Wulff had his own pistol out by then, putting a shot through the open space up the hatchway.

Inside he heard a scream, then the sound of thrashing. The pilot's pistol hit the floor of the copter with a clang, and Wulff stretched, then leaped, got a handhold on metal, and one-armed himself into the abscess of the copter. Here in the spokes of dim light coming from a distant part of the field he saw his assailant flopping like a fish on the floor of the cabin. Moaning. "Please," the fish said, "please, now."

Always the same. They would kill you fast or slowly; they would kill you like a fly, construct your death out of indifference and then walk away laughing, but at the moment of confrontation when the weapons were stripped from them, when their own death was imminent, they would break open. They had done it that way, all of them. In San Francisco, Boston, New York, Havana, Lima, the tough men had opened up screaming and pleading. But this, Wulff thought, this was not necessarily anything against any of them because their own cruelty and terror (he understood this now) came not from a contempt for life but out of excess respect and for love of that fragile light which was conveyed through their bodies.

"I had to do it," the bearded man said. "You would have done the same thing, you know it; we're no different you and I. What could I do?"

Well, maybe yes and maybe no. Maybe he would have done the same thing and maybe he would not, Wulff thought; he might well have done it if positions were reversed, although he liked to think that he had not changed so much during his journey, that in many ways he was still a cop and took the cop's dictum: only necessary force. There had to be a level at which a man could be spared simply because of the value of life itself, call it the sacredness of life to reach for an odd term. Then Wulff felt a backlash of bitterness because looking at the bearded man he understood that life meant so little to this creature precisely because he had never understood it. The thing on the floor understood nothing and therefore it had no reverence.

If life was death for this creature, then death was merely a transition. The thing was crawling, flopping before him, and Wulff felt nothing; this was merely another body, more meat to be conveyed from one part of the slaughterhouse to the next. Life was a slaughterhouse with a lot of cubicles and only one exit out to that great yard of decomposition. Wulff thought, drugs were perhaps the best conduit for a lot of dead meat, and the thought was a flare of revulsion, a bright spot of rage out of which the pistol kicked twice, his body shaking with recoil.

The man died silently. Nothing came from him but the sound of escaping air, his bowels voiding. He lay quietly, a neat, almost imperceptible entrance hole in his neck, a somewhat slighter exit wound to the side of the head where the blood was already puddling in its murky escape. He had no sensation whatsoever. All of the feeling had left him a long time ago.

Wulff put the gun aside shoving it deep within his pocket and then he leapt from the copter for the second time, careless now of his angle of descent (killers had luck; he was a killer again), hitting the ground hard on the shoulder blades as he went into a roll. He came from that roll slowly, gaining his feet, dusting dirt and death from himself, moving casually and purposefully through the dark to reclaim his prized sack of shit. That was why the bearded man had shot at him. There could have been no other reason. Wulff himself would not have been worth killing.

Wulff walked away, Santa Claus with his sack, blanking his mind. So many yards to the far side of the field, so many more yards, perhaps, perhaps not, to a highway on which he could flag down a car or hijack one if necessary. So many miles to the car until the next stop and he had an idea where he was going to go from there.

Not Chicago. Not to Calabrese.

He was not ready. He needed to rest, to recoup, to plan his next and final campaign against Calabrese but he could not bait that tiger now.

He found himself thinking of Tamara.

Well, it had been a long time, quite a time since he had seen the girl, almost as long since he had last spoken to her from Las Vegas. There had been a time when she had reached him, another when he thought that he was beyond reaching and that what had happened in San Francisco was just a brief collision of the bodies . . . but now she had touched him again. He realized that he wanted to see her.

So be it. He was entitled at this stage of the game to the integrity of his impulses. He would see her then. See her, and finally Calabrese.

Wulff walked through the darkness of the abandoned airfield, moving toward the far side. He had killed four hundred and fifty men, most of them fairly prominent at one level or the other of the international drug trade. Four hundred and fifty in four months. He had swept from New York to San Francisco, Boston to Havana, Vegas to Peru and most of these centers would never be the same again, not in relation to the drug traffic, maybe not in relation to anything. He was thirty-two years old. He had a girl behind him and a girl ahead of him. He had a dead man in a cockpit and a couple of other corpses almost as fresh to the far south. He had a lot of bodies ahead of him, still moving, breathing, fucking, drinking, that had his name on them too.

III

"Get him," Calabrese said over the phone. "Get him. I don't care about the cost, I don't care about the risk, I don't care what kind of troops you have to bring around. Get the bastard."

"You should have gotten him a long time ago," the voice on the other end said calmly, "I could have told you, I—"

"Shut the fuck up!" Calabrese screamed. He felt the blood working its dangerous way through the channels of a network, pressing to burst free, moderated himself with a few even gasps of breath. He was not worth dying for. No son of a bitch was worth a stroke. "I know that," he said more quietly, "I know all about that now. Don't get into that again."

"All right," the voice said. He was a professional subcontractor, working out of the coast area, not really part of the organization at all, which was the only reason that he could get away with talking to Calabrese like this. If he had been almost anyone else Calabrese would have touched him with death right then. "You see the trouble you make for yourself, Calabrese? You see the fucking time and expense? It's your own goddamned fault. You had him and you should have killed him."

"That's in the past," Calabrese said, "the situation has changed."

"You bet the situation has changed," the voice said almost meditatively. "This is a hell of a job you've given me, Calabrese, I want you to know that This man is no clown. He's no fool."

"I know that," Calabrese said, "don't you think I fucking know what we're dealing with? But at least he surfaces easily. You won't have any trouble fingering him."

"I know that," the voice said, "in fact he's already surfaced. He's in LA, do you know that?"

Calabrese paused deliberately, reacting against screaming into the phone. Two more breaths and his control had returned. "Sure," he said, "I suspected that."

"We've got pretty good information where he is and what he's doing. Word gets around about him pretty fast."

"So why didn't you go after him?" Calabrese said. "Don't you know there's a bounty on him already?"

"I was waiting," the voice said, "waiting for you to call. I'm no bounty hunter, I'm a professional. Besides, I figured that we could do better in direct negotiations than working any bounty and I was right, wasn't I? I'm usually right. I'll be in touch," the voice said and hung up.

Calabrese held the empty receiver in front of him for a while and then very slowly, very neatly he placed it down. He stood, walked from the desk, turned and looked out at the spaces of Lake Michigan for a while, and then he turned back, very slowly reseated himself, ripped open a fresh pack of cigarettes and began to scatter them, one, two, three, broken butts and edges over the room.

I should have killed him when I had the chance, he thought. I had him and I let him get away. So it's my own fault but what does that mean? What does any of it mean? Fault or no fault, you have to go ahead.

I'm losing my grip, Calabrese thought, and I'm getting old, and it's all starting to move away from me, but one thing is sure; one thing is absolutely sure; I'm going to get that son of a bitch before he gets me and I'm going to stand over his corpse and I'm going to spit and laugh. And then I'm going to kick his eyes out of his head.

Sure, he thought, and broke another cigarette, that will be very constructive.

IV

Wulff had been a New York police narco for three years. They had thought that they were doing him a big favor on his return from Vietnam, giving him a job with the ones who were considered to be the golden boys of the department in those days. Only the vice squad could come near it for sheer fun in the sun but the vice squad was in the process, in those late sixties, of falling apart whereas narco just got bigger and better all the time. J. Edgar was gearing up his Federal Bureau for the final assault on the international drug merchants at about that time, and surprisingly the new federal money and interest just made things better for everyone in the racket. There was no competition between the bureaucracies, there was just fallout.

Wulff was on the squad for three years. Considering his state of mind when he got the assignment it might have been something of a record; longest time in a job held in highest state of revulsion.

He had come back from mid-sixties Saigon in a total rage, a rage which was only partly compounded of war fatigue, mostly it was the clear intimation that here it all began. Saigon was the living, beating heart of the world's corruption, and it was this heart that was being used by the blood of America to test out the most advanced forms of death. Here funneled the poisons and from them the poisons spread out again through the trunk and limbs of the world and much of the poison was junk. Saigon was awash in drugs.

Wulff had seen whole platoons wrecked on hard shit; he had seen hundreds of men, boys really, who had been sent to death by shit, and all the time that he was living and seeing this and keeping his own hands off in horror the trade was going on. He could see its map streaked out in a thousand Saigon faces every day and when he came back to New York, finally, it was with the feeling that he would either have to single-handedly put shit out of the world, or failing that, would have to get as far from the racket as possible so that he would not have to think about it. In more ordinary circumstances he would have gone the latter route; Wulff was angry but he was not *that* angry, and war did things to a lot of people's heads that eventually got pushed away back in civilian life. Or drove them to suicide.

Wulff might have settled for the comfortable, easy way but narco wouldn't let him. He couldn't escape the war frame of mind. New York *was* war. He was in the middle of it every duty day.

He saw the informers: smiling, empty men with the shit stashed in their own back pockets, the informers who were working arm in arm *with* the arm as the saying went, selling their brothers on the streets down the line for a nickel bag and a little less heat. He saw the periodic sweeps when the inspectors would move in from headquarters in response to the newspaper campaigns demanding arrest, and the narcos would go out to pick up truckloads of smiling, willing, nodding informants. In with them today, out by the middle of the next morning, all charges dropped for lack of evidence. He saw the other empty, smiling men in their big cars cruising by the distribution depots at midnight, a last check before turning in for the wife and kiddies and home. He saw the look on the lieutenant's face when a rookie had been stupid enough to have busted one of the Eldorado men. Wulff got a good taste of all of it.

Well, Vietnam and Harlem; they were both places in the same city. When the dusk began to crawl they even looked the same; combat zones. It made no difference, shit was the name of the game, over here, over there. Fight to keep America free for shit. Twenty-forty a bag or fight. Don't give up the shit. It got Wulff angry, all right. It got him pretty damned mad.

Finally, he got mad enough to bust an informant in a bar for possession. He collared the son of a bitch and took him into the local precinct. The informant must have had six decks sticking out from his jacket and back pockets. Smiling, nodding, bullshitting Wulff along, just daring him to do something because he knew that Wulff was the man and the one thing that the man never did was to break the rules. Wulff wasn't going to put up with it. He had his limits, too. So he brought the informant into the precinct and lost sight of him for four hours. He was sitting around the record room, filling out his reports like a fool, bullshitting with the sergeant, until the lieutenant came in finally and said that Wulff had made a false arrest. No evidence. All evidence had disappeared. How could Wulff have brought in a man who was not holding? The lieutenant was very serious when he said this; he was even able to meet Wulff's eyes. If there were any drugs in the informant's possession he must have managed to ditch them somehow, somewhere between the bar and the precinct when Wulff had not been watching, the lieutenant said. Wulff had been watching. The lieutenant was a liar. Still, what was he going to do about that? Bust the lieutenant himself?

There would be an investigation, the narco supervisor told Wulff when he came on for his next TDY. Something about Wulff fucking up. In the meantime, though, they had no choice; false arrest was a very bad thing for the department's image and they were going to send him back to a patrol car. The narco supervisor at least had had the decency not to meet Wulff's eyes when he went through this but maybe he was not the old hand that the lieutenant was.

Well, going back to a patrol car was a bitch as they conceived it but it was all right with Wulff. He would have taken a beat for that matter except that about that time the department was phasing out the beat policy. Patrol was fine with him. After three years in narco, hustling family disputes and bar hassles, delivering a couple of babies or pegging numbers, runners would have looked like a good clean job, and he found himself looking forward to the assignment as if it was actually some kind of an honor. Which in fact it was. It was fairly rare to get bumped down in the PD for making any kind of an arrest.

But the gig that he had been looking forward to turned out to be his first and last TOY pulled that way because on duty, riding sidesaddle with a black rookie named David Williams, Wulff had stepped into a blind tip about an OD'd girl in a tenement on West 93rd Street. When he, as the sidesaddle, had sprinted up the five flights of the premises to do the honors he found a girl named Marie Calvante lying in the middle of the room, absolutely OD'd out, all twenty-three years of her,

her eyes fishlike on the ceiling trip.

Seeing a pretty white girl OD'd out in circumstances like that would have been bad enough for Wulff, hardened ex-narco, combat veteran and all that, but the Calvante call had been even tougher because, unfortunately, Wulff knew her. He knew her very well. In fact, he and Marie Calvante had been engaged to be married within a couple of months, earlier if he could push her, and it was hard for him to believe that she was lying on the floor of that tenement unless someone had put her there. Someone personally interested, not so much in the girl, but in Wulff. It all tied in pretty clearly, he thought, to the informant bust. Cause and effect. Chain reaction. It was nice to think that at least this was one murder in New York which wasn't senseless.

All things considered, Wulff had taken it pretty well. Pretty professionally. He hadn't cracked up, he hadn't pulled any dramatic shit like throwing himself across the body, he hadn't sworn vendetta. That kind of crap was for the movies. All that he had done was to move out of the room right away, almost immediately after David Williams, the rookie, had come upstairs to find out what was taking Wulff so long for verification. He had told Williams very quietly where they could take their police department and stick it and then he had gone onto the streets past the patrol car (Williams had left the keys in, the motor still running, pretty stupid, Wulff had noted professionally) and chucked his badge and credentials into a sewer. In this way he had resigned from the department immediately without bothering to give them the benefit of notice. Loss of pension, of course; he would have to swing his own way after the twenty. But Wulff did not expect to get anywhere near the easy twenty now. He doubted if he would make eleven.

He went out to murder the international drug trade.

He had wanted to do it ever since Vietnam. That was for sure. For a long time a lot of things had held him back, all of those things wrapped together under that deadly, all-inclusive word *system*: the good twenty was system and busting the informants was system; the thirteen grand a year plus increments and benefits and graft was system, too and system with a capital *S* had been the gentle girl named Marie who had really hooked him in with pictures of the house they were going to buy, the babies they would make. Nobody in the house-buying, baby-making bit was going to attack the shit-dealers when he had something like that to protect, but the murder of the girl after what they had taught him in the precinct house the night before carried the message for him pretty well. They weren't going to let him play after all. He was going to have to go outside of it.

Well, he thought, why not? Why not fulfill an old ambition now that the furniture of life had been carried out for him? He might as well try to put all of them out of business. One at a time. Face to face.

The funny thing was that they all denied it.

As Wulff cut his path across the continent, starting in New York, sweeping his way to the coast and then back to Boston, into Havana and Vegas, out the pipe to Chicago and then to Peru, spreading death in bright, broad strokes, there were a lot of system men he met, most of them at the point of his gun or theirs, and none of them would admit that the organization, if there was such a thing, had had a thing to do with Marie Calvante. They had never heard of her. It must have been ten different people was the consensus, because no one in the organization killed anyone on the sidelines, particularly relatives or close friends of antagonists because that could only put things into a newer and uglier context where it could, by implication, become open season on everyone. Marie Calvante had been an unfortunate accident, then. Some freelancer might have done it, maybe the girl had secretly been a junkie and ran into very bad luck on West 93rd Street. But Wolff should understand the protocol of the trade the systems men had advised, averred, insisted, articulated, slobbered, begged, gibbered across desks, back seats of cars, open fields. Wulff should know that the organization had its own code of honor more stringent than anything in the outside world.

Wulff killed them anyway.

What the hell, they were all liars, and responsible for the girl or not, they had killed a lot of innocent people. Directly or indirectly. It was a good philosophy. There was nothing wrong with killing when the enemy was dealing from a stack of cards smeared with blood.

There had been a girl in San Francisco who had given him back a few particles of life; there had been a copter pilot in Havana who had turned out to be a bastard but had taught Wulff a few things first; there was the rookie cop, David Williams, who had pitched in and made himself useful a couple of times before he got hit in the stomach checking out a methadone center in central Harlem. What would cautious Williams make of his precious system now? Wulff wondered. So every now and then you met a few people who were not as bad as most but essentially it had been his own trail. He had played out his own hand without expectation of help and in the conviction that he was going to die soon anyway; why not, then, take all those he could down with him? Peru had been the roughest of all the stops so far, but he had even managed to get out of Peru with a big bag of shit, so what the hell, what the hell indeed . . . maybe his luck would hold to the end of the trail after all. But Peru had been a rough one.

Peru had damned well not been on his list to start with.

Peru had been the decision of a Chicago boss named Calabrese. Chicago had been on Wulff's list all right and finally in Chicago he had run up against something really major league, something that possibly was not within his capacity to handle, although he did not want to truly accept this. Chicago, in any event, had been the stomping ground of an old, deadly man named Calabrese, a man in his early seventies who lived in an estate on Lake Michigan and who was so far ahead of the rest of them that he could almost operate out in the open. He virtually did. Calabrese had insisted to Wulff that he, Calabrese, was simply a legitimate businessman trying to make it in a very tough world. He had almost killed Wulff twice, this legitimate businessman. The second time, locked in his office with Wulff, he had laughed in his face, said that he guessed he would not take Wulff out of the game for the time being because he was interesting, he gave Calabrese something of a charge and a challenge just knowing that he was around and functioning.

The idea, Calabrese, that deadly old man, said, was to get Wulff out of the picture for a while but only to a place where he would remain under Calabrese's control. Peru had been the choice then. He had dumped Wulff into the Hotel Deal in Peru where Wulff had met an ex-Nazi named Stavros who was trying to work his own figures around Calabrese, and although Stavros had been Wulff's exit ticket from the country, Wulff had been the ex-Nazi's undoing. Stavros was dead. His pilot who had flown Wulff into El Paso was dead, too.

Almost everyone with whom Wulff had been dealing was dead, come to think of it.

Still, that was one of the breaks of the game. If you administered death you were going to get caught up in it, sure as hell. Wulff found that he didn't mind it that much. After awhile, for high purposes or low, killing could be almost as much fun as sex if you put it in the proper perspective . . . which was easy. He had nothing, personally, against killing. As a tactic against these clowns it beat all hell out of busting informants in prearranged sweeps to get headquarters and the newspapers off your neck.

Wulff, carrying a big bag of shit with Stavros's odor still on it, cut his way out of the border town of El Paso. He had a pretty good idea of where he wanted to go and who he wanted to deal with. But the girl came first. Los Angeles came first. Too much action, too much impacted in too little; he needed a stopover before he could gird himself to take on Chicago again.

So take the show to LA. There was the girl and he wanted to see her
. . . and maybe LA could use a little bit of his action, too. He had the
bag. He had the bag of shit and that would suck them in.

It always did. Vermin loved shit.

V

He had the gun in his hand when he yanked the door open, of course.
That was routine procedure; anybody who opened a door to a blind
knock without a pistol in his hand was asking for a shot in the gut
without reply. But it was not the gun that saved him so much, it was
what he did after he had flung the door open; he kicked it back into
the wall with an ankle, slamming it hard, feeling it rebound, and
simultaneously with the crack against plaster, he was rolling, diving,
bringing up the gun for a shot.

There was only one man in the hallway. He could see all that in the
stop-action of the roll, but his attention was fixed less on the man than
on Tamara, the sheets gathered around her, the look of her as she
arched up in the bed, a palm like a bud against her mouth as if
screaming into it. She did not make a sound. The girl had guts, there
was no question about it; call it guts or class, maybe it was the same
thing but there was something unbreakable there, and he knew it,
recognizing this almost idly, absently in some pocket of the mind as he
pumped a bullet into the assailant, then another one, still rolling.
There was a sound of flesh hitting wood, then the man was down, the
gun leaping from his extended hand, spanging off a wall, and then
coming to a stop next to the bed. In that moment the girl looked at it
incuriously, hand extended, all of her attention seemingly drawn to
the gun, and then her hand came away, disinterest or fear overtaking
dispassion, and she leaned back against the headboard. She was still
naked. So was Wulff. Remarkable accomplishment, to rear from bed
and murder, but he did not think of that now.

He found a towel, draped it around himself as he leaned toward the
man on the floor. One eye closed, the other cocked open at the ceiling
in a horrid wink that even as Wulff stared, diminished, filtered itself
away. One final sigh and then the eye closed, the man lay dead on the
floor. He was simply dressed: killing garb you might call it, a
sweatshirt and tight-fitting pants. This meant that he had probably
come into the lobby with the gun exposed; there was simply no place
to conceal it. Surveillance at the Colony Quarters was not too good; a
man could walk into that lobby at any time in almost any condition,

caveat emptor. But this, Wulff thought vaguely, was ridiculous. He turned to the girl. "He's dead," he said.

"I know he's dead."

"There was nothing else to do." He felt vaguely apologetic. "I had to kill him."

"I know that," she said. She had been silent and accommodating since he had met her; now her mood had not shifted. She held the sheet up against her neck, her sole impulse seemed to be to keep herself covered. "It all comes back to me," she said.

Wulff stood, kicked the door closed, went back toward the bed. "I don't even know who sent him," he said. "He could have come from Calabrese but then it might have been someone else. I won't know."

"It's all the same," she said. What he had said did not seem to have registered with her. "Nothing's changed since I saw you in San Francisco."

"How could it?"

"The killing," she said, "the killing goes on."

"It has to."

"It never stops. I thought that it would, but it didn't."

"I had no choice," Wulff said, "I have no choice at this point. None at all." He looked at her abstractedly, then through her, his mind already scuttling away at some perilous angle. Just a moment ago, a few moments ago, he had been totally involved with the girl, concentrating on probing her body, working out through her flesh some dark necessity that he had not even known to be there until she had capped it free . . . but now it was as if she was not even in the room. Whatever passions had driven him toward her had been transitory, he realized. They did not count. The main thing that counted was the quest.

"I've got to get out of here," he said. "I didn't think they'd find me so quickly."

"Yes you did. You wanted them to find you."

He shrugged. The idea of arguing with her was pointless. Looking at the outline of her body behind the sheet he wondered what had driven him to her in the first place. Whatever it was, whatever she had meant to him, had been so thin that it was now gone. The corpse on the floor was leaking blood. "We've got to get out of here," he said. "I thought we had some time but I was wrong. There's no time at all."

"You like to live this way," she said. There was no accusation in her voice; it was a calm, flat statement. "I really think that you do."

"That doesn't matter."

"When you saved me, when I was with you back in San Francisco, I believed what you were saying. I thought that you were in a bad situation that you hadn't been responsible for, that really wasn't your fault at all, that they were closing in on you. But I see now that I was wrong. You enjoy it."

"I don't enjoy any of it."

"Oh," she said, "but I think you do. I really think you do."

He looked out the window then, looked out at the range of Los Angeles; no smog on this day. Peculiar, the smog was supposed to be the dominant characteristic of this landscape and yet the air was a complete, uncharted, transparent mass around them, the view from the Colony Quarters stretching far out toward the mountains which seemed to be close in on them by some freak of vision, not miles out there but only a few hundred yards away, and then his attention shifted back to the bed. She had dropped the sheet, was sitting there exposed to the waist, her breasts hanging like teardrops, much lower than they would have appeared in clothing, almost brushing her navel but for all of that there was no impression of heaviness or flab, rather the breasts seemed merely to curve on that angle. She was an attractive girl. One could see where she in herself would be responsible for an itinerary. She stood, her legs tensing underneath her thin but surprisingly strong, little muscles jumping in her calves.

"I'm going to get out of here," she said, "I'm going to get out while the going is good." She looked at the corpse and then away from it, walked toward the chair against the wall on which her clothing was propped. "I see the way that this thing is going," she said, "and I don't want any part of it. I know that you saved my life and all that, and you can be sure that I'm grateful, but on the other hand, I'm really not up to this any more. My wild times are behind me. Actually, since I got back home after you took me there things have been very quiet and dull and I find that I like it just fine. I wish that I had gotten into the dull life years ago. I may even go back to school in the fall." She reached for her sweatshirt from the chair, standing on tiptoes to avoid any contact with the corpse, then shrugged the shirt on quickly, casually. "I'm a little old for school, but on the other hand there are worse places to be. This is really wild you know," she said, taking her pants off the chair, inclining on a toe like a dancer and digging a foot in, then pivoting for the other leg. "Dead men on the floor, people all over the country out to get you, mob bosses who carry your photograph around, triggermen, what not. It's a wild life, but you've got to get out of it, you know. You can't go on this way."

"Listen," Wulff said, turning back from the window, going back toward the bed, "you can't just walk out of here. It's ridiculous."

"Why is it ridiculous?"

"For one thing we don't know who may be waiting down the hall or covering us on the street. He may have a backup man, there may be other people carrying out surveillance on the building who know who you are. You can't just walk out into this. You don't know what you may be walking into."

"That's all right," she said, "I'll take my chances."

"No," he said, "it's really ridiculous, I can't permit it. We'll get out of here together."

"I don't think you understand," she said, turning, facing him, her eyes blank and yet somehow knowledgeable. In this aspect she looked something like the girl that he had pulled out of the San Francisco apartment in a speed jag months ago, although she did not look damned much like her. There were now whole layers of experience seemingly interposed over her attitude and also the softness of that girl that he remembered had gone. "I agreed to meet you, I was glad to hear from you because I felt I owed you something for what you did and also because I had to test something out in myself. I was pretty hung up on you, you know that, don't you? I guess you could figure that out; the man who was my savior, ex-New York City cop, the lone wolf battling all of the bad men, and so on, and I don't exactly love the drug pushers myself. I had to see you again, I had to test myself and also, really, I'm grateful for what you did, but you see," she said, looking once again at the corpse and then putting a small hand, a surprisingly delicate hand for a well-proportioned girl, on the doorknob, "it's definitely over now. Whatever it was I had to find out, I had to get it out of my system, I did. I can't go on this way. It's too dangerous. I'm twenty-five years old. I'd like to make it to twenty-six and I'd rather have a long, boring life than a short, exciting one. Please, don't come with me. I want to get out of here myself. I just don't think I want to have any more of your luck riding along with me."

The girl opened the door, went out into the hallway, closed the door, and left him there standing with a dead man in the middle of the room, her footsteps at first almost imperceptible in the hall and then soundless. As he turned to the window to try to follow her out of the building he realized that the room was looking out on the other side and that there was no way in which he would be able to see her. If someone was lying in wait for her out there she would not have a chance; there would be no way whatsoever that he would be able to protect her.

He stood there poised, listening for the sound of gunfire but there was none, and after a time, Wulff could not calculate exactly when, he knew that she had made it through safely and that he was now alone.

Alone with a dead man. He dropped the towel from its position around his waist and slowly, wearily began to dress, feeling as if he had aged years within the last moments, as if some foreshadowing of his own senescence and decline had dropped around his shoulders like a cloak. He hadn't expected it. He simply hadn't expected that it would go this way.

The dead man, lusher in his death than ever in life, was leaking fluid through the thin, cheap covering of the floor. Looking at him, Wulff realized that if he did not do something quickly he was likely only to have dead men for company in the near future. They had their merits, dead men did. For one thing they had no ambitions and for another they did not struggle for possessions and show the uncommon perversity that living ones did, but on the other hand it was perhaps better to hold onto life for the time being; it was a known quantity. Also, he had a job to do and he was not finished yet.

It was strange, but apart from these two cited reasons he could not think of one other basis for not pitching it in right now and joining that creature on the floor.

VI

Williams heard about the Evans-Finch double murder the night before he went back on duty. Almost every cop in the city knew about it within two hours, but Williams was still at home so he had to pick it up from the late edition of the *Post*. To the paper's credit they gave it a great deal of play, centering a close-up of Evan's covered body lying on Lenox Avenue with a lot of theorizing out of headquarters as to whether this had been a planned slaying or an impulse killing, but Williams wasn't having any of it. It was obvious as hell what had happened here. Evans and Finch had probably been in the middle of taking a narcotics bust when the guy on the other end of the score, keeping September 1st in mind, had decided it was better to take a chance on capital for killing a cop than taking sure life for dealing, standing, and letting the two cops put the cuffs on. A week ago the murderer or pack of murderers might have stood still for the arrest, just possibly. Five years for dealing, with the possibility of parole after twenty-two months, would have looked a little more promising than sure death if they got nailed for cop-killing. But with the new program, all bets were off. It was going to be open season in the arena of the shooting galleries from now on; God help any cop who tried a dealing arrest without a gun in his hand and a strong backup across

the street. Even that might not hold them. Credit the governor for the
new narcotics law; he was going to drive all the dealers out of the
streets all right. He was going to disperse them all over the country
doing their wonderful work, all except the few who would be starting
up a new death row, that is. But the governor didn't believe in pill-
taking of any sort, and goddamnit, if he wasn't going to take even an
aspirin for a headache no one in the State of New York, if he could help
it, would be able to do the same. At the rate the governor was going,
Williams figured, aspirin-taking without a prescription would itself be
a felony within the next four years.

He thought about it quite a bit that night. He wondered if it would
change his decision to take the desk job that the precinct had offered
and go back on duty at least for a few months while the gut-wound
healed completely and he decided what he wanted to do with the next
forty or fifty years of his life. If his wife had been around Williams
would have discussed the thing with her again, but she was not.
Things had been deteriorating between them since the knife that had
put him in the hospital had struck. Four days ago, after a particularly
vicious disagreement, she had packed up an overnight valise and
moved over to her sister's place in Flatbush; just for a few days, she
said, until they cooled off and got some perspective. But it had been
longer than just a few days now and she still had not called nor had
he. Williams supposed that he couldn't blame her. The knifing he had
taken checking out the methadone center in Spanish Harlem had
changed his perspective on a lot of things; had imploded all of his neat,
previously held ideas about the system which would protect him and
hold him in place as he climbed narrowly up the ladder of the white
man's world, sneering at all of them. Now, having been knifed in the
gut, having taken what he thought of as the white man's knife for the
privilege of protecting him, Williams was not sure about the system.
It was a massive trap, a sinkhole, that was what it was; it existed for
the convenience of a very few who lied to the vast percentage of fools
and failures out there so that they, too, could find their way inside with
perseverance and luck, the principle of the lottery, a chance for all
takers . . . but it just didn't work out that way.

No, maybe Wulff had the right idea after all. He had been skeptical
about Wulff, more than skeptical. He had taken the man to be crazy
with his attitude that the system sucked right down to the bottom,
that the system was dedicated to neither good nor evil but simply to
its own preservation, and that that preservation would lead it
inevitably to more wrong choices than right ones. The idea that a man
could go outside of the system deliberately was bad enough, but when

it involved a quest as monumental as putting the drug trade out of existence . . . . Well maybe, Williams had thought when this all began, the right thing was to take up some kind of collection for the guy's hospitalization.

But maybe Wulff had a point after all. Certainly he was doing more in a matter of months than the narco squads, the DA's, the President's Council, and the border operators, to say nothing of the FBI and the late J. Edgar had been able to do in ten years. Williams could read the headlines; just a look at the front pages of the newspapers some days was an indication of what Wulff was up to and how he was going about it. A freighter fire in San Francisco, two hundred dead. A townhouse blown up on the East Side of New York, an important figure lost in the rubble. Someone shot to death in Wall Street. A fire in Boston. Yes, Wulff was making an impression; he was making the rounds. Williams had been able to help him a little bit, too, give him an insight into a weapons shop here, a lead into a missing bag of shit there. But Williams had now heard nothing from Wulff in several weeks. Only the calls from Calabrese, the boss in Chicago, asking Williams where the hell Wulff had gone, were indications that the man was still in the picture. Williams knew Calabrese pretty well if only third-hand. If Calabrese was looking for Wulff that meant that the man had really reached the big leagues, was starting to dig in at the highest point, because Calabrese came out from under his rock only once every ten years and then usually only to sneer at a grand jury or something.

But the problem was not Wulff right now; the problem was Williams and what was going to become of his life. The decision to go back on duty had been easily formed, had been inevitable even though he had done it for the wrong reasons at least according to his wife. "I'll hang in for a couple of months and really get well," he said, "and maybe I'll get hold of some files and data and information and when I'm back to myself I'll do what Wulff did, I'll quit them and I'll really blow them up." She hadn't liked that, not the part about going back, but the part about blowing it up. She was eight months pregnant now which made him doubly a bastard for letting her walk out, he supposed. She was all for the house in St. Albans and the system. That was what he had offered her when they were married and that was what she was in it for. At that level her loyalty was unquestioned. But when the very prerogatives shifted, when it turned out that he was interested in something he had never talked to her about, all bets were off. He supposed there was at least a chance that they would never get back together again.

And then the business with Evans. Still, what the hell could you do?

The governor was fucking things up right and left. The governor should at least have thought about the choices that he was giving the dealers and the cops when rammed down to confrontation, but the governor, of course, did not give a shit; that kind of thinking was too abstract for him. The governor was a first-class shit at least on this count, Williams thought, but then again he knew nothing about the ins and outs and intricacies of politics. Maybe the governor thought that he was ramming through a popular program and New York City *was* shit capital of the world as everyone knew. Anyway it hardly mattered to him except in the abstract sense. He was going to go back on desk duty.

Williams lay in bed unable to sleep for a long time, thinking about what had happened to him and what was going to happen next. His gut still ached in certain positions, little slivers of pain like cold radiating through him, and he had to adjust himself repeatedly, trying not to think of what that pain meant, some refraction of his death, the pain of his own death, refracted some fifty years down the pike. He was able to touch his death in the darkness, feel it as a companion in his bed. Instead of a wife, now he had death lying in his bed and this knowledge brought him upright in the darkness, the realization cutting through him as that knife on Lenox Avenue had . . . and when the phone rang he seized it gasping, groaning, shouting into that phone as if it was only further confirmation of that message.

"Yes!" he said. "Who is it? What is it?" The thought occurred to him in that breathing space that it might be his wife, contrite, willing to come home, or maybe his sister-in-law to tell him that he had a son, but the pause stretched out and he knew it was neither. "All right," he said in a more restrained way then, "who is it? What the hell is it?"

"You know who this is," a voice said, "don't you?"

He guessed he did. Williams guessed he did. "Yes," he said, "I know who it is. Where the hell have you been?"

"That's a long story," Wulff said. "Where the hell have you been?"

"I've been in a hospital and then I've been home. There are a lot of people querying your whereabouts, Wulff."

"I know that. I know that damned well. You okay? You've recovered?"

"Parts of me," Williams said, "parts of me have recovered. I'm supposed to go back to work tomorrow."

"How's that wife of yours?"

"That's another story," Williams said. It was funny how after a lapse like this he could fall back into the same, odd rhythms of the relationship he had established with Wulff. Nothing changed. Nothing changed at all; at least on the outside. That seemed to be a truism.

"That's another story altogether."

"I'm in trouble," Wulff said.

"That's okay. I'm in trouble too."

"You want to help me out?"

"I don't know," Williams said. "I don't know about my sources of information anymore. I don't know about anything."

"I mean more directly," Wulff said, "more directly than information."

"Where the hell are you?"

"I'm in Los Angeles. Half the country is looking for me now."

"You wanted to take on the system. That's what happens when you take on the system. A lot of people begin to get interested in you."

"It's too much for me," Wulff said, "it's a little too much even for me. I need some help here. I don't think that I can hold them off single-handed."

"I got a knife in my gut," Williams said. "I almost died up there on 137th Street. I'm lucky to get out of it alive."

"All right," Wulff said, "it was just an idea. The hell with it."

"I didn't say I wouldn't go. I don't see what I can do for you, though. I'm supposed to go back on duty tomorrow. Desk job."

"Desk jobs are all right," Wulff said. His voice was thin and high through the continental transmission, not quite as Williams remembered it. Some freak of receptors, of course, unless it was something else . . . unless he was talking to a man different from the one he had last spoken to. "You're a system man, Williams, remember? You ought to be happy."

"I don't hold no truck with the fucking system," Williams said, "I'm in a different position now."

"Then come out," Wulff said, "come out and help me. I can't handle this alone. I can't do it anymore."

"I'm still on light duty. They don't want to put me behind a desk because they feel sorry for me. I'm not able to get into heavy stuff."

"You'll come out then. You'll help me."

"I don't know," Williams said. "I'm about to have a child. She's into the ninth month."

"Then it's still the system. The ninth month and a desk job. That's all you're telling me."

"No," Williams said. He shouted again. "I got nothing to do with the fucking system. I almost died on 137th Street, man, don't you know that? And she's not living with me any more. She walked out."

There was a long pause; Williams could hear Wulff breathing on the other end but for an extended time there was nothing but that breath. "I'm sorry," Wulff said, "really, I'm sorry about that. I hope I didn't have anything to do with it."

"Not much," Williams said. "Not much."

"I have no right to ask you anything then. Listen, you get back with that woman. You—"

"It's too late," Williams said sharply, and realized in saying it that it was the truth. Of course, it was; it must have been from the beginning. He knew that there was some reason that he had not tried to call her and now he knew what it was. They were simply past that point. "Too late for any of that crap. You're in a lot of trouble, right?"

"I'm in more trouble than I've been in my life. I don't think I can handle this myself. I thought that if you wanted to come along for the ride I could use you but if you're not able to handle—"

"I'll handle it," Williams said. He clamped the phone in his hand, feeling that hand moisten to the contact. "If I can be of any help I'll handle it. Where are you? Just tell me where the hell you are."

"Well," Wulff said, "I'm at one hell of a place, one hell of a place, old friend." And he went on from there, giving Williams exact details as to where he was and in what section of Los Angeles and how to get there and what to do when he came in. "Not that it makes any difference," Wulff finished up, "they have this place under such tight surveillance probably that you'll have a hell of a lot of trouble getting up here unmolested. I hope you know what you're getting into, that's all. I just hope so."

"I think I do," Williams said, "I think I do." And then there was suddenly, awkwardly nothing else to say. He told Wulff that he would try to make it out soon, within a day anyway, depending upon airline schedules and he would do what he could after that.

"You'd better bring some pieces," Wulff said. "I mean, both service revolvers and anything else that you can get hold of. What I could use, tell you the truth, is a fucking machine gun."

Williams said that he doubted that very much, for one thing it was a hell of a job to get a machine gun onto an airplane these days. Wulff said he knew what he meant about that and then he hung up because there was simply nothing else to say.

Williams lay there in the dark for a little while. In a vague way he was astonished at himself; how quickly he had seized the bait, how happily he had collaborated with Wulff. His revulsion with what had happened must have been even greater than he had calculated if he could abandon it so quickly. But then again merely the idea of a desk job might have been what had touched him off; he was no ornamental cop, no play cop with toy armaments. If he was going to do the job he wanted to do it on the front lines or not at all. Funny; he could admit that now. Funny what you sometimes learned about yourself only in the worst of circumstances. His gut was still shuddering but somewhat less than it had before; constriction had overtaken that looseness of uncoiling and he was able to stand and move without pain. He did so. It made no difference now; there was no point in waiting. He got off the bed and packed a suitcase shoving in both service pieces and he left the ranch-style home in St. Albans, New York.

Poising at the threshold for a moment, Williams thought of calling his wife, at least telling her what had happened and where he was going but he did not. It would not be worth it. There was nothing to say to her and the less she knew of his whereabouts the better off she would be if Calabrese decided to put the pressure on. Nobody was going to mess with a woman pregnant in her ninth month, not even Calabrese, and his sister-in-law would take good care of her. He would only be a liability at this time; he would only contaminate the child. I'm sorry, he guessed he could say to her, I'm sorry, sorry about everything, but even this would not have been true. He simply did not know what, if anything, he should feel sorry for. None of what had happened was really his fault. It had all been inherited; inherited pain, inherited destiny.

Maybe the path he was taking now had been the only solution from the first. He would see. He would just see about that.

Williams walked to a corner and hailed a cab, went out to the airport. His wife had taken the Montego when she had split. There were ten payments still due on it. The shocks were gone and the transmission at seventeen thousand miles had already begun to slip. Junk. *Junk.*

VII

Wulff, '62 Cadillac Sedan de Ville, and a small trailer checked into the Idle Time Trailer Park in the San Fernando Valley about twelve hours after his phone call to Williams. Wulff did not look like Wulff any more, wearing a false beard and sideburns which he hoped would make it through the night. The '62 Sedan de Ville looked like no Cadillac conceived by the mind of man since the golden days of the automotive age, and the trailer was a horror, a rotting construction that he had picked up along with the Sedan de Ville from a junk lot, the best he could get on short notice. Only the gift from Peru was the same but that was stashed in a corner of the trailer, folded in upon itself, covered with scraps of newspapers, and hopefully no one would be able to tell the difference. If they could find that bag so much the worse for him . . . but if they could find that bag, Wulff thought, it would only be because his cover was completely blown and in that case it simply did not matter. He had a couple of carbines, too. He would make it very unpleasant, at the least, for anything less than a small army. He did not think Calabrese would send an army out after him. On the other hand, you never could be sure. He was top priority now; he knew that.

The Cadillac, the trailer, the trailer park were out of character, of course. What the hell was Wulff doing underground anyway? But it was a simple calculation of possibilities. Dealing with Tamara after the man had burst in, talking with Williams and then the understanding had finally broken upon him that he was in too deep. He could take on the world, maybe, but he could only do it in small groups, sequentially, over a period of time.

Calabrese had the whole fucking world after him.

Not only that, but organization security could be conceived to be as fouled up as security anywhere. If the word was out through the organization that he was top priority then it would long since have leaked out . . . his picture, his biography, his probable whereabouts and methods, as well as the goods he had on his person . . . all of those would be available by now to almost any ambitious freelancer with the price of a gun and a train ticket in his possession. A man could do worse than to go after Wulff at this stage of the game. Killing him would be career-making. Getting hold of the goods would be something more than that.

It was just too hot. He was too deeply in. Surfacing to pick up Williams, if the cat got to LA, was as far as he wanted to go at this time. Even that was a risk. He needed to continue his quest, he needed to kill Calabrese—they were the same thing after all—but right now most of all he badly needed to get underground. Discretion was the better part of valor. Common sense was the only preservation of the courageous man.

"You can be thrown out on an hour's notice, my notice," the man at the check-in office of the Idle Hour Trailer Park told him. He looked at the trailer and the Cadillac with revulsion, then reached under his arm and brought out a pamphlet, gave it to Wulff. "These are the rules of the park," he said, "read them. Any violation and you're out on your ass." His eyes would not come off the trailer. "Where did you get that shit?" he asked.

"I picked it up at a garage sale," Wulff said and turned to go back to the car, the engine still idling.

The guard pursued him though, leaned against the door, blocked Wulff before Wulff could make entry. "How long are you going to be here?" he said.

"I don't know. I paid a month in advance up front."

"That didn't answer my question. You think you're going to be here a full month?" The man was in his fifties, a transplant, Wulff thought. He was wearing California costume but the look, the face, the eyes were all New York. Probably he was a civil servant, maybe even a cop, who was living on his pension; enjoying the good trailer life in the San Fernando. Sure. Sure he was enjoying the good life.

"Could be," Wulff said. "I went all through that in the office."

"Office don't mean shit," the man said. He reached under his arm again, felt something, not the pamphlets he was holding. Probably he had a gun in there and likely he had fantasies of using it. Wulff fought for control, opened the door slowly, finding a foot of space between him and the man, and squeezing himself through. The gaseous odor of the car interior rose, enveloped him; looking down at the floorboards he could see the suggestion of wires, gutted steel peering up at him. The car was idling unevenly, at least five of the cylinders dead, choking out clear dribbles of gas he could see in the open spaces purling beneath. He did not want to antagonize these people. Trailer parks were the last frontier. But the urge to smash the transplant was full within him.

"Tell me," the guard said, "you in any kind of trouble?"

"Not that you should know of."

"Plenty of people with trouble, they think that they can use this space as a stakeout, a hideout. No address you know, just a lot of trailers." The man motioned down the path; Wulff following it could see the trailers, many colors, grouped close upon one another. Nesting pattern. "But that's a goddamned mistake. We report everyone who comes in here to the cops for a routine check. Any troublemakers, the cops come in and bust them up. Also," the man said, "also, we got our own security forces."

"That's nice," Wulff said. Gently he closed the door, eased the Cadillac into gear. The transmission slammed, bucked, more metal fell off from somewhere. "I'll keep that in mind."

"Anyone we don't like," the guard said, still scratching at the place in his armpit, "gets thrown off the land on an hour's notice like I said. And you lose your whole goddamned deposit too. That's the way we run things around here. You don't like it you can move your ass right out now."

"All right," Wulff said, releasing the brake, "all right." He let the car roll; it parted the mud, and he brushed the guard out of view, the car moving, the old, yellow trailer lumbering behind him. He was aware that the guard was standing, following him all the way down the path but whether this was real curiosity, something about Wulff in the heavy disguise which had provoked him, or whether it was the natural hatred which this transplant felt for all people, people who mucked up his grounds, impinged on his territory, Wulff did not know. Nor did he care. He was desperately tired and beginning to feel for the first time now that he was approaching the limit of his possibilities. Always the pursuer, Calabrese had him rammed now into the posture of quarry. He did not like it.

From the road the Idle Hour had looked something like a camping area, a rather bucolic one, set off by fringes of trees and little signs. But now as he penetrated the area in which the trailers were actually parked the bucolic nature went away and Wulff found himself inching down an ever-narrowing path, trailers of all colors parked crazily in every direction, a few forms sitting on those trailers or wandering in the spaces among them in a dishevelled condition, barely enough room now on the declining path to keep the shaky Sedan de Ville properly pointed. Here, he thought, here was the new slum, the new disgrace. Harlem, the agony of New York and the central cities were thought of as the slums in the popular mind but they reflected a reality which had existed seventy or eighty years ago, an industrial reality, say. The slums of today's New York were little different from the factory towns which had sprouted in the Midwest . . . the diseased sinkholes that the great cities had been by 1900 . . . but the trailer park was something new, a post 1950's invention coming out of an America whose new mobility had merely enabled it to spread its poisons further and thinner. So here in the Idle Hour were the thin segments of agony brushed over the landscape, the same thing really: Harlem, the Idle Hour, miserable areas carved out of the landscape presided over in the one case by landlords and corporations who milked it dry, in the other by small-time entrepreneurs like the guard and his brother who were squeezing a living out of the Idle Hour in a kind of tyranny. But if it ever became profitable, truly profitable, why then the corporations would move in here just as they had moved into Harlem and really make it pay. Wulff smelled over the odor of the car the denser smell of the trailer park: too many forms huddled together in these demolished woods, the tangled odors of fires, washing, human feces. Something within him balked, really revolted. He brought the Cadillac to a shaky stop in the first open area that he could find and hit the brakes hard, the yellow trailer behind slamming against his bumper bringing him into the windshield, and the car stalled. He sat there in mud, little rivulets and trickles of foul water running on two sides of him, a welter of trailers of all sizes closing him in on three sides. The man up front had said something about finding a spot with plumbing facilities, hooking into flush toilets and running water. But where? Where the hell was he supposed to go?

He didn't know. He supposed that he could worry about that later, if it made any difference. He was not here for plumbing, hot water, conveniences. He was here for the same reason he guessed that everyone else was: to get out of it, to find some cover, to get the hell out of America. But looking through the bitter, bitter landscape, the faces peering through the windows of the trailers, dirty children playing somewhere in the piles of mud, the plumes of exhaust as someone down the line revved his stinking motor . . . it occurred to Wulff that you could never get out of America, not ever, not if you had the remotest connection to this diseased country . . . and that when he had been out, in Havana, in Peru, nothing had motivated him so much as the need to return.

You are your world, he thought wearily and went back to the trailer to see if the goods were still there. They were. He wondered if he was simply renting out space.

VIII

Williams was on US 90, halfway across Nebraska, when the first ambush team hit him.

But a lot had happened in the three days before that, so much that it made the ambush almost inconsequential. Not that that was the right way to take it . . . because the men at the roadblock were really ready to kill him. Still, it was something of an anti-climax after what he had been through. He was proceeding through Nebraska in a rented Ford, behind the Ford was a U-haul closed to the world and loaded to the hilt with mortars, grenades carbines, automatic rifles, pistols . . . more ammunition than he had ever seen in his life outside the barracks of the police academy. It would be more than enough to get Wulff back in business again. It might have put the Eighth Army back in business again.

But coming by it had not been easy. Williams had scratched right away Wulff's suggestion that he pick up what he could carry in a large suitcase and fly out to LA. That was crazy; his old friend was not really thinking right, the pressure was obviously getting even to Wulff. What with the federal surveillance of luggage and passengers, in light of the hijacking problem, Williams would not even have been able to sneak a water pistol through the loading areas at Kennedy. And even if there had been no surveillance what would he have been able to take on a plane, a couple of rifles at best, a few compact grenades, a scattering of pistols? No, if you were going to get into something like this you had to do it right. You had to get the real stuff and in quantity on a do-it-yourself basis . . . and you had to do your own trucking and hauling.

Williams was going to go into it. There had never been any doubt in his mind from the moment of Wulff's call. In a sense, he now understood, he had probably been waiting for that call for a long time, many months, even before he had taken the knife in the gut. But putting down the phone he had gotten past his wild first impulse to grab a couple of pistols and make it out to LA. That wasn't going to help Wulff a hell of a lot. It wouldn't have helped him much either. He had to do it right or not at all.

So Williams waited until the next day and then he made a few phone calls. He had a pretty good idea of whom to get in touch with, a black cop had really decent contacts if he wanted to cultivate them, and Williams had done so. Also, being a black cop was an advantage to get through to sources like this because if you handled them the right way they thought of you as less of a cop and more of a black. He knew that he would have to go outside of conventional channels to get his hands on what he was seeking. He found himself set up for the meeting in a basement on 139th Street between St. Nicholas and Eighth Avenues.

The man he had come to see wore flowing robes and had a religious aspect. That was quite natural; he was working behind a storefront, labelling the basement as the ALL SOULS DIVINITY AND BROTHER'S CHURCH, just another of the thousand storefront churches in Harlem; religiosity and disease mixing there as in no other country in the world. Perhaps they were the same thing. Not anything to think about now. The man's name was Father Justice. He was about thirty years old and held a prayer book. The basement had a small altar thrown up against a bleak wall, a few benches lined up behind the altar serving as pews, a couple of collection plates lying on racks to the side. Standing in here, looking at Father Justice, Williams could hear the music.

"Yes?" Father Justice said. He had a quiet, flat voice. "There are no services. Services are at seven, evensong at nine and—"

"Michael sent me," Williams said. Getting through the door had been easy; the key was supposed to be the word *Michael* after you were already through. Father Justice's expression did not change. His eyes, however, slowly kindled with light.

"Michael?" he said.

"That is correct." Williams held his ground, tried to lean against the wall to show control, put his hand in his pocket where ten thousand dollars lay in rolled up hundreds. Seed money; his inheritance. Someday it was going to pay off the house if he ever needed to pay it all off in one chunk. He had pulled it out of the bank this morning. The other ten in the account he had left for his wife. Fair enough. Fifty-fifty split. William's father had made absolutely no provisions; it was his to do with as he saw fit. What would his father think now? Williams thought wryly. The old man had died just six months ago, time enough to see Williams inducted into the force but very little else. The old man had been proud. Well, moderately. "Michael," he said again.

"Ah," said Father Justice. He moved behind Williams delicately with motions as graceful and imperceptible as the wind, closed the door of the storefront behind him, came to Williams's side. "We do not believe in violence," Father Justice said. "Violence is a very terrible disease in this society. Furthermore, it is a slander on the name of the Lord."

"That is true," Williams said.

"The ways of the violent are corrupt and their ends disastrous. Those who live by the sword must die by the sword. Always throughout generations this has been the word of the Lord."

"I know that," Williams said. "Violence is a terrible disease within our society."

"On the other hand," Father Justice said after a little pause, his eyes opening and closing ecstatically, his hand clutched in his robes, tugging at them, "we are confronted by a paradox. For who is to say that the man of decency must not turn to violence just as must the evil man to counteract those deeds? What can speak to the mighty but their own weapons, their own greed and evil?"

"I've thought about that."

"Truly the oppressor must die by his own sword, truly the oppressed must inherit the earth. But how are they to inherit the earth if they do not have the means to do so? The Lord counsels moderation and a benign spirit, the turning of the other cheek to the aggressor, and submission to the wicked. But the Lord has also counseled us to know thine enemy, to extract justice, to avenge the meek and mild, and to bring about the era of justice."

"Yes," Williams said quietly, fascinated. Father Justice's eyes were round and luminous, his expression had shifted from the ecstatic to keen intelligence. Slowly Williams dug his hand into his pocket, slowly then he extracted the hundreds tightly rolled into one another like a deadly little grenade, and showed it to the father. The man began to rock back and forth on his heels, making little noises.

"An offering," Father Justice said, "an offering to the All Souls and Divinity, to the mission itself, to the holy purposes."

"Freely given," Williams said.

"Freely given and from a generous spirit. Happy is he," Father Justice said, "happy is he who gives kindly from a kind and benevolent nature for he shall be known and be celebrated by all the mingled angels of Heaven." He backed away from Williams, moved to a small door against the other side of the room adjoining the altar, reached into his robes to extract a large key, and then with a flourish opened the door. He motioned to Williams. "Happy is he who walketh with the Lord," he said, and Williams went to him, went under his beckoning arm and into a back room which looked like a munitions factory. Williams had never seen anything like this in his life.

Well, he had seen a lot of things he had never before seen in his life: he had seen men wounded, men killed, blood running through the streets of Harlem, a generation destroyed and dying, but still there was some place in the lexicon for the simple wonders of technology. On the walls hanging in racks were rifles of every size, of every description. Between the rifles, like flowers, hung pistols, on another wall were grenades and cartridge belts, a third wall was devoted to machine guns and clips, and then instead of a fourth wall ahead of him directly behind the altar, there was a long tunnel opening up into a musky abscess in which once again Williams could see the glinting of ordnance.

"It has to be cash on the line, and I'll pay fifty percent for whatever you bring back," Father Justice said in a different tone. "The stuff is mostly good, it can't be traced that is, but I'm not letting any machine guns go out of here unless I get a lot better from you than 'Michael sent me.' 'Michael sent me' is all right for pistols and rifles; I might even give you a grenade or two on a 'Michael sent me,' but as far as machine guns that's definitely out unless I know a hell of a lot more about you and right now I know dammed little. I know that you're a cop or an ex-cop and that you want to ship the stuff out of town to do a job on some drug guys. That's okay with me, I want to get the shit-takers as much as anyone around because they're just cutting into everything here, but a 'Michael sent me' is not for machine guns." Justice coughed hoarsely, wiped a hand across his mouth, heaved his shoulders. "This is more of a rental than a store as you can see," he said. "I want to have as much of the stuff returned as possible; I don't have an unlimited stock here and there's more of a call for it all the time. If you return it in good condition I might be able to give you fifty-five, even sixty percent back, depending. For the unused stuff, stuff that's just carried along for insurance, and I can tell if it's unused, it might be seventy-five percent. Now tell me about yourself, if you want some machine guns and what else you want, and let's get out of here." Justice's shoulders were twitching, seemingly out of control. "I tell you I don't like it," he said, "standing back here, looking at all that stuff, it gets me very, very nervous." He lifted a finger, wiped some sweat off his forehead neatly, deposited it in an unfurled handkerchief. "It's a goddamned violent trade," he said.

It was a goddamned violent trade all right, but Williams was able to get out of it what he wanted with only a little haggling over the thousand dollars apiece that Justice wanted for machine guns and clips. That was too much if he was going to get the rest of the stuff, and when Williams explained in more detail than he originally intended who he was and who he was working with and what they had in mind, Justice came down to four hundred apiece and knocked the rifles down to two hundred dollars for the automatics and fifty for the old M-l's, fully restored.

"I know about Wulff," Justice said, "*everybody* knows about Wulff now and as far as I'm concerned I'll risk a loss on him because he is on the right path."

Still, it had eaten up far more of the ten thousand than Williams had expected it to, leaving the barest safety margin for the rental and expenses getting cross-country. God willing, Wulff had his own sources of cash out there. He already had the U-haul and the Ford, of course, and it was simple enough to back them straight up to the church. It turned out that that long hallway in the back room instead of the fourth wall led to a boarded-up wooden door around the corner near a vacant lot. No one was on the street at this hour at all and the U-haul was able to come in flush to the wall so the armaments were not exposed to sight for even an instant. Still, it was hard, heavy work, Justice helping, the two of them sweating freely in the dark, Harlem air and when they had finished Williams wanted nothing so much as to sink into one of those pew-benches in the Brother Divinity and just sweat for a while.

But Justice had become very nervous. "You must go, my son," he said, adopting or readopting his ministerial manner the moment that they had come out of the street. "He who travels with the Lord travels as if with the wind; his feet are speedy and his heart is light but he that will tarry, yea, he that will tarry even in the name of the Lord will do so with a great burden because in His service there may be no delay." That seemed to clinch the issue fairly well, at least from Brother Justice's point of view.

He had given the reverend eight thousand three hundred and four dollars and had gotten into the Ford and gotten the hell out of there as quickly as a man could when he was leaving a place of the Lord. Driving south on St. Nicholas he had done so with the vague feeling that he might never see Harlem again, that he never would see Harlem again, but that was merely an illusion. The only way that he would fail to see Harlem again would be if the two of them got killed out there. (He could not think of Wulff dying and Williams lucking through alone.) Otherwise he would be in Harlem for the rest of his life. Any black man in America lived in Harlem no matter how far he journeyed, and that was the truth of it.

So he had the U-haul loaded and the next thing was to call his wife; at least tell her where the ten thousand was and that it was hers and he had to get out of town but he found that he simply could not do it. He could not face it; more than likely he would find if he called that she was giving, had given, birth and that double-connection, son (he knew it would be a boy) and wife, would have been too great. As far as he had gone, he would simply never make it all the way out of here if he learned that he had a son. So instead he simply wrote her a letter, a flat, businesslike delivering-the-message letter which he mailed to her in care of her sister, saying nothing about the way he felt or what it meant to leave her, saying that he would be back and this time, somehow, they would make it work. It was a lie, he knew it was, but at this time it was the best that he could give her, the only thing that he could give her.

And then, the letter mailed, the blinds drawn, the house locked up, the few items he thought he might need rolled into a suitcase and hurled into the back of the car, the armaments themselves under double-bolts which he spent half a day working on, Williams got out of there as quickly as he could. Staying there, staying in the little house in St. Albans with a U-haul full of ordnance in the neat, white garage would have been criminally stupid for anyone . . . but it was not only that. If he stayed in this house, even with the phone pulled out of the wall, which he did, the memories were going to get him, the feelings composed of rage, loss, abandonment, disaster . . . and he might never move. He had to move. If he did not do it now he never would. He would stay in St. Albans with a healing knife wound in his gut and he would die slowly, thirty or forty years maybe, sinking into his own revulsion. What Wulff offered him was at least quicker and cleaner. It was a chance to confront the enemy whole, to seize and see the face of the nightmare.

He would take it.

So he got into the Ford and pulled the U-haul out, getting only one suspicious glance on the George Washington Bridge from a toll-taker who thought that he heard something rattling in the back. If he had been going east, where the toll booths were, they might even have stopped him but west the toll booths had long since been abandoned, double-fare, get you on the way back (he might never be back) and the toll-taker, peering down the line at the jouncing truck, obviously calculated and then decided that it was not worth it. He was not going to be any goddamned hero on ten thousand eight hundred dollars a year—Williams knew the feeling—and besides the U-haul would probably turn out to be full of pots and pans. Who the hell needed it?

Over the bridge and onto Route 80. Immediately, just three miles, less than that, out of Manhattan the road, the flat, dead spaces, and sensation of the interstate highway overtook him, a road that was everywhere and nowhere, the same ruined landscape that would confront him for three thousand miles already at Teaneck, Little Ferry, Hackensack, Paterson . . . and deeper then to the breakoff on 46 where 80, not yet completed, fed into the state highway for a while, fighting for space and air with trucks on all sides. Then another patch of 80 and the death of interstate again. He did not know which was worse, to choke and fume on a road with character or to be lost in the emptiness of the interstate . . . back on 46 again for a little while to figure it out, make a final decision (he never did). And then on 80 for real now, rolling toward the Delaware Water Gap, into Pennsylvania, on Pennsylvania sections, the night falling fast, cars passing him at a hundred and a hundred and ten miles an hour on these unpatrolled segments, the Ford stumbling and missing around seventy-five, the little trailer chattering behind him. On through Pennsylvania all night, poking on into Ohio by the dawn's early light, his first stopover in a cheap motel in Ohio for a five-hour nap, uneasy dreams of the U-haul exploding tumbling through his mind. Then to the road again, Ohio the same as New Jersey, Pennsylvania, Ohio the same as Illinois and swinging then outside Chicago, the hookup with 90 leading across the flat, dead plains states. Then the real interstate began: mile after mile, hundreds of miles of gray, empty space, sometimes the Ford surrounded as he picked up commuter traffic off the city belts, most of the time almost alone on the highway pushing it as close to seventy-five as he could, the motor cutting out thunderously once at seventy-eight, loss of power steering and the U-haul jackknifing, almost hurling him ass-end first, off the road, but he was able to save it. That was the only exciting thing that happened for twelve hours as he decided to get the best he could out of the five hours' stopover and see if he could make it all the way into the far western states before the dawn. In and out of transmission belts, the radio flicking on and off, his mind submerged somewhere below attention, Williams kept the pace up, after a while almost locked out of the world, the perimeters of the Ford the perimeters of existence, everything happening only in the car.

Then he came up against the roadblock, locked into that hypnotic state, yanking the wheel, smashing the brakes almost at the last moment, coming to a rearing, terrified attention as he saw men pour from the sides of the road surrounding the wooden sawhorses. There were guns in their hands.

These were not cops.

Williams saw it all in one burst of attention, then, the car idling, he was already diving toward the floorboards. The first shot came high, too high, smashing the safety windshield, putting little plasticine pellets down around his shoulders. And then the second, more intense series followed, the shots skittering off the hood, dumped into the driver's compartment. If he hadn't hit the floor they would have had him. But even on the floor Williams was calculating, he was coming to attention, could feel himself beginning to function. Then he got the gun up and at a seated position raised his hand, pumped out two shots, then ducked again as response bullets tore their way again through the windshield, falling around him like ball-bearings.

Too much, too much; these guys had to be crazy. Who would set up a roadblock on an interstate highway and what did they think that it would profit them? Even if they were able to nail him in this trap, didn't they understand that traffic was going to pile up rapidly behind him, even on a seemingly empty highway, three cars a minute passed a given point . . . and as if in confirmation far beyond Williams heard the dull pounding of a truck, the hiss of air brakes. The knowledge that traffic was then already beginning to form behind him, that he was not functioning in isolation, gave him the courage to rear all the way up and from this position, peering over the dash, he saw the situation in true perspective for the first time; everything had happened too fast before. There were just two of them, a Chevy van over on the side of the road, the sawhorse slung crudely across the two lanes as a block. Another bullet came, but Williams from this vantage point was already beginning to feel invulnerable. He got his gun up and out and put a clean shot into the near man, a shorter type holding a sawed-off shotgun. The man fell across the hood with a scream, the shotgun firing, the pellets misdirected, and the second man loomed behind him then. Williams saw a man in his forties wearing an odd, double-breasted, gray suit, some archaic aspect coming out of the fields of Interstate 90 to kill him, and in a slow and terrible calm he pointed the pistol at the man and shot him in the throat. The man had not even fired a shot; apparently the death of the man first in line had shocked him. He fell straight to the concrete, spread-eagled, little objects falling from his pockets scattering on the highway; pieces of paper, a few dollar bills, jolted loose by the impact. Breathing heavily, Williams leaned against the door of the Ford, got the handle up from memory, and went out onto the roadway.

Behind him a huge diesel, motor idling unevenly, had come to a stop just a few feet behind the Ford. The truckdriver, a thin man concealed behind enormous sunglasses and cap, was looking out the side. "What the fuck is this?" he said, pointing, taking in all of it; Williams, the roadblock, the two dead men lying on the concrete. "What the fuck is going on here?"

"I don't know," Williams said, "I don't know." And he meant it. Little knives of Nebraska heat filled with dust and light went through him. He put his pistol away and walked toward the sawhorse. The near corpse was bleeding thickly, dribbling blood into the concrete in a Rorschach pattern. Williams kicked it aside and put his hands on the sawhorse, bit his lips, heaved it upward. Surprisingly light, the contraption came up easily. He staggered to the side of the road, holding sixty pounds, dumped it on the shoulder, came back to the Ford noting abstractedly that there seemed to be bloodstains on the hood. Well, that was to be expected, wasn't it? He had shot, let's think about this now, the first man close on the hood, getting him in the throat, or was that the second man, but anyway it had been a bloody shot and of course at that proximity to the Ford he would have.

"I think we better get the cops, friend," the truckdriver said, still leaning out the window. Another car was lumbering up, a black shape just coming over the horizon. Behind it Williams could see a few more like insects, slithering, stumbling along. There would be five or six cars here in a minute; behind them another five or six more. Traffic was sparse but not all that little; even in Nebraska people still got on the highway, if only to get out of Nebraska, of course. "Really," the truckdriver said, "we ought to get some cops in here; find out—"

"Right," Williams said, "right you are." He got back behind the wheel of the Ford noting that his hands were shaking nicely. When you came right down to it these were his first two kills, weren't they? The business near the methadone center didn't count; that went the other way. "Right you are again," he said, turning, reaching for the door handle, slamming it, turning on the ignition. "I'll just get down to one of these phone booths and call in," he said and he slammed the door, locked it, floored the accelerator, and got out of there at sixty-eight miles an hour for the first quarter of a mile, a hundred flat for the first half. Yes, these Torinos, even with the emission devices, could accelerate, it seemed.

The hell with it, Williams thought, the hell with it and another thought on top of that: well he was really in for it now. Really in for it, yes sir, he was committed up to his black ass and beyond.

The scene behind him, perceived through the rear-view mirror, diminished, became miniscule, became inconsequential, vanished. He prowled on through Nebraska. He had no idea who the road-blocking guys were looking for. Maybe they had had him tracked all the way from New York.

And just maybe—this was the more frightening thought—just maybe they were looking for someone else entirely and had walked into something that they had never expected.

The hell with it.

The hell with all of this shit now.

He was really in for it.

IX

The ad in the personals that he had been looking for for a week was there that morning—ALL HECTOR LOPEZES: HECTOR LOPEZ CLUB FIRST ANNUAL MEETING SANTA ANITA RACE-TRACK, THIS AFTERNOON—was in and Wulff was there; in the grandstand at Santa, twenty minutes before the first race, pacing between the five and ten dollar win and show windows, checking the time as it came on the tote every minute. They were supposed to meet down at the finish line, that had been prearranged, just before the first race. All right then. Williams had made it; somehow the son of a bitch had gotten through and not a day too soon because Wulff did not know how much longer he could have held on. The Idle Hour trailer park was bad enough; it had turned out to be even worse than he had expected but the hell with the trailer park; he could have done that kind of duty standing on his head. What he could not take was the clear feeling now that they were closing in on him; that even this cover had run out its chances and that it was only a matter of time, very little time indeed, until Calabrese's forces or the freelancers had him nailed to ground. There were too many strange people poking around the place. There was too much traffic moving in and out. After five days he had pretty well mapped out the residents of the Idle Hour and there were people coming into the place now who had no trailers there. How much longer did he have? He had a huge bag of shit and light armaments, no way really of procuring more. How long could he have taken it? The net was tightening. But Williams had made it, somehow the son of a bitch had made it and put in the agreed-upon personal and maybe now he was at the end of this. Or at the beginning of something else. Wulff did not know. He simply did not know. It was the feeling of helplessness which he could not take, the rage, the slow feeling of entrapment. Somewhere, he knew, Calabrese was laughing at him.

Santa Anita. It was the richest racetrack in America, that was what he had read. The purse distributions were the highest, the per capita daily attendance and handle were on top now that the New York circuit had collapsed under the same government that had given New York the drug law, and Santa Anita stood or squatted alone, huddled in the mists around the valley, a vast pocket in which thirty-five thousand men, women, and children, most of them wearing dark glasses, came every weekday to throw their money against the tote, screaming. It meant very little to Wulff, horse-racing. Never had, never could now, but pacing here looking at the track, waiting for Williams, the son of a bitch, to show or not show, he could understand a little of what was going on here, what drove people to the track. Craziness. They were beating at the cage of possibility, the cages of the windows here, like insects. Heightened to rage, these people discolored the voice of the track announcer heard through all the megaphones. For all the information it was giving on weight changes, change of jockeys, scratches it could be giving out funeral information.

Well, it was very much like heroin. Then again, it was nothing like heroin but maybe it had the same outcome. People were looking for the same things from both: a passage out of the world and into some space where possibilities and accomplishments could be spliced, no difficult passage, easy conjoinment. Wulff did not want to think about that too much, standing under the tote hung from the ceiling of the grandstand, horseplayers scurrying around him, the heat and noise of the track rising to clamor now with ten minutes to post. The horses first taking the track, he was thinking, instead of the sack of heroin, rolled up, stuffed into the trunk of the Cadillac in the parking lot a quarter of a mile from here. That was probably stupid, bringing it out into plain daylight if even under cover; a clear target where anyone could get a shot at it, but on the other hand what the hell could he do? He sure as hell could not go lumbering around the grandstand of Santa carrying a sack like Santa Claus nor could he leave it in the trailer at the Idle Hour. That would have been classically stupid because Wulff was pretty sure that back at the Idle Hour trailers were ransacked in the owner's absence, possessions were gone through pretty quickly by the staff there. It was a police state was the Idle Hour, tight surveillance, all lights out at ten o'clock, stiff deposits paid when entering, a penalty fee paid as removal charge if one wanted to get out before the end of the month, and a list of rules and regulations which as far as Wulff could deduce made anything impermissible, gave the owner all the options and the residents simply one . . . to pay and pay subject to the whims of the owner. It was a nice, tight little slum there all right; a slum with the further virtues of a jail. That was an American characteristic anyway; there was something about people in this country that made them enjoy putting themselves in jail, made them delight in the restrictions they imposed upon themselves. Americans, it seemed, only derived their sense of identity from being imprisoned. The Idle Hour, a perfect little South American nation carved out of the ruined landscape of California, was as perfect a working example of oppression as Wulff had ever seen. There was a whole generation of people now who were living this way, living in the Idle Hours of the country, and although they grumbled and complained a bit the Idle Hours were flourishing. The trailer park business was certainly a growth industry. What it came down to, Wulff thought, was that people liked it. If they had not had the abuse they would have taken to thinking of all that space, all that possibility, and the human mind, or at least the human American mind, was not equipped to take it. A man was looking at him.

Odd that even in all this heat, this swirl of crowd, Wulff could pick up one clear focus of attention, but police training, whether you wanted to remember it or not, was always there. Leaning against a shutdown fifty dollar window about ten yards away, a tall man wearing a hat, a Racing Form folded and shoved into his armpit, was looking at Wulff with a steady and rising interest, a glare of attention so pure and clear that Wulff knew that he had been recognized. Slowly he adjusted his position under the tote, then turned and went into the line behind the five dollar window. The man's eyes followed him. Seeing Wulff's sudden reaction to him, the man very slowly took the newspaper from under his arm and feigned reading it, his eyes peering out above the paper with intense interest. There was a slight bulge on the left side of the jacket near the heart. The man was armed.

Well, Wulff thought, that was wonderful. That was just wonderful, but then what had he expected? A disguise was only as good as the degree of interest you had aroused and he had aroused a good deal. The tall man seemed to know exactly who he was. Standing there, the line shuffling forward slowly to the window like a group of penitents waiting for assembly-line communion, Wulff instinctively patted his own inner pocket where the point thirty-eight caliber rested. It was no defense. Assuming that the man was after what he supposed he was, you could not take out a pistol in the grandstand at Santa and start shooting. That kind of thing just wasn't done. Also, there was no assurance that the man was working alone.

There were three people ahead of him now in the line. Wulff looked up at the tote; three minutes now until post time. If he and Williams had worked it out properly Williams would almost be down at the finish line now, would almost be ready for the meet, but he resisted the impulses to lunge from the line and walk down there. One had to remain cool; one had to force a sense of control of the situation even if that control did not truly exist, because if you lost the handle, if everything came apart inside, then it would come apart on the outside with the same alacrity. The owners of the Idle Hour knew all about that kind of control. A small man shambled away from the window looking at the tickets he had bought with a bemused air as if not sure that he even remembered having done this, and Wulff told the seller, "Number five," and put a ten down on the counter. Five was as good a number as any, he supposed; he was at the five dollar window, wasn't he? The man over by the closed fifty window had now put away his newspaper and was slowly ambling toward Wulff. The ticket came out of the machine, lay in front of him. With a kind of exhausted tilt to his head the clerk slowly counted out five singles, held them, finally put them down next to the ticket when it became apparent that Wulff was not going to leave. Behind him, with the flash down to two minutes to post (but the tote always worked a minute ahead to build the action of the last-minute bettors to early frenzy) the crowd was mumbling and cursing. Wulff took the ticket, took the singles, stuffed it all into his right pocket and began to move slowly toward the great doors that opened out to the concrete lawn, the lawn running up to the rail and beyond that to the earth of the track. It was cool and pleasant today but it had rained the day before; that meant that the track was a holding, hard surface bad for come-from-behind horses, good for early speed, or so Wulff had heard around the grandstand. He did not give a damn. Horseracing meant nothing to him; he was dealing with a much deeper, darker history of chances. The man was still behind him as he worked his way through the crowd toward the finish line.

No doubt about it now; he had been spotted. There was always that small possibility up until the moment that they pursued you that it was all in your mind, that he had been functioning at the edges of attention for so long that innocent people, innocent gestures, became transmuted to menace. But this was unmistakable; as Wulff increased his pace dodging through the crowd, the man behind him, afraid that he might lose the trail, also extended his own stride. For the first time Wulff could see, looking back in little glances that the man had abandoned his posture of inattention and was pushing, really pushing frantically, trying to keep him in sight. Wulff put a hand inside his jacket pocket, checked the point thirty-eight. To use it in the infield would be crazy, of course; he simply could not do it. But would the tall man have similar consideration?

He did not know. Down at the finish line where the rail of the infield joined that of the paddock there was a crush of bodies, hundreds of people leaning against the rail staring out at the horses, who were now dots on the backstretch wheeling to turn into the starting gate for the six-furlong sprint. Wulff could not see Williams. For a moment he thought that it had all gone to pieces—there was also the chance that Williams, similarly spotted, might have been intercepted—but then he saw him, the tall black man at the furthest point of the conjoinment wedged tightly into the spot where the rails met, looking back at the crowd with bright, staring eyes. They must have recognized one another at the same instant; then Wulff was using his elbows to prod his way through the crowd, really shoving now. Williams extended a hand, and then his reserve returning at that instant, elaborately turned and looked back toward the track. The tall man was somewhere behind Wulff now but he could not for the moment see him. Momentary respite, that was all. He was closing in.

He poked through bodies, then came against Williams. The man was looking out at the track, still with that elaborate unconcern, but the fingers of his left hand were jumping and there was a tremor in his cheek. "Yeah," he said quietly as Wulff came against him, "yeah," a short emission of breath making the word a sigh . . . . He smiled in an intensely private way and then wedged himself yet deeper into the rail, looking out at the backstretch. "Who do you like, man?" he said. "I think the one horse has got this; he's got the early speed for the conditions but seven to five is no bargain, not for cheap shit like this. I've been making a study of the conditions," Williams said quietly.

"I'm being followed."

"Oh," Williams said. He held himself steadily against the rail. "Oh, shit."

"Somebody in the grandstand spotted me."

"That stands to reason," Williams said very quietly. The track announcer said something about post-time. "Just one of them?"

"So far. Maybe he's a spotter, maybe he's got partners. Don't know."

"You're in deep, man. You're in very deep."

"I told you that over the phone. You get some stuff?"

"Yes," Williams said quietly, looking in his cop's way carefully through the crowd without his eyes lighting on any specific individual; it was clever, the rookie was a good man. Always had been. "I got a lot of stuff. I don't see anyone looking at you."

"Can't tell," Wulff said quietly, head down, hands in pockets. Through the megaphones Wulff could hear a thump, and then the black dots, far in the distance were moving freely, scurrying down the backstretch. The noise level around the two of them began to build; they were able to talk under it, moving close together. A fat woman to Wulff's right was jumping up and down, cascading sweat. Wulff flicked the drops off him. The five horse seemed to have taken the early lead.

"Let's get out of here," Wulff said.

"No point," said Williams. "Couldn't move in this, anyway." The noise level was terrific, waves of sound beating at them like surf. "Wait till the race is over, then they scatter."

"Let's go now."

"You don't know shit about racetracks, do you?" Williams said with a little smile. "When the race is on nobody moves. Somebody spotting us, he'll pick us up right away. After the race there's plenty of movement, we can get lost." The five horse was still holding the lead coming into the stretch. Williams leaned over, grasped the rail, inclined his head down the track surface. He seemed to be saying something but with the noise Wulff could not hear. *Come on, one*, he lip-read. The son of a bitch had a bet down.

Well, that was his business. In the fifteen seconds during which the last furlong and a half was run Wulff suspended his attention, turned on the crowd, saw in that crest of faces all of them pointed toward the track: begging, pleading, shouting. He saw that the man who had pursued him down to the rail had vanished. There was no doubt of that whatsoever; he had positioned the man in his mind, known exactly where he had been standing, understood his intention . . . but in those moments since he had made the meet with Williams the man had somehow ducked out, gone away from there. It would not have been difficult. As Williams had said, who during the running of a race watched anything but the race?

They should have gotten the hell out of there already.

The horses had gone by; Wulff turned, saw their rumps passing the finish line, some bunched together, a few strung out. From this angle there was no indication who had won but Williams, hunched over the rail, had taken a ticket out of his pocket and was busily shredding it, cursing. "Fucking one," he said. "Fucking son of a bitch lays off the pace; if he had only chased that cheap speed—"

"Let's get out of here," Wulff said.

Williams jerked his head up, his eyes round. The idea of getting out seemed to be a new one to his consciousness. "Yeah," he said, "yeah, I guess we could do that."

"He must have thought he blew his cover," Wulff said. "He's gone."

"Gone? Gone? Oh, you mean the guy—"

Something seemed to have happened to Williams' cerebral faculties. Call it the racetrack itself, he guessed. "Look," he said, putting a hand on the rail, then gesturing as numbers started to appear on the tote, as the announcer began to babble something about the results not yet being official. "Look at that. The five horse won it."

"Let's get out of here," Wulff said. "I think that we've got a few minutes' grace; I don't know who the guy is with though, or what he might be carrying—"

"Yeah," Williams said. He shrugged rapidly several times as if cold, "yeah, we ought to get out of here. Okay. The five horse won it A forty, fifty to one shot." He squinted, looked at the tote. "Fifty to one on the last flash," he said, "that means a minimum of a hundred and two dollars. That's wild."

"All right," Wulff said, putting a hand on his partner's shoulder, guiding him through the crowd which was indeed breaking up into little clumps, most of them babbling curses. "Let's get the hell out of here." A continent, four months, three thousand miles for this reunion . . . and all Williams could talk about was the five horse. "I don't know how much time we've got," he said. "They're closing in. It's bad."

"I know it's bad," Williams said, following Wulff now in a rapid scuttle, pulling alongside of him when they broke into an open area under the grandstand, damp gusts of air propelled by fans hitting them. He was not walking quite normally, Wulff noticed, the knife wound that Williams had taken had hurt him obscurely, badly, changed him. Williams no longer looked twenty-four; he might have been forty. "Don't tell me how bad it is. I almost got fucking knocked off in Nebraska."

"Yeah," Wulff said, "I almost bought it in a few places too." The announcer was now saying that the result was official, dim groans were coming up like steam around them as they walked rapidly downstairs to ground level toward the parking lot. "Quite a few places." He looked around him. The tall spotter was nowhere in sight. All right. All right, then, he had been right; there were at least a few minutes lead time. "Let's get back and unload," he said, "you got the stuff?"

"In the parking lot. Oh my, yes indeed, I would say that I have the stuff."

"Good," Wulff said, "good," throwing his ticket onto the concrete of the parking lot, the ticket fluttering behind them. It only occurred to him a little later when they were already on the road toward the Idle Hour, forming a little caravan, Williams trailing him tight, the U-haul wobbling in his rear vision, that he had bought a ticket on the five. The five had won the race. He spliced the two facts dimly, obscurely; in this gelatinous mix they moved together. What had Williams said? Fifty to one? One hundred and two dollars minimum?

Well, how about that, he thought, fighting the wheel of the diseased Cadillac. Son of a bitch, they talked about Onan casting his seed upon the ground. What would they say about him?

Probably very damned little. There wasn't going to be much of a history. And since the guys from the winning side wrote the history books, there probably wouldn't even be a mention of it.

The hell with it, anyway.

X

Billings was willing to be patient. The plan to Billings was beautiful; two million dollars' worth of shit, if that was what the guy had on him, was certainly worth a hell of a lot more than fifty thousand bounty or whatever crumbs Calabrese would throw at him. Probably not even that; the old man was a cheap bastard. Better go after the shit, he thought, even if possible try to make contact with the guy, arrange a straight split of some sort in return for Billings's advice and counsel. Wulff would have to know by now that he was a dead man. Everybody in and out of the country, every organization man, every freelancer was out to get him. The guy would surely have to be at the point of listening to reason now. He was a tiger but there were limits.

He had picked up the trail at the trailer court and he had followed the guy into the track, laying back all the time, taking his chances, taking it slow. On a straight kill he might have been able to have taken the guy in the Cadillac out on the highway. Why not? That disguise and cover weren't fooling anyone and if Wulff thought that they were it was only diminished alertness. The instructions filtered down from the top were very clear, shoot on sight, get him at any cost, but Billings had decided against it. If Calabrese wanted this man dead there would have to be far more guarantee than a bunch of vague promises passed down third-hand through a Los Angeles enforcer. No. He followed the man into the track. Take your time. Wait.

He didn't know if he was still working for Calabrese or going freelance. It was hard to say; it depended upon conditions. Through forty-three years of life, some of it disreputable, most of it dull, Billings had cultivated one attitude: you went with the tide not against it. If it seemed the only way he could use his knowledge of the man's whereabouts was to score him out then he would do it and settle for the low money, the hundred dollars and a bottle of Scotch that he would probably wind up with from the old man after the organization's various levels had finished cutting in. On the other hand, the basic plan was to get out of this at the highest level possible; that meant freelancing if he could get away with it. Get away with the goods. But above all you remained flexible, you changed your outlook to suit the conditions, and you never panicked. Panic was deadly. There was always a way out if you could find it.

Billings used to shoot heroin but with great difficulty he had kicked it. He had decided ten years ago that horse didn't pay; even at discount rates the habit was too expensive and it was undercutting his ambition. So he had gone into screaming fits in cold isolation for two weeks and walked out of the rooming house with the habit kicked but with the sullen knowledge that he would carry the desire for shit around him as long as he lived. All right. You could live with that, too; better wanting it all the time and living, being able to carry on, than having it and not wanting it and winding up OD'd out or in a sewer somewhere before your thirty-eighth birthday. But his years on horse had given Billings one overpowering insight which would not have been available to him otherwise: he knew all about the stuff. He could understand why a man or woman would get involved, would wind up dedicating the meaning of their whole lives simply to picking up the next shot or the next. It was powerful stuff. It beat all the hell out of ordinary living for the ordinary people and if he had had a choice he might have stayed on it. But no good. No good at all. He would have wound up dead and who would there be to funnel out the shit if all of the shitsellers were on the stuff themselves? That made simple sense:

stick to hard liquor and sex, look for kicks anywhere else, but stay off that stuff. He had managed it for over nine years now, nine years, six months, two weeks, four days exactly and there had not been a morning of his life once in all of that time when he had not awakened, alone or with a woman in his bed, aching for one poke of the needle. So live with it.

He picked the big bastard up at the grandstand at Santa. He thought that he had lost him in the parking lot and that was a pretty panicky feeling, stumbling out of luck with the same haste with which he had stumbled in. But when he came frantically into the track convinced that he had lost him he had almost walked up against Wulff underneath the grandstand tote, the big man holding a hand in his pocket, looking nervously up at the tote every thirty seconds or so, which meant that he was waiting for a meet of some sort. Billings had measured the guy; he had looked rough all right but not quite as difficult as rumor had it. When you came right down to it he was just another man, another human being, and Billings knew all of the pressure points. Jugular, groin, nape of the neck, solar plexus, they all went down in the same way to the same trigger and they took bullets in the same way too, blood spreading out like flowers from the ruined flesh no matter who they were. That was the secret: all men were the same in the way that they died and Calabrese knew that secret too, this probably being the center of his power. Billings had looked him over, planning it, plotting it, deciding on the best approach. What he wanted to do, of course, was to find the shit and kill him straight off but since finding the location of the shit probably involved not killing the guy but instead dealing with him in some way, Billings calculated it from that angle. There had to be a level of approach. He would find it.

The guy was alert though. He was goddamned alert; well, maybe that was one of the advantages of having been an ex-cop, he sensed a tail, he sensed cover, and Billings became quite aware, early on, that the man had somehow become alert to the cover. Nothing to do then but to fade away; either that or kill him then and there with the silencer and better than an even chance of sneaking away through the crowds, but Billings had decided to wait on the silencer. He could do that anytime. If you were willing to pay the price, that was what the cliché was, any man could kill any other man anytime. You couldn't stop killings, you could only punish them and by the punishment set a discouraging example. Maybe. The law had not had too much success with that concept for a couple of thousand years but you couldn't blame people for poking ahead still trying.

Then the guy got on the window line, shuffled slowly forward, made a bet, went out into the crowd on the lawn. Billings had by that time faded far back, moved out of the guy's range entirely, and he had almost lost him in the crowd, then he had picked him up, head bobbing, as he had gone toward the finish line. Billings closed in again. Here, possibly, was the place to do it. The audacious answer might be the right one. Shove a gun into the cat's ribs and abduct him right on the spot, disarm him, get him to the parking lot or wherever the hell the goods were, and then dump him right there. It seemed reasonable and Billings who had never liked the racetrack was beginning to become jittery with the crowds, the heat, the light, the noise. Better get out of here. Maybe it would be better to kill the guy here and get away cleanly than to mess with him, he thought. It tempted him. But he reminded himself that this was only old Santa, pounding its madness into the bloodstream. Better not take this seriously. If he did something like that he would be panicking.

Then the situation had suddenly taken another turn. There was a black guy down at the finish line and this Wulff was talking to him. Suddenly the picture came clear to Billings, this was the meet that Wulff had been waiting for, that was no idle chatter, no black-white relations and understanding going on down there. The guy had a partner of some sort, the black guy must have been the one, and somehow looking at this and the way that the two of them were talking the situation became infinitely more dangerous to Billings; it was not just a question of doubling the antagonists but rather geometrically compounding the odds against him. The black guy was bringing something into the equation that had not been there before, the black guy was obviously some kind of a key to what Wulff was doing here and where he would go from now on because he could see that Wulff was looking for an exit hatch almost as soon as he had started talking to the black guy. He had accomplished what he had come here for. He wanted to get out as quickly as possible. It was the black man, probably more interested in horses than Wulff, who insisted that they stay, that was obvious. Billings felt a profound disgust looking at this but he also felt the beginnings of calm and understanding. They would be coming out soon now. They might stay one race, they might somehow stay even two, but they were going to come out of here shortly and there was only one exit from the grandstand into the parking lot, one into which all of the alleys and corridors of the grandstand staircases fed. He could cover it easily. He could wait. He faded out of there.

Waiting, one hand on his gun, leaning against a gate, covering everything carefully, the thought occurred to him for the second time that he was probably in too deep. This might be a job for Calabrese after all; Billings had his advantages and talents but the odds were enormous and if he blew this one it meant that not only Wulff and the partner but Calabrese himself was going to be after him. It meant that even if he was successful he would just misdirect the heat meant for Wulff onto him. Better by far, maybe, to take a shot when he had a chance. They would be coming out of here soon. Okay. They would be coming out of here soon and with the silencer he would have a clear, clean shot and a good chance at escape before anyone even noticed that something was wrong. Who the hell looked at a couple of losers coming out of the track after the first or the second? At that time, the main flow was still the other way; hope money being toted in for the third, the fifth, the eighth, or ninth races. Take his shot and be done with it.

But he was in too deep, Billings thought. He had already made a decision and besides that, besides that he would admit it: the thrill of the hunt was upon him and beyond that the thrill of the ultimate hit. The two million dollars' worth of Peruvian goods which this character had with him were authenticated, that much was clear. Calabrese would not call this level of attention into play unless it was true, because Calabrese was cheap. So there was two million dollars for the taking, and damned, Billings thought, if he would relinquish it so quickly. He had scuffled on the margins all his life while worse men had gone further. Now it was his turn. He kept his hand on the pistol and he waited.

After a while, as he had expected, the two men came out of one of the doorways, poked their way through the flowers and greenery of the track, and came onto the path facing him. Billings ducked behind a tree holding his pistol; he was completely concealed then behind a bench but the two men simply kept on walking, kept on talking. For all the difference that Billing's presence made at this moment he might as well have not been there. Well it was obvious, Wulff had deduced inside the track that he was no longer being covered and now Billings was out of mind altogether. They were deeply involved in conversation; the black man was telling Wulff something. Good, better, best. Billings fell behind to a distance of two hundred yards and then he trailed them.

Coming into the parking lot the men split, the one heading off into the distance, the other, the black man, getting into a Ford sedan with a yellow U-haul behind it. The shit might be in there, Billings thought with vague excitement, it was quite possible, but he kept his eyes on

Wulff who was trudging on, seeing him go at last into a beaten-up car of some sort parked all the way down, separated from the other cars by a gap of ten to twenty yards. No, Billings thought, no, the shit isn't in the U-haul, that's something else. The shit is in Wulff's car and he parked it away from the others for that reason but he's a goddamned fool because it just brings more attention to him. He watched as Wulff struggled with the trunk, opened it, looked inside, then closed it. Checking. The Ford with the U-haul was already backing out of the lot. Billings, hunched over behind a row of cars watched that one move, watched Wulff's car move, and then as the two met somewhere in the exit path forming a file, he stood and sprinted to his own Volkswagen, not cautious at all now of being seen, simply desperate to reach his car, make the hunt. This was no time to worry about being seen. It would be insane to have gone this far, to have seen this much, only to lose them. He knew. Billings knew now. The shit was in the trunk of Wulff's junker. And if he knew anything about this situation the U-haul was full of something else, rifles maybe. The black man was bringing in the ordnance. They were a beautiful team all right; oh boy, they were one magnificent team. Kill them both. Billings thought wildly, double your pleasure, grab some guns *and* shit. He picked them up on the highway outside of Santa.

Here, they had slowed, had tried to blend inconspicuously into traffic but that bright yellow U-haul stuck out like a needle from a junkie's arm; Billings had no trouble at all picking them up then hanging back in traffic, letting the gap widen but never enough so that he lost direct sight, just hanging loose, digging in, and waiting to see what was happening. The trouble was that he was driving an unwieldy Volkswagen, not the car to take in the dense, alternately fast-and slow-moving traffic of the freeways. The four-speed transmission drove him crazy and it was impossible to set the car into a given speed range and track them. It was shifting up and down, cutting across lanes, changing speeds all of the time, and he had the panicky feeling twice that he was going to lose them as he got himself into a jam just as the U-haul broke free of it. It was stupid of him to have rented a car like this for the job. He should have gotten something larger with an automatic transmission but he had thought that a Volkswagen would be relatively inconspicuous. Live and learn. Everything was a process of learning, Billings thought. He was in trouble now, no question about it: he might have been able to take Wulff alone, risky business but despite the man's reputation at least possible, but the black man, the black man was a new element altogether and a dangerous one. Billings was convinced that the U-haul was filled with ordnance. It was the only explanation that made sense. But what the hell did they plan to do with all of this stuff? Blow up LA? Make a frontal attack? They were in no position to do so . . . but Wulff was crazy. Everyone knew that; his track record was one of constant attack when he should have been mostly on the defensive.

Billings couldn't figure it out, but then again, he thought, there was no reason why he should. Five miles out of Santa the traffic thinned, he was able to set the car down at fifty miles an hour, and track them easily. He would follow them where they were going. Eventually they would get there and then he would decide. Then he would decide what he was going to do. He did not want to get in touch with Calabrese for instructions—the fact that he and only he knew their whereabouts and had some inkling of what was going on was like a rare precious pearl in his grasp—but maybe he would have to contact the old bastard after all. Two million dollars was better than five hundred, sure . . . but life was better than death, too.

XI

Calabrese said into the phone, "I do not bargain. I do not negotiate. That is not my policy. Tell me where they are and the matter will be handled from there on in. If the information is correct you will get your share."

The voice said, "I don't think that's good enough. Their whereabouts are worth so much to you; there ought to be something on the front end."

"Front end?" Calabrese said. "You do not even identify yourself. I'm talking to a disembodied voice without a name or a location. What do you think that this is worth to me?" He began to tap on the desk restlessly. The man who was sitting in the room with him stood, looked at Calabrese with some nervousness, and began to pace. Calabrese focused his attention on the phone. "You must think I'm a fool," Calabrese said.

"No," the voice said, "I don't think that you're a fool. I respect you a great deal."

"You have to take me for a fool," Calabrese said. "You won't identify yourself, you say you have definite information on their whereabouts, you ask for some tribute paid immediately, and yet I don't even know who to send it to. What am I supposed to do? Send you a money order care of general delivery someplace?"

"No," the voice said, "that wouldn't work." If Calabrese had intended any irony here the voice seemed to have decided to pass it over. "Obviously you can't send a money order general delivery and Western Union doesn't work anymore anyway. What I suggest is that you have someone meet me, carrying some money. I'll identify myself, he'll turn over the money, and then, afterwards, after I've gotten back to a safe place I'll call you and tell you where they are. Originally I was going to try and take them myself but it's too tough. It's out of my class; I think that they've got enough weapons now to fuel the Seventh Army for a month. It's a job for you."

"And how do I know your information is trustworthy?" Calabrese said. "How do I know that you have the location of these people, that this is not a double-cross simply to extort money from me?" He tapped the desk again. The man in the room stopped pacing as if shot and looked at Calabrese with stricken eyes. "It's ridiculous," Calabrese said, "just ridiculous."

"Listen," the voice said, "I obviously know something because I know you want him and the other one and I know your number. So I've got information, you can tell that." The voice paused, seemed to swallow, then went on. "This is the only way it's going to work, Calabrese," it said, "the other way, a payoff after you hit them is too chancey. I won't get a dime of it."

"All right," Calabrese said. That was the way you had to be if you were truly able to run a shop; you had to be able to follow your instincts, work with the moment, obey impulse. "All right. I won't argue with you; you're right. I want them very badly. Tell me where they are."

"Bullshit, Calabrese. Cash on the line. I'm not giving you a thing over the phone."

"What am I supposed to do? Stuff the fucking bills through the receiver?"

"No. I didn't think that would do it. Let someone meet me out here; have him wear an identifying mark so that I'll recognize him. Tell him to bring money. He pays, I tell, you move in."

"I don't like it," Calabrese said, "I don't like your plan of action at all."

"You don't have to like it. I didn't ask for any opinions about it at all. The question is, will you do it?"

"I don't know," Calabrese said. He looked up at the pacing man, made a violent gesture with closed hand, and the man stopped pacing, looking at Calabrese wonderingly, then settled into a couch at the side of the room. "All right," he said after a pause, "All right, you're giving me no choice every step of the way. You cross me, I'll kill you. I'll find out who you are and you're done for."

"Fine. That's a chance to take. I'll write it down as a business risk."

"Give me a description of yourself. Tell me where you want to meet."

"No way. No way you'll get a description. You have your man wear a blue suit with a black tie; let him be carrying a brown attaché case in his left hand. We'll meet in front of the *Times-Mirror* building."

"And how will he recognize you?"

"That's no problem," the voice said, "that's no concern. He doesn't have to recognize me, I'll recognize *him* and that's sufficient. I want ten thousand dollars in hundred dollar bills."

Calabrese inhaled, held the phone away from his ear briefly, then brought it back. The man in the room looked at him incuriously, his eyes dull, then looked down at the floor, broken, defeated in spirit. Everybody he dealt with was, Calabrese realized in a sudden flare of insight; he had surrounded himself with men who offered him no challenge. In one way this was good; standard organizational practice but in another . . . well, in another it left him improperly prepared to deal with characters like this one he was speaking to. Maybe he needed to deal regularly with a few people who would not break down so easily . . . but no, he thought, no, I'm seventy-three years old and at seventy-three the battles have got to be behind me; it's better that way, just give me Wulff and I'm finished. I ask for very little, almost everything I've wanted I've got, just let me get this one cold and I'll call it quits. I'll never ask for anything again. "You are not a modest man," he said into the phone.

"I know you want him. You've got him now. The information is probably worth three times as much to you."

"Yes," Calabrese said, "the information is worth a good deal; everyone knows that, but how do I know that I can trust you?"

"It's mutual. How do I know that I can trust you? This way, meeting your man in a public place I've got just a little bit of a chance. Not much but a little. I'll be there at ten o'clock tomorrow morning and if I were you, Calabrese, I wouldn't try any maneuvers. You'll get me but you'll lose him, and Wulff's the one you really want, isn't he?"

Yes, Calabrese thought, Wulff's the one I really want but you too, you son of a bitch, I want you too. You're quite right not to trust me; in ordinary circumstances you deal like a gentleman. You might have but not now. I'm going to get you, you bastard, I'm going to make you pay for this. "All right," he said flatly, "ten o'clock tomorrow morning my man will be there. You'd better be there."

"Oh, I will," the voice said. "I definitely will, Calabrese, the only thing is you'd better be ready to go in attack force because the one thing I guarantee is that they can't be counted on to stay there long. Not too damned long, time is catching up with all of us," the voice said and hung up. Calabrese held the phone in his hand, feeling the damp welling off his palm, noting that the phone now seemed to feel lighter with the weight of the voice out of it. An illusion, of course. Everything was an illusion. He put the phone down carefully and looked at the man who was in the room with him, the man with his hands clasped, looking down at the floor like a penitent, or like someone with a serious disease holding down space in a doctor's waiting room. "We're ready to move," he said. "We're going to move now."

The man sitting there said nothing. There was, of course, very little for him to say. Calabrese knew the problem. Once you got started talking there was sometimes no end to it and this man did not want to make waves of any sort. Calabrese looked at him shrewdly, eyes narrowing, and then he had an inspiration. It would do. It would certainly do. The man lacked a certain energy but he had loyalty and fear and those were the more important qualities for a job like this. The world was full of energetic types. Some of them even wound up making phone calls like the one he had just received.

"Can you make it out to Los Angeles by tomorrow morning?" Calabrese said.

The man looked up quizzically.

XII

At first, holing up in the Idle Hour trailer park wasn't too bad for them, at least it wasn't too bad for Wulff. Williams was so screwed up by that time Wulff figured that anything would have set him off; he was racked by guilt about his wife, worried as hell about the ordnance piled into the U-haul which he was convinced was under surveillance, and most of all he was bugged by the conditions of camp life itself, which he took to be oppressive, a concentration camp in fact. "People live here the way the black man lives all over the country," Williams took to saying and when Wulff said that there was nothing racist about the attitude here; everybody, white or black was being screwed equally, Williams said mysteriously that that was the point and let it go at that. Also, the people who ran the Idle Hour weren't crazy about a black man moving into Wulff's trailer, and they had solved that one only by offering a rent increase of seventy-five dollars a month flat, which had brought them around sullenly although they suggested that Williams stay the hell inside the trailer as much as possible and not let people be exposed to him. That would have been the case anyway; they were functioning under very tight wraps. As a matter of fact, they weren't going to go anywhere for awhile.

So it was a bad time but Wulff found it better than it had been being alone; in a way he found being cooped up with Williams better than almost anything he had gone through since he had left New York. At least there was someone to talk to now, someone who he could feel, even incorrectly, was carrying the burden with him and he and Williams had a lot of catching up to do. Williams wanted to know every detail of Wulff's mission which he had picked up only half-assed through various sources and the misinterpretation of the press; Wulff wanted to know exactly what the hell was going on in the department and specifically what changes were being made under the new drug laws. Williams said that all of the changes were for the worse and all of it was full of shit and then went into the Evans business but all of this was strung out over several days. There was plenty to talk about. There was a brief period during the first week when it seemed that their conversation was literally inexhaustible and Wulff allowed himself to succumb for the first time in many, many months to a feeling of leisure, to a feeling that things would work themselves out next week or the week after that, and in the meantime they were out of his hands. It was a good feeling; it was the way that most people lived. Also, at that point it made a lot of sense to calculate that way because coming out from under tight hiding in the Idle Hour, no matter what amount of ordnance they had, would probably have been disastrous. They had lost the guy who had trailed them from the racetrack. ("We should have killed the son of a bitch," Williams said, "goddamnit we should have pulled over on the side of the highway and nailed him; I don't want to live with that cat hanging around.") But that was only temporary; somewhere the guy was around, in the picture, going to make a move sooner or later. Also, there were a hell of a lot of other people looking for them, both of them by now. Really, there was nothing to do but stay there. Wulff figured that it would have to be a month before they could push out and cautiously venture east. He had an appointment with Calabrese.

But by the end of the second week, things had begun to fall apart. The conversational topics had been gone through over and over again. Williams, increasingly guilty about his wife, was getting irritable and sometimes even aggressive and Wulff, looking at the walls of the trailer, making small trips to the outrageous commissary where residents were compelled to make fifty dollars' worth of purchases of overpriced goods every week, found himself beginning to palpitate with tension, his body shaking at odd moments, turning and turning in the well of sleep, images of blood on his mind. It was quite obvious already that they would never hold out the full month; they would not manage it without, insanely, turning upon one another. He was not geared for inaction. Williams had not travelled cross-country with a U-haul full of death to hang around a wretched trailer park and leave the next move to the enemy. No, Wulff decided toward the end of that second week, it wouldn't work out. They were going to have to break out.

"That suits me," Williams said, "that suits me," pulling aside the frayed curtains of the trailer, peering outside, looking out on the same view of miserable, rutted path cutting between the trees that they had looked out on, once every few waking minutes, for twelve days. "I told you it was a bad idea. We can't sweat them out, man; we're just sitting here and leaving them make the moves. The longer we stay here the more time they have to get a good fix on our position. You think they won't find us sooner or later? We're just sitting here, waiting to be mopped up."

"It seemed like a good idea," Wulff said, "I knew the pressure; I felt it was good to get under—"

"Get under?" Williams said and began to laugh a little hysterically. "Get under what? That's the question I want to ask, what the fuck are you going to get under? You're a marked man, you'd have to get under Mount Everest to find something big enough to cover you, and people climb up Mount Everest. The only way you got this far was by making your moves before they could make theirs; now you've changed your pattern but that's just goddamned stupid. I didn't drive cross-country, I didn't get involved with that lunatic in Harlem, so that we could sit holed up in a plantation and let them fuck us over."

"It won't work," Wulff said suddenly. He stood, walked away from Williams, leaned against one of the thin trailer walls, feeling it buckle and give. Nothing worked like it should in this country filled with junk. "Now I understand the problem. We can't move together."

"No?" Williams said.

"No. I thought it would be a good idea; I thought that I had gone as far as I could going it alone and that I needed real help but I see that it's all wrong now. That's why we've just been sitting here instead of moving. I've been afraid to move."

"Oh. How's that?"

"Don't you understand? There's no mobility and we're so goddamned recognizable that there's no cover either. Calabrese knows who you are; he's been in touch with you, he's made the connection between the two of us. We might be twice as dangerous as a team but we're also twice as visible and they've got us nailed. One man is a guerilla army; two are a division." He sighed, shook his head and looked levelly at Williams. "We're going to have to split up," he said.

"Split up? How?"

"I mean I'm going to have to work on my own. We can't go it together. It was an idea and I was at the bottom, it seemed to be a solution. But it's no solution; it's no goddamned solution at all."

"So I'm out on my ass," Williams said. His face was peculiar, impassivity and expression chasing one another across his features, his eyes shrouded. He looked much older than Wulff would have ever thought he could look; at the beginning, in the patrol car, Williams had had one of those rookie's faces that seemed to literally resist the effects of experience. But that had been a long, long time ago. . . . "You're pitching the black man out on his ass," he said.

"Oh, come on," Wulff said, "don't be ridiculous." He bounced off the wall, the trailer shaking a little and went over to Williams. "It's just that I'm in too deep," he said quietly, "don't you understand that? I'm on the bottom now; I'm so far down that I'm probably on the way out. Why drag anyone with me?"

"I don't know," Williams said quietly, "why drag anyone with you?" He slumped over, clasped his hands, leaned on the knuckles. "I never did think of us as a team," he said.

"I can't be a team with anyone."

"You were right about the system though. The system sucks. The system is what makes it all possible; I found that out. So what am I supposed to do? Go back on the force? Get a nice desk job with security and a pension plan? Don't you understand how deep in it I am?"

"Go back to your wife," Wulff said suddenly. What he had said caught him by surprise; he found himself looking around the room to see if just possibly someone else had said it. No one had. "Go on back. She's a nice girl. You've got a child by now. You're a father. You've got something to go back to."

"Don't you understand?" Williams said. "It's too late. I'm closed off. I did the same thing that you did; I walked out. They all know who I am. You think that they're not after me the same way they are after you? Shit, man," Williams said violently, standing, kicking the wall, "it's too late for all of this crap. We're in too deep. It's no fucking time to turn sentimental."

"Isn't it?"

"Don't give me that shit about a wife and a child," Williams said. His face contorted suddenly, grief and rage merging into a quality which was neither; call it simply gelatinous, little pores and spaces falling that way. "Don't you give me no hearts and flowers right now, you son of a bitch. You were the one who turned me against the whole wife and child bit, you remember?"

"I did nothing."

"You said the system sucked and you were right: it does suck. So don't cop out on me now, man, say go back, tend lawn, grow up strong and straight in St. Albans, Queens, New York. It's too late for that now, you motherfucker." Violently Williams yanked his shirt up, showed Wulff the thin scar implanted by the knife; months later it still seemed to glow, turning subtle colors in the dim illumination of the trailer. "That's my mark," he said, "that's what the system got me. That's what it gives anyone at the bottom who takes it seriously." He brought his shirt down, the ends dangling, closed in on Wulff then, fists balled. "I could punch you out, you son of a bitch" he said.

"Don't do it."

"Don't do it! Don't do it! Everybody knows what to do or not do and I'm fucking sick of it," Williams said and then insanely, ducking low, threw a fist into Wulff's mid-section. It missed the plexus but still it hurt, the unexpectedness of the cheap-shot sending little groping fingers of pain up and down Wulff's body. Instinctively, Wulff brought an open hand down, wedging the side of it into the back of Williams's neck, just dropping it at the last instant so that instead of hitting the killing area near the medulla he struck him on the bony part near the nape of the neck. Williams gasped, sprawled on the floor, rolled against the wall, then got up slowly, his face holding an expression that Wulff had seen many times before . . . but had never expected to see on Williams's face.

"I'm going to kill you for that, you son of a bitch," he said.

He rushed Wulff then, coming in at him straight and low, Wulff angling away from the mad dive only at the last moment so that Williams pitched into the wall . . . and at that moment, outside, there was a dull roar, the earth under their trailer shifted, Wulff, too, went sprawling toward a wall, the trailer rocking, flame all around him. Dimly, he could hear Williams's bellowing. It looked like the world had blown up. The second explosion came, then.

XIII

Billings had been in front of the *Times-Mirror* building fifteen minutes before the meet, checking out the scene; five minutes before he went into the lobby where he had a good vantage point on the street, a good controlling view of everyone walking, out of sight himself. Calabrese would have taken him for a fool if he had done anything else, Billings thought. His maneuver might be risky here, entirely risky when going up against someone like Calabrese, but there was one thing he definitely was not and that was stupid. He figured that Calabrese would send at least two men into this meet, one of them dressed as per instruction, the other one supposed to merge into the crowds until the last moment and then emerge to overpower him . . . but he could figure at least one move ahead, at least at this primitive level. That he was ready for.

Anyway, Calabrese did not know Los Angeles if he thought that a man could be merged into the street scene here. In New York it would have worked well, Chicago too: there was always plenty of traffic on the street and in the middle of those eddies figures who simply loafed around, peanut vendors, bums, junkies, hippies cruising a handout, pimps, all of this was part of the downtown scene in the great metropolitan centers . . . but Los Angeles had no center, it was not a city. There were no crowds. The presence of a second man could not be concealed. So when a stranger had set himself up in an uncomfortable position across the street two minutes before the meet, shifting from one leg to the other, smoking a cigar, scratching himself in an armpit where a big Luger probably was holstered . . . Billings knew exactly what he was and even under the tension of circumstances was able to grant himself one thin grin. Calabrese was smart all right, the smartest of the old-line bosses, one of the true greats . . . but he had worked this one out along traditional lines. Billings had had him figured. Sure you could figure out these bastards; their reputations meant nothing, they had the same tricks that anyone else had, just a little more originality in the switches, that was all. Calabrese leaned tightly against the lobby, no movement here either, 11 A.M., lunch hour for no one, no traffic coming in, and a man in a business suit wearing a blue necktie came out from some abscess of the street and stood in front of the building. He had a high, dedicated look, the kind of look that a man might have, Billings thought, if he was about to sacrifice himself in the line of a better cause, or maybe it was merely the expression that the horseplayers at Santa Anita took on somewhere around the eighth race, the beginnings of the knowledge that they were battering themselves against the tote, the impermeable machineries of chance, but still, what could you do? It beat working for a living. Billings slowly disengaged himself from his position, moved through the doors.

The man in the blue suit looked at him and at the same time something else happened; the other one, the man across the street who was supposed to be part of the scenery except for the problem that no scenery existed, looked from right to left in a nervous, distracted manner and then began to pace, his arm moving within his clothing, drifting from chest to waist, then nestling in a pants pocket. Son of a bitch, Billings thought, they wouldn't be that audacious. Still, on the other hand, when you were talking LA, who noticed? There was, strictly speaking, no street scene whatsoever in LA. If there was a murder right here, the few pedestrians, the people passing by in cars would probably take it as part of a shooting script, on-location shooting. With the breakup of the big studios, after all almost everything was being done on the cheap, on a shoe-string, in far-flung areas of the globe. A company could move out and try to get some location shots in front of the Los Angeles *Times-Mirror* building while a couple of extras sprouted fake blood. Why not? Everything was going into the countryside, Billings thought.

He had his hand on his own gun, the hard surfaces of the point thirty-eight whickering into his hand as he came from the building. The man in the blue tie and the black suit regarded him with steady attention. Then as Billings closed the gap he was already turning, making some kind of obscure motion to the man across the street. That man was trying to cross now but they had not calculated on the traffic; a pack of cars sprinted free from a traffic light up the block and began to overtake one another, moving for a little borrowed space as they hit the center of the block, and the man across the street was unable to get to the other side. He stood there, shaking his head, hands on hips, spitting and cursing. Well, Billings thought, these little frustrations were entirely natural. They were all part of the great game of life, which you tried to play right down to the end, as if it mattered. Maybe it did. That would be the joke: if life really counted, if it was serious, if everything that took place here did add up to something after all. That kind of thought could drive a man mad if he dwelt on it. Better to juggle the odds on the tote and to deal with the Calabreses. Nothing was serious.

"All right," the man in the blue suit said in a hoarse, high whisper, "all right, all right." He was in his fifties, modest, inconsequential, but his eyes rolled in the purest of drug spasms. Be damned, Billings thought with some amusement, but then again in this city of wonders you could take nothing for granted. Maybe, Billings thought, maybe Calabrese kept his forces stoked on shit as a fringe benefit. There were stranger things. An army of freaks. "All right," the man said again, "have you got the stuff?" His hands moved restlessly, like little animals, through his clothing. "Here I am, have you got the stuff?"

Billings closed in on him; now they were almost belly to belly. The man across the street was still unable to cross, tourist buses moving side by side in the near lanes were tying up everything. "I've got what I need," he said, "have you got what I need?"

"I don't know what you're talking about."

"I mean ten grand," Billings said. Sometimes it was best to be indirect and then again sometimes you had to come right to the point. Coming to the point could sometimes be the best tactic of all because these people were often not prepared for it. "I'm looking for ten grand."

The man in blue shrugged. He looked despairingly across the street, then back at Billings, eyes still rolling. "It works two ways, doesn't it?" he said. "You're supposed to have something for me."

"Yes, but yours comes first."

"I don't know anything about that."

"You'd better know something about it. Ten grand," Billings said, "I'm waiting for ten grand."

The man in blue cast another desperate glance across the street. "He'll make it," Billings said, "the light is going to change up above and he'll be fine. But that's not going to change the situation. You owe me ten grand."

"Ah—"

"Make an independent decision. Stand on your own, for once. Sooner or later you reach a point in your life where you've got to lay it on the line, where you've got to come to terms with yourself. Come on," Billings said, "let's do it."

The other man, spotting gaps in the traffic, had begun at last to move across the street. The traffic had humbled him, the roar of the buses' exhaust, the choking fumes which had spread through the air lying heavily now a few feet above street level. He might have been older than the man in blue but he moved more slowly in a gimpy stride. The man in blue gave him another desperate glance, then faced Billings. "Where are they?" he said.

"You'll find out. Give me the ten."

"I can't do that until you tell me where they are."

"He says he can't do it until I tell you where they are," Billings said as the other man came up to them, still limping, his face drawn with tension. The skin of the cheeks was like canvas stretched with a very uneven strain. "But you know he's full of shit," Billings said, "you're the senior operator here; he's just carrying the bag. So tell him to pay up and be reasonable."

The other man shook his head, made gestures with his fingers, said nothing. Billings put his hands on his hips and looked at him in disgust. "Come on," Billings said, "be reasonable."

"That won't get you anywhere," the man in blue said. Suddenly he seemed almost cheerful. "He's a deaf-mute. He doesn't hear and he doesn't talk. All that he does is watch."

"That makes sense," Billings said, "he sure as hell isn't going to break silence to anyone, isn't he?"

"I don't give a shit," the man in blue said. "That doesn't matter to me. Maybe he talks to other deaf-mutes. I have definite instructions; you tell me where they are and—"

"And then I get shot in the gut," Billings said, looking at the deaf-mute who was fondling something in his pocket. "No way. Give me the ten."

The man in blue sighed in disgust. Starting at fifty, he now looked sixty. He reached into his pockets, fumbled with something, keys clanking, then came out with a rolled up wad of hundreds. No one was looking at them at all. There was no one on the street. Another avalanche of traffic came from the far corner and staggered by them.

"Here," the man in blue said, "now you tell me where they are." Billings shook his head in disgust, reached for the wad, took it out of the man's hand. It came reluctantly, bulging, greasy. Slowly he began to count it.

"It's all there," the man in blue said, "goddamnit to hell, what kind of an operation do you think this is?"

The deaf-mute began to make croaking noises. After a fashion they could make sounds; it was pretty much a myth that they were silent. He reached out, pawed the man in blue on the shoulders, then made menacing gestures with his free hand at Billings. The eyes were cold, private, reserved, the other hand still out of sight. Billings counted the hundreds slowly, patiently. There were quite a few of them. He got up to forty-five, then stopped counting. The uncounted amount seemed to be slightly larger than what he had already gone through. All right. The deaf-mute continued to regard Billings with unusual, acute interest; he felt a fix in those eyes of unusual intensity, sucking him in. Calabrese ran a hell of an operation all right. A stupid man might think that he had sent incompetents, a deaf-mute and a panicky type, to this assignment but that stupid man would not have seen the genius of Calabrese's calculation. There were a substantial number of corpses floating or lying around who had thought that they could outsmart Calabrese.

"All right," Billings said, stuffing the money into a pocket, "I'll take you there."

The man in blue said, "What the hell is this?"

"You got a car?" Billings said. "I've got a car. We've both got cars. Everybody has a car and I'll drive you to where they are, point out the spot, and take off. You don't think I'm just going to tell you now, do you? I'm not stupid. For ten grand I'll take you to where they're holed up, point out the place, and then I'm taking off. Call it safety reasons."

"Those weren't my instructions. That's not what you're supposed to do. You're supposed to tell me where the fuck they are."

"I will," Billings said, "I definitely will. But this way everybody's protected. You get your payoff and I get the hell out of there."

The man in blue turned, looked at the deaf-mute. Oddly, the deaf-mute seemed to be the leader of the two. He was looking at Billings now with a low, cold expression, dementia at the edges. Deaf-mutes, Billings thought, weren't supposed to hear anything, right? They were *deaf*, that was why they were called deaf-mutes. Also they couldn't talk. But this one seemed to have taken in everything. The man in blue made vague signals with his hands. The deaf-mute nodded impatiently, not keeping his eyes off Billings.

Billings turned. "All right," he said, "let's go," and he then began to walk. This was the risky part of the deal, all parts of it were risky, but this was the most dangerous aspect because if he hadn't handled this just right it was possible that Calabrese's men would panic, become impatient, perhaps do something really impulsive and dangerous. If he could clear this moment. Billings thought, he could probably carry it off all the way, but this was risky. There was a vague itch between his shoulder blades right in the place where a bullet would be most likely to hit him. He shrugged it away, kept on walking. His car was parked up the block, he had it within vision now and he went into his pocket, burrowing beneath the bills, finding his keys, carefully extracting them without causing the bills to fall, flapping, all over the pavement. That would be really bright. That would be exactly what he needed.

Nothing happened. He got to the Ford, walked over to the driver's side, slowly opened the door and wedged himself behind the wheel. Only then, the door slammed, the lock button depressed, did he look up. The two were coming slowly toward him staring intently, communicating in some way with one another, making no erratic moves. Billings sat frozen behind the wheel, let them draw up to him. They stood on the pavement outside the car for a while, watching, then they slowly moved on.

Billings suppressed a wild impulse to turn the key in the ignition, floor the accelerator, get out of here, and make a run for it. That was human nature; he had to understand that the impulse was within him but under no circumstances could he do it. No, that would blow everything; so far he had handled this right with the correct measure of courage and calculation but the wild, panicky flight out of here with ten grand in his pocket would be the foolish thing to do. He simply would not get away with it. They had gone along with him up to this point simply because they did not know what to do, probably had no specific instructions for this, but he could not blow it now. Also, he thought, there was no chance to get back to higher levels, get some advice. They were playing it on their own; they were as disconnected as he was. For the moment they were all freelancers.

The men began to move again, trudged slowly down the block. Billings sat there, palm flat to the cushions, not thinking, not reacting, simply waiting. He had no intention of not delivering. Delivering on the promise was the key to the deal. Only a fool would not deliver. But it was better, it was much better this way. Not only did he have some protection, a chance to get away clean . . . but there was also a thin chance that the two of them, Wulff and his companion, might be able to get away through no fault of Billings or his information.

He was forcing Calabrese's men into a premature move.

He sat there in the car. After a while, a half-demolished Impala, two forms huddled inside, poked its way through traffic and came parallel to his window. He rolled it down, looked across, exchanged a look with the man in blue sitting in the passenger's seat, the deaf-mute driving. Was that legal? he wondered vaguely. Deaf people weren't supposed to drive; they couldn't hear horns behind them, train whistles, officers' commands, whatever, the state motor vehicle bureaus had laws against that kind of thing. But then again maybe the deaf-mute wasn't really deaf and then again, being able to hear nothing while driving would certainly instill a certain calm in a man, a tendency not to get rattled.

"Don't cross us," the man in blue said flatly although there was a little tinge of uncertainty back of this, "that's all I can tell you."

"I won't cross you," Billings said, "do you think I'm crazy?" He wrenched the wheel, pulling the car slowly out of the space while the

Impala drifted up a few feet beyond, gave him clearance, allowed him to pass, and then settled into a steady pace behind him. Thinking no, he really wasn't crazy, not at all. He had no intention of crossing them. He would take them to the trailer park, point the way in, leave them to their devices, and get the hell out of there with his ten thousand dollars. He doubted if they would follow him, and even if they did, he figured that he could outrun them in this thing, particularly considering the condition of their car. He would take the ten thousand on the front end. After all, the front end was best. Let Calabrese do the mopping up. The shit would only wind up in his hands eventually anyway, and these two men, Wulff and the black partner, were doomed. No matter what happened, matters pivoted around those two constants: Calabrese getting the drugs, the two men dying. Take your ten grand and get out.

He put the car into a steady, grinding forty, showing nothing of the potential for cornering, the accelerative power that the three hundred and ninety c's under the hood gave, lulling the men behind, maybe, into the feeling that he had a junker. He was swinging in and out of the lane, driving easily, pausing every now and then while idling at traffic lights to pat the ten grand in his pocket. Ten grand in cash was nothing to Calabrese but it was the largest amount Billings had ever had altogether in his life. Out of the miniscule downtown area the roads opened up, traffic thinned, he and the Impala formed a caravan that way. They closed within a mile of the Idle Hour in only twenty minutes. That was good; much longer than that and they might have gotten very nervous and restless, thought that they were being conned in some way. That was one of the reasons why he had arranged to meet where he had. A short drive. Give them little time to think.

They were in the junkyard of America now: used car lots, fast-food franchises, miserable motels slammed up against the low hills of the landscape. The first sign for the Idle Hour came up; it was on the right, hitting him so suddenly that Billings instinctively gasped with surprise, the drive much shorter than he had thought. It must have seemed longer the first time around, stalking them, because he had been terrified that they would detect his tail at any time and pull him off the road; then, too, the careful drives that he had made here subsequently to see that they were still tucked away had been made under similar conditions of tension. It had been a risk all of those times, a terrific risk, but he had ten grand in his wallet and that payoff reduced the tension a little, even in retrospect. It had been worth it after all; ten grand was nickels and dimes to Calabrese, not much probably even to these two clowns trailing him, but to Billings it was plenty. It could finance a new life. He looked back into his rear-view mirror, seeing them come up closer behind him, pressed the hazard flashers to show that he was slowing, and then motioned with his right hand off the wheel. Five hundred yards up the road there was a small arrow under the lettering IDLE HOUR: TRAILER PARK, and then taking off the hazards he cut slowly into the shoulder lane bumping along at ten miles an hour, his right flasher indicating the turn.

His idea had been that they would fall back into line behind him, at the entrance to the park he would quickly accelerate, spinning out and getting away from there at fifty miles an hour, leaving them to their own method of figuring out where Wulff was in the park, which trailer was his. That had been his plan and figured out coldly beforehand it had been a good one, had made as much sense as not leading them here until he had the money and was in his own car . . . . But these men worked for Calabrese, even if they were fools they would not be total fools, there was some aspect of professionalism and anticipation in them after all, Billings realized . . . because the Impala sailed along in the right-hand lane, closed alongside Billings, and then almost casually cut him off, the mute yanking the wheel imperceptibly, the Impala sliding crosswise. Billings braked desperately, cursing, the Ford sliding along on the gravel almost swaying into the Impala, but even as he was pounding the wheel the man in blue on the passenger side had rolled his window all the way down, was shouting out to Billings. "All right," he said, "where are they?"

"They're in there," Billings said, finally contriving the sedan to a halt, his palms so damp that they almost came off the wheel. He pointed at the sign. "Right in there."

"Good," the man said. "Lead us in."

"I don't have to lead you in. That wasn't part of the deal. I told you they were in there and that's enough. They're in there."

"You must think we're stupid," the man said. If he had been confused and taken by surprise on the street the drive had, seemingly, given him plenty of time to bring himself together again; the uncertainty was gone. "How do we know they're in there, how do we know that this isn't just a big rib?" A bus came lumbering in the passing lane, traffic behind it already clumping up as the slow-moving vehicle had been forced to the outside. Faces like flowers peered out of the cars, looking at them coolly.

"Lead us in there," the man in blue said. "Show us where they are."

"That's no deal," Billings said, "no deal at all," and reached to roll up his window. There was a gun, suddenly, in the man's hand. A miniature, it glinted at him from the cave of his palm, held almost casually.

"Please," the man said, "you've fucked us up plenty already. Don't fuck us up anymore, okay? I don't want to kill you. Take us in there, point out the trailer they're in, let us make a quick check. If it's as you say it is you're out of this and ten gee's richer." He gestured with the gun. "People are starting to look," he said. "Be reasonable now. Don't be a fool. Cooperate."

Billings nodded slowly, reached out to crank up the window. "No," the man said, "no, no, don't think of that. Leave the window open. You need the breeze for all that sweating you're doing. Just drive. Drive the car, that's all I ask."

Billings nodded again, feeling very old, feeling at bay, and dropped the car back into drive. The wheels spun on the gravel, then lurched the car forward; it crawled down the shoulder at five miles an hour. No way to get out of the box; the Impala was still wedging him in, crowding him over on the left. He had no choice, he had to lead them in and that knowledge, that acceptance coming through him finally, resulted oddly in a relaxation of the tension, even a faint wisp of exaltation. It was always that way when you knew you were committed passing any point of refusal; had he not known it a thousand times, the needle sliding in cooly, past the dark veins, into the bruise of the body itself? Of course, he had been there; he had seen it all before. One way or the other it would be over soon. If nothing else, that could be counted on, five minutes, ten minutes, and it would be done. He would be out of this with ten thousand dollars and a new life opening in front of him at the age of forty-seven or he would be dead. No more middleground. People dwelt in the middle, on the margins, all of their lives: that was death, that was what was killing them more than mortality itself, the slide toward emptiness, the absence of clear choices, but it had never been that way for him. Once again he was in a high, clearly-defined area where the right would happen or the wrong would happen but he would never be the same again. Yes, he thought, that was what might have driven him to the needle in the first place; that might have been precisely it. The need to cut loose, the need to take the high, deadly ground. The need to get off the margin forever.

He was bumping down the miserable road of the trailer park now, the guard nowhere to be seen, the barricade off-angle, crazily on and off the road. A stroke of luck this, the guard not being here, because he knew that the men behind him would almost certainly have killed him to gain entrance. That was the way it was. Behind that spot,

angling off to the right, just barely he could see the top of Wulff's
trailer, the yellow U-haul parked beside it linked to the Ford sedan,
the ruined Cadillac a little further on.

He leaned across the seat, turned to the Impala which was turning
close, gestured violently toward the trailer, pinning them, giving them
the signal . . . and then he yanked the wheel hard left, looking for the
sweeping U-turn that he could just make and which would carry him
past the Impala, up the path to safety . . . but he never made it.
Something hit him in the neck, stinging and then dull, a feeling of
wetness, and as he was sliding into the seat thinking, son of a bitch,
son of a bitch, they shot me, more in amazement than anger, he had
had this fully calculated. *Why would they shoot him now?* As he was
sinking to the seat a roar hit him and then another roar, a whole series
of implosions battering and battering away through the blindness
that was his sight.

And the world blew up.

XIV

The first explosion sent them locked together, sprawling on the floor,
the second lifted them as if in a gigantic fist and hurled them across
the tilted floor and into the wall, but it was Williams, more alert than
Wulff, who was screaming, "Christ, Christ, they'll get the ordnance,"
and Wulff was able to break the hold, then, fighting to do so, coming
off Williams's body, their contact gelatinous in retreat. And then yet
another explosion hit them, this one breaking in the walls of the
trailer and sending little fragmentation pellets through the opening
pores. Wulff rolled on the floor, absorbing the impact, the world
shaking, body shaking, then came up with the pistol in his pocket to
find that Williams had already, using the stock of the one rifle they
had brought in here, battered open the door. They looked out into the
damp air. They looked out into horror.

A junk Impala was lying down the path fifty yards or so, next to it a
Ford had skidded completely around breaking the path of the Impala,
but then again it might have been the Impala hitting the Ford
broadside. In either case the Impala was surrounded by little puffs
and plumes of dust, and even as Wulff looked another grenade,
unmistakably it was a grenade, came sailing from an area behind the
car, turning lazily in the air, heading toward the top of the trailer.
Wulff could see it all happening; the grenade would hit, it would
explode, force would drive it downward, breaking the trailer in five or

ten pieces, those pieces imploding around him. There would be one shrieking, burning instant of torture in the last blaze of which he would see Williams . . . and then they would be dead . . . both of them. The panorama cleared again; no trailer in the landscape but the grenade did not hit the trailer. Something caught it in the angle of flight, maybe a breeze, most likely a prayer, and it hit the ground some ten yards in back of the trailer still rolling, turning like an egg on the ground, rolling into a small clump of trees which went up with a dull roar, the foliage catching the fire and fragmentation. Flat dud, flat failure, the grenade captured by the earth . . . and by that time Wulff, too, had his pistol out, was firing in the direction of the car.

Williams, following the rifle, allowing the rifle to guide him more than he exerted control, was coming out in front of the trailer now, the stock of the rifle buried deep under his armpit, the recoil causing him to groan and give a little ground reciprocally as he got off three, then four shots in the direction of the rear of the Impala. The trailer itself was on fire, little crowns and plumes of haze surrounding it, but Wulff was not concerned by that; he was not concerned either with the faces that were beginning to peer out of the trailers, the dull threads of scream that he heard intermingling with the sound of ordnance. No, the thing to do was to get to the source of those grenades before yet another one could come . . . He heard a scream then, something behind the Impala hit, and a man leaped up from behind the car as if on strings, his face contorted, blood coming from all the crevices, then disappeared behind the car.

"Cover me!" Wulff screamed to Williams over the noise. "Goddamnit just cover me, I'm going in there." He went into that terrain in a low crawl, holding the pistol over his head, clearing it from the dirt, thinking that this was insane; he was asking for cover from a man who not two minutes before he had been trying to pound into unconsciousness, who had been trying to do the same to him . . . but Williams could be trusted, he knew that, what had happened in the trailer had nothing to do with what was happening now. It was from an excess of knowledge, too much realization that they had attacked one another and now that was over; the real enemy lay before them.

He heard the whine of Williams's rifle as another shot was put down and then he was into the middle of it, crawling behind the Impala. Two men were lying there. One, a tall man, was playing stupidly with a grenade between his crossed legs as if it were a toy of some sort, trying to formulate a series of gestures which were appropriate to the grenade but failing, muttering to himself, spittle coming from his lips. A bright bloodstain was in the center of this man's forehead and

without thinking about it further Wulff doubled the blood, raising the
pistol, pumping a shot as near to the hole as he could get it. The man
grunted once, almost gratefully, Wulff thought, spun and fell over the
grenade, his body holding it like a cup. He had taken a shot in the
cerebrum, Wulff thought, that had destroyed the higher intellectual
faculties but with his last energies he had still been trying to figure
out what the grenade was for, exactly what to do with it. A good
organization man to the last. Next to him, a man who might have been
immaculately dressed a little while before, wearing a blue suit,
bloodstains on his tie, was squealing and mumbling, trying to raise a
revolver, not quite able to make it. His body glistened with a thousand
cuts and violations; somehow a grenade had gotten hold of him and
torn him open but he too was still determined, still trying to get a job
done and the higher intellectual faculties with him seemed to be
functioning nicely as he raised the gun in slow-motion, sweat coming
out of his face, mingling with the blood, trying to level the gun down
on Wulff.

"Son of a bitch," the man said, and each word was a breath, each
breath a further explosion of blood. "Dirty son of a bitch." His finger
was looped around the trigger and only then did Wulff, waiting it out
until the last moment, shoot the gun out of the man's hand. It spun
twinkling downrange, the man in blue caving forward again, lying on
the earth, pounding his fist against it like a frustrated child. "Son of a
bitch, son of a bitch," the man was saying, and uprange Williams's rifle
went off again. A bullet came across the distance and smashed into
the small of the man's back. Little fingers of blood sprang out. The
man screamed weakly. Wulff aimed the pistol carefully and shot the
man in the head. He died quickly, gratefully, the pistol flying away
from him.

Wulff stood up slowly, giving Williams plenty of time to see him then,
giving the black man plenty of time to adjust himself to the realization
that it was over. If Williams was going to shoot him this would
certainly be the time, but he had faith. He had a complete and sudden
faith in Williams; the man was working with him, not against him, he
was not going to shoot Wulff. Slowly he waved his arm, standing to full
posture, motioning toward the ground, and from the trailer Williams
exposed himself, holding the rifle at port arms, then raising it slowly
above his head.

Up and down the path now there were little flames. Wulff could hear
the sound of their faint crackle and behind that he thought that he
could hear the sound of voices as well. Not the proprietorship, of
course. If anyone was going to get killed in the Idle Hour it sure as hell

wasn't going to be the owners who would surely have taken cover, but it would instead be some wretched tenant who had booked space next to a travelling assassin. That would be just about the way it would go, but Wulff did not want to think of the voices now, let them react to this as they would. His time in the Idle Hour was most certainly completed now. Most of the grenade fires were starting to go out on their own. There was a ragged glaring blaze up beyond in a grove near the gate, but some men had already come out of one of the trailers, a bright, blue job, and were throwing coffeepots and frying pans filled with water on it. That was not the problem. Wulff waved the all-clear to Williams again, stood, looked at the two corpses on the ground bleeding thickly into the foliage, red and green smeared throughout and then he went to the Ford sedan where he thought that he had seen something moving just a few minutes before. He peered in through the window. A man lying flat on the seat, head under the steering wheel, looked back at him. There were small bloodstains around his ears and hinted at behind the neck, but Wulff could see nothing mortal. The man tried to raise a hand with effort, finally got a finger moving. Late forties. There was a gun on the floorboards to his right.

"I think I've got a broken back," the man said, "you've got to get me out of here."

Wulff looked at him, said nothing.

"Didn't you hear me?" the man said in a high voice. His speech faculties were certainly unimpaired. "I said, I think the sons of bitches broke my back. I've got to get some help. I'm paralyzed."

"Who brought them here?" Wulff said.

"What? What's that?"

"I said, who brought those men here?" He looked back at the Impala and the two corpses.

Even in paralysis, the man's eyes turned cunning. "Brought who here?" he said. "Brought what? I was just driving in here. Then there was some shooting. They started to shoot at me and then they were throwing grenades. You saw the whole fucking thing."

"You brought them here," Wulff said.

The man's cheeks began to twitch like frog's legs. "Get me out of here," he said, "you want me to die? You want me to die in this fucking trap? It's not right, you've got to help me—"

"You brought them here," Wulff said, "you led them in. You spotted us for them but you weren't able to get clear. You got caught by surprise. They double-crossed you. You were on the kill list, too."

"What the hell does that have to do with anything? Goddamnit,

I'm dying."

"I recognize you," Wulff said, "don't you think I know who you are?"

"Listen," the man said, "that doesn't have to do with anything. I didn't want anyone to get hurt. I wanted—"

"Santa," Wulff said. "Santa Anita. The grandstand. You think I'm a fucking fool?"

Williams was waving at him from the steps of the trailer, apparently trying to indicate that someone was coming. All right. That would be the next thing to deal with. He could already see, inclining his head, the guard trudging his way toward the trailer very slowly, holding a rifle extended. Pick him off here? He thought, well, that would be a pleasure. If he had to do it he would without a second thought. Still, it might not be necessary just now.

"I'm no fool," he said, turning back to the man. "I know exactly what's going on. I know what the game is; I know what you had in mind. You were going to finger us and take off. That was all."

The man on the seat tried to move. The effect was perhaps an inch of elevation, holding his buttocks off the seat, but for what this was costing him it was obvious that he might as well have been beaten with clubs, slashed with razors, the agony came out of him in little gasps and tiny screams. "Please," he said, "please don't do it." He looked at the revolver in Wulff's hands. "You wouldn't—"

"I wouldn't?" Wulff said. "I wouldn't? You died in the accident, remember? A couple of guys came in here, no one will ever know who, and started to throw grenades around. Unfortunately you got in the way of one and got yourself badly mangled. Maybe you tried to intervene and they had to put a shot through your throat." He levelled the pistol. "There's got to be an end to this," he said. "Somewhere along the line it's just got to stop now."

He shot the man in the throat.

Pain, death restored the man as the efforts of a hundred surgeons might not have. He flopped around on the seat like a fish, his face, despite all of the agonies of the body, strangely composed, the eyes welling inward as if for strength. His hands squeezed once, reaching down toward his belly as if there were something that he could grasp; he seized his navel, pounded the skin, twitched and gathered it together and then rolled, fell to the floor of the car, his legs, comically held by the steering wheel, coming straight upright. Wulff looked at the soles of the man's shoes, ripple-soles, encrusted with little pellets of dirt. They lashed out once, those shoes, like a laboratory animal already dead and dismembered being given a testing electric shock, and then the man lay very still on the floor doing nothing. Wulff, meaning to fire a single precautionary shot, found that his hand locked on the trigger and he put two, then three, finally four shots into the corpse, firing spasmodically, gasping with the release as the bullets went in, watching the body flop around through death with an almost sensual pleasure. Only when the gun was empty did he stop, the gun falling away, his hand lolling open-palmed against his waist. Then slowly, slowly Wulff trudged up the hill back toward the trailer, feeling much older suddenly, feeling that he had learned something about himself that he would rather not know, a knowledge that he could not quite bear and yet which he would have to internalize along with everything else because not to do so was to lie. He would not lie to himself. If nothing else he would hold onto that.

But he had learned what he would rather not have known.

He was just like them. When it came right down to the confrontation he probably enjoyed administering death just as much as they did. Because it was a condition of the business.

As a narco he had suspected it but there was a lot of knowledge you could duck in the police department, and besides that narcos never had to use their guns. But it had caught up to him now. It had caught up to him good.

There was less and less difference between him and the enemy.

The guard was screaming at Williams.

XV

There was no way to settle it. There was just no right way, no decent way to settle it, and so they had done the only thing that they could have to make the situation work at all; Wulff had pulled a gun on the guard. The pistol was empty but the guard would never know the difference. "Shut up," Wulff said, "just drop the fucking gun now," and the guard had dropped the gun. He had raised his hands, backed away from them in a spasm of reluctance as once again the faces in the trailers had disappeared, shutters and shades coming down. This was a wonderful place, the Idle Hour, you could probably have ritual sacrifice in the middle of the trailer court and risk nothing more than a note from one of your neighbors a few days later suggesting that you keep the racket down.

"No fight, no fight," the guard was saying in a whimpering old man's voice, "anything you want you take, I don't want to make any trouble, I just didn't know what's going on here."

Williams stepped forward, holding his pistol butt-end, hit the guard a ferocious blow in the cheekbone and the man went into the mud, into the spaces where the fires had been. "I've been waiting for weeks to do that," Williams said to the man on the ground and then kicked him hard in the ribs, the guard screaming and snaffling, then burying his head into the mud and sobbing. Williams spat and then with sudden disgust lurched away toward the trailer, Wulff following. "They turn you into them," Williams was saying. "You like to think that you're different, that you don't play their game, but shit, the game is that *you become them*, and that way they always win because it's always they who are still on top." He raised his pistol and threw it into the woods in an enormous sweep, coughing, spitting, then leaned against the ruined wall of the trailer, the wall crumpling, looking away from Wulff. "I've had it, man," he said, "this has been coming a long time, I knew it was coming, I knew what it was going to be but still you're never ready, are you? They turn you into them."

"All right," Wulff said. He looked back at the three bodies now in the grove, the guard thrashing on the ground. "We've got to get out of here," he said.

"You're bloody fucking-a right we've got to get out of here! I know that."

"Someone's going to reach the cops."

"*We* are the cops," Williams said and began to laugh hysterically. The laughter turned into sobs and he spat again violently. "We've got to get out of here," he said, "I know that; I know you're right. We've had it. Our cover is blown."

"Now," Wulff said, "right now."

"I don't even know if that fucking thing will drive," Williams said, pointing toward the U-haul. He seemed calmer, now that the sobs were out of him. "It's got scars all over it; they might have hit the axle."

"We've got to try," Wulff said, "we've got to try to get out right now; it's no good. We can't hold out here."

"Look at that son of a bitch," Williams said, pointing toward the Sedan de Ville. The flak had pitted even deeper holes in the body frame; parts of the roof were literally torn open. "Look at that; you think that's going to drive?"

"Your Cadillac is a quality car," Wulff said, "they're built with quality, they're serviced carefully, they're your best value in a used car, don't you know that?" wondering vaguely if he were a little mad even as he started toward the car. The trailer, tilted crazily, shed some more strips of fragmentation, little steel joints collapsed into the mud. "Can't get anything out of that," he said, "let's go."

"Go where?"

"Get out on the highway," Wulff said. "Follow me. We get thirty, forty miles, maybe we'll be able to stop. Don't you understand?" he said, and suddenly there was a siren whooping in the distance. "Don't you see? We can't stay around here; they'll nail everything."

"Yeah," Williams said, "yeah." Wulff got into the Cadillac thinking it was sure a fortunate thing that he had stashed the sack in the trunk, done that a couple of days ago on a vague impulse which he could not understand, just a feeling that it would be better in the car than in the trailer. Prescience, foresight, some word like that. As he had expected the motor turned right over, the transmission caught, the car began to roll.

Watching Williams maneuvering behind him Wulff went into a long, shaking U-turn and headed out toward the highway.

The siren was closer but not close enough. They turned south and began to move away at a slow, even, regular pace, leaving three dead men behind them.

XVI

The report got to Calabrese within thirty minutes. If nothing else, he thought, he had intelligence. His intelligence sources were excellent. A man with his intelligence sources could sit in a room high above a drive and do nothing except to give orders and hear results; he would certainly never have to go out into the world. That was fine, not going into the world; after seventy-three years Calabrese had had quite enough of it. But now the world was turning against him.

Surprisingly, he was able to take it calmly. He would not have thought so himself but at some level of foresight he must have seen how this would go, what was going to happen, he must have already dreamed the failure. Three men dead in a trailer park, the pair escaped again. There seemed to be no reason for there to have been three men; the deaf-mute and Parsons were a team but where had the third man come from? Cross and double-cross? Who knew? Eventually he might find out but it was in the category of ancient information already. It simply did not matter. None of it mattered; it was esoteric. The sons of bitches had gotten away again.

At least he had them nailed to the ground now. He had suspected that they were in the coast area but nothing was certain. He had had to fan out the alert all through the country, had had to diversify his forces but now he had them nailed in, in a pocket. He could bring down everyone in the Los Angeles area, get them into a net, sweep them in.

He knew it. It stood to reason.

So it was for the best. It was for the best that three men had been lost, a trailer park blown up, Calabrese frustrated and defied once again. He wanted to look at it in that way; really wanted to feel that the disaster had done him a favor but Calabrese could not. He simply could not take satisfaction in it. Time and again he had had this bastard cornered, time and again there seemed no way that he could have gotten loose . . . and yet he had. Peru was an enormous box; he had had him tied in Peru with a ribbon. And yet the bastard had hijacked his way out. It was mystical.

No. No, it wasn't mystical, Calabrese thought. It was retribution, that was all that it was. It was retribution for that moment in Chicago when he had had the man in this very room, had had him positioned for a kill order . . . and had let him go because he liked the excitement of having danger within compass. Liked it because he was an old man, losing his grip; that was why he had liked it. Walker had been right, the son of a bitch. He had killed Walker for saying it but it would not take away the inescapable truth of the matter. He had acted like an old fool, he had missed his one real chance and now there was no recovery. He would never have that chance again.

He would never have it again. The thought was chilling; it sent a thrill of dread through him and Calabrese stumbled away from the desk from which he ran the world, went to the concealed liquor cabinet and taking out a bottle of scotch he swilled a good fraction of it in a series of choking swallows, handling the scotch like beer. It went down into his gut like a wound, then spread out into lazy, indolent fingers which poked through his esophagus. He belched.

The man who had been sitting in the room throughout all of this, sitting silently, looked at Calabrese wonderingly, then looked away. *No questions*, his expression showed clearly. He was a bodyguard; he was here at the old man's request; that was where it all ended. Think not and you don't get hurt. Now he took the gun out of his inner pocket, played with it, his eyes glowing with a faint light. The man loved guns. He loved everything about them. That was why Calabrese had brought him in here.

"I've been a fool," Calabrese said.

The man said nothing. He hunched over the gun, considering it. If any man came into this room to try and hurt Calabrese he would kill him; if Calabrese ordered him to go out and do a job he would do that. Otherwise he would do nothing at all. That was clear. He shrugged, looked at the floor.

"I've been a goddamned old fool," Calabrese said. He took the bottle, proffered it "You want some of this?" he said.

The man shook his head.

"Come on," Calabrese said, "it's only a goddamned bottle of scotch, it's not going to kill you."

The man refused for the third time, his eyes glowing just a little. "Peter denied Christ three times before cock-crow," he said, "I couldn't do it a fourth."

"Don't," Calabrese said, "don't do it a fourth. Don't call me Christ, either." He passed the bottle over; the bodyguard took it, put away a few neat swallows, smiling to himself in a private way, then handed the bottle back. Calabrese put it on his desk. Drinking and bullshitting with a religious bodyguard. That was what it had come down to. All of the power, all of the roots and interconnections put down over forty years, the struggle, the manipulation, the control . . . all for this. There was something very wrong with it.

But on the other hand, he couldn't think of a goddamned thing to do otherwise.

"I want him," Calabrese said. "I want him badly. I want pictures. I want pictures of his corpse."

The bodyguard shrugged.

"I'm a goddamned fool," Calabrese said again and picked up the bottle, wiped it, put down another drink, "but if you ever take that news out of this room I'll kill you."

The bodyguard shrugged, showed his hands. "It's okay," he said, "it's okay by me. It's none of my goddamned business, believe me, I don't care, I won't take nothing away. I'll do whatever you say." He looked sidewise at the scotch bottle. "You got me started," he said, "if you don't mind—"

"Oh, no," Calabrese said, "I don't mind. I don't mind at all."

He handed the guard the bottle.

And then for a long time, the two of them just sat there, seventy-three and forty, getting drunk in the cool chambers of Calabrese's throne room.

XVII

Picking up Route 80 at San Francisco, heading east this time, the U-haul flat behind him and filling the rear-view mirror, Williams, alone, had an insight: the men who had waylaid him in Nebraska had not been looking for him at all. They had merely been freelancing, shopping around, seeing what they might be able to get off the road in the same spirit that fishermen would toss a net into promising waters. It would have been less horrible, somehow, if he could have thought that they were organization men and they had had a tracer on him but even the organization was not that sophisticated. No, these men had merely been on a fishing expedition. The roads, with the closing of the continent fifty years ago, were now the last frontier; the last space in which the highwaymen, pirates, freebooters, sharks could roam. That was even worse. It meant that in addition to worrying about everything else on his three-day haul East he'd have to think about walking into some freelancers again.

Still, he thought, it was the only thing to do. Wulff and he had discussed it; nothing else made sense. They had to split up and he had to go back on his own; together now they were twice the target, not twice as deadly. It had become quite apparent to Wulff from the moment of the attack in the trailer camp that they would not be able to stay together; Williams had seen it even before that. Not if they were jumping each other the way they had. No way. The fight in the trailer, just before the grenades hit, had been terrifying because it had not really been anyone's fault. It was just the way that the situation had developed. "Go back to your wife," Wulff had said to him on the vacant back road into which they had pulled their caravan, "get the hell out of this while there's still time. I'm a doomed man now but you can still get away."

"They know who I am, too," he had pointed out, "they got me spotted; I told you Calabrese knows—"

"They only want you because you're with me," Wulff said. He spoke slowly, softly, with the determination of a man who had sifted through all of the choices in his mind a long time before and now had gone long past indecision. "Otherwise you don't matter. It's me they want."

"I'll stay with you."

"Can't," Wulff said, "can't do it. We can't operate together." He smiled in a strange way, stared at Williams intently. He was leaning out the window of the ruined Cadillac, Williams having come from the Ford to talk to him. "You see what happened."

"Forget it."

"I can't forget it. You don't really want to be here. I don't see why you should. There's no way to fight it together. I've got to be on my own."

"I can't go back to being where I was," Williams said, "it will never be the same again."

"What is? What the hell is? You get out of bed in the morning; you're never going to be exactly the same as you were. Everything changes moment to moment. But you can still pick up the pieces. You can get back somehow the way it was before." Wulff shook in the seat, pressed his back then against the rear and restored control so quickly that if Williams had not been alert to it he never would have suspected anything. But for just a moment there had been a real aspect of pain in the man; now he was impassive again. "I can't do that," he said, "I can't ever get back near to how it was. It's all the way to the end now."

"So what are you going to do?" Williams said, looking nervously beyond the cars toward the road. No traffic; they had picked a gutted local highway here running parallel to the interstate. Twenty years ago it had been filled with gas stations, diners, used-car lots, people . . . now it had been abandoned. "What's your next step?"

"That's simple," Wulff said flatly, "I'm going to get back to Chicago and kill Calabrese."

"Are you?"

"*My* way. I've got to be alone."

"You'll need some fucking ordnance," Williams said, looking at the U-haul.

"No way. No way at all I'm going to be able to go in with that stuff. I've got to travel light; that's the only way. Load myself down with that, and I not only restrict my mobility, I risk turning it over to them. They could use it; you've got half an army in there."

"So what to do? Take it back?"

"Take it back," Wulff said, "take it back to your Father Justice, argue for ninety percent. Most of it's unused, untouched even, he ought to settle for ninety percent. He's a businessman and he'll see the value of renting out merchandise that wasn't even used."

"Shit," Williams said obscurely, shaking his head, "shit, I thought we could have done something—"

"I did, too. But we can't. We couldn't It wouldn't have worked out, I see that now. So we've got to settle, cut our losses." Wulff bent over the ignition, cranked the car. The Cadillac started with a gasp, idling unevenly. "I'm sorry," he said.

"I am, too."

"But you see what happened."

"Yeah, man, I see what happened all right."

"If they hadn't attacked then they might not have saved us from ourselves," Wulff said softly, and raced the engine, the valves clattering, then threw the Cadillac into reverse. The tires spun, then caught softly.

"Wait," Williams said, throwing up a hand, "what next?"

Wulff braked the car, the frame shuddering on the chassis. "What do you mean by that?" he said.

"Is this how it ends?" Williams said. He found himself being betrayed by an odd kind of sentiment, it was not loss exactly, nothing in circumstances like this could be called loss, but then again it was not sheer eagerness to get out. "Never again?"

"I don't know," Wulff said, leaning out the window again, "this can't go on much longer, you know."

"I know that."

"It's been this way but it can't continue. I've got one more job to do before it's over."

"Calabrese," Williams said.

"Calabrese," Wulff said nodding, "Chicago and Calabrese. The stakes are too high; one man can't carry this alone. It's a one-way ticket on a death trip, don't you know that?" He revved up the motor again, the Cadillac starting to reverse. "Go to Father Justice," he said. "Get a refund, see what percentage you can have returned. Go to your wife, go back to the force. Be happy. This isn't the answer either, don't you see that? You can't beat the system, make it work, but you can't go outside of it either because that way you just get crushed out. There's got to be another way, but I don't know what it is. If I find it I'll send you a telegram," Wulff said, "I'll send it to you back at home." And then the car was moving over the ruts on the highway, lumbering out of his line of sight, Wulff trailing a hand out of it for a long time until the car was invisible. Leaving him alone with the U-haul, the Ford, and himself. As he must have known from the beginning that it would have to be.

So here he was, picking up eighty, moving as fast as he dared and thinking about the hijack team in Nebraska as he locked the Ford into its seventy-five miles an hour thruway pace again. There had been nothing personal about that team, they had perhaps been as impersonal, basically, as the way in which Wulff and he had fallen upon one another back at the trailer park, doing it simply because there was nothing else to be done, because they had tuned themselves, been tuned, to fighting pitch and there was simply no one else to fight. It all ate shit, that was the point, anything stunk, whatever you did wound you up in the same trap, brought you to the same outcome. Whether you pounded it out in St. Albans for twenty years looking for the good time and the pension-and-out, or whether you started roaming between the coasts and to foreign counties looking to confront the enemy whole and destroy him . . . it all caught up to you. Whatever you did it was the same and the sudden knowledge filled Williams with fury. He pounded the steering wheel, aware for the first time of his mortality, of the limitation of his possibilities, of the trap into which life itself had brought him. You couldn't get out: the system was a lie but trying to beat it was also. Look at Wulff, look at himself, and he felt his lungs blowing and dilating with rage as he thought of this, then settled the car down to sixty, shaking his head. Can't do this, he thought, got three thousand miles to go, got to go cross-country, start carrying on this way and it's no good at all. I'll blow myself out before I get into Utah, got to be calm, got to look at the long view . . . and behind him in the rear-view mirror he saw something growing. It looked like a hearse, a long, black, gleaming car shifting back and forth on the two lanes of highway, coming on him at a hundred miles an hour or more, he thought. He could see two bodies in the front, hunched down, and at that same moment Williams knew exactly what had happened to him and what was going on.

There was nothing to do. He was caught in a trap so profound that his very movements were as predictable as if they had happened a long time ago. He floored the accelerator, urging the Ford to ninety miles an hour and took over the center stripe of the highway, hugging it, the car rocking with speed. He would have to try and outrun them, not because he had any chance, not because a Ford with a U-haul could outrun a new limousine with a determined driver . . . but only because that was the way the game was played; that was the nature of the scenario . . .. Knowing this Williams pounded that accelerator, moving his foot on it back and forth like an organist, trying to urge a little more speed, the U-haul beginning to sway dangerously behind him now, the U-haul trying to pull off the road with its own torque and he fought back against it, lashing the car from side to side to set up a counter-torque of his own which would carry him against the thrust of the U-haul. It worked, although perilously. Now the following car had closed upon him so that it was invisible through the rear-view mirror, shut out by the U-haul. He had to use the side mirror to see it . . . and looking through the side mirror he could hardly lose it. The car was a 1970 or 1971 Lincoln town car, what did they call it, Mark something or other, the jobs with the Rolls-Royce ripoff grilles and the opera windows, perfect for bulletproofing. The car gave less open glass area to its occupants than any production car made in America. The car, now insolently on his back bumper seemed to come off then, slid back almost arrogantly allowing Williams to open up three or four car lengths. They were toying with him.

Either toying with him, he thought, or waiting for the road to be absolutely clear. He could see nothing coming up behind him but then, of course, he was at a partial disadvantage. In the other car they would be able to get a clear view back on this flat, undulating terrain, looking back a mile or more, and they would want to make absolutely sure that there was no one behind. Made perfect sense. Murder, even highway murder, was a private thing. Even the vast crackups of the interstate seemed to happen in an enclosed space, attacker and victim, walled off by their disaster from the fact of the road itself. There was something very private about dying, always: no matter how you came to it, what life you had led to get there, it seemed to happen in a black tube or funnel stuffed with cotton, just you and the act and the emptiness outside.

Wasn't it always that way? Williams thought bitterly, holding the wheel with shaking hands, keeping the Ford at a savage, desperate, almost losing-control seventy-seven miles an hour. Maybe the pictures they drew were different but it was always the same: here he was, an American Negro, getting his black ass chased all over the continent, a bunch of white men in a big car behind him. That was the way it was: they reamed you from dawn to daylight, they stalked you all of your life. They trailed your black ass, stalking you from birth through the middle years, and then sooner or later, in a white, blank, staring space they got you. That was life, face it, breathe it in: he was running guns for the white man, moving in the white man's service, and another group of white men were coming out to kill him. Did it matter why the one had sent him out with the guns, why the others wanted to stop him? It was just whitey, that was all; he was a rat in a trap, carrying out matters for whitey, fetching and carrying for whitey, and now they had decided to kill him. He shook his head, cursed, spat neatly through the spokes of the steering wheel. He saw what the Panthers meant now. He saw very well what Malcolm, that stoned priest, had been shouting from the pulpits. You carried out their shit all your life, mucked up their floors, did their dirty work for them . . . and then they killed you. The only solution, the only way to come to terms with it, Malcolm and the Panthers had said, was in recognizing the enemy, seeing him whole, realizing that when the enemy outnumbered you seven to one every black man would have to be your brother. Instead he had opted for the system. He had gone into the coils and wires of the network thinking that he could bury himself in it so deeply that he would not only be doing the white man's work, he *would* be a white man. Well, that would show you. Oh, yes, indeed: live and learn, twenty-five years old, all the living and learning done, and now he was ready to die.

He had hung all this time in the passing lane; streaking near the flat valley between the two panels of highway, not in any hope that he could outrun them but only because it might be a shade more difficult to pass him on the right than on the left, particularly with the waggling, U-haul duck's ass behind him. But now the Mark came up beside him, lunging out of the rear view, reappearing to his right with the same insolent control and rapidity with which it had dropped back, the car coming belly to belly against the Ford. He could see the men in there for the first time, two of them hunched in the front seat, the driver holding the wheel rigid, hands stroking the wheel of the thing, shaking with the effort to control the car at this speed. The other one, obviously the one who he had to fear, looking at him sidelong in a strange, demented way somehow seeming to smile at him. Slowly, the Mark began to drift over to him then, crowding Williams in the lane, forcing him over to the shoulder. In a box, he tried to drive his way out of it but once again as the speedometer got past eighty the trailer began to slew dangerously behind him; he could feel the damned thing slewing, setting up a force that would, if the angle of the rock continued to expand, force him into a ditch. There was nothing to do then but to come off the accelerator, the car hanging back to seventy, then drifting to sixty-five. With that same insolent burst of power, the driver leaning forward in the seat, the Mark pulled away from him, drifted over and drifting lazily, gracefully, everything suddenly quite low at these speeds, the big car cut him off.

There was nothing to do but grab at the brakes and pray. Williams did so screaming, yanking the wheel right, drifting toward the other side of the road, the car looking for space on the shoulder. But the Mark, devastatingly maneuverable for all of its size, was there still. It was in front of him, crowding him into a panic-stop and nothing to do then but to come down on the brakes hard, harder, hardest, the Ford in a full-dive, almost out of control. Fighting, Williams could see that he was going to hit the big car, then the realization and the impact itself became spliced. He slewed into it, hit the rear quarter panel hard, the Lincoln slewing across the road. The Ford chased it, the U-haul waggling and hit it again, and then somehow the two cars were linked together. Just as he and Wulff had been tearing at one another in an embrace so now were the two cars, twisted, screaming metal, and they spun, turned, and came off the road, the U-haul clattering into them, beginning to roll as they came off the side and finally they came to a stop. Williams hit steering wheel, windshield, dashboard, bouncing off their surfaces like a ball, slamming around the car, the wheel braced in his hands only slightly lessening the jolting impact, not cutting it off and finally, he did not quite know how, he sprawled to a stop, lying on the seat, staring up at the ceiling of the car, at the gutted, ruined surfaces of cloth which had covered the struts. The car seemed to be resting on three wheels, bearings had snapped, the left front wheel was completely off the ground and he was watching it spin. Little puffs of smoke came from it. Someone was yanking at the passenger door.

He arched himself on the seat, saw that it was the man who had been in the passenger seat of the Mark, and weakly dove within his clothing trying to get his gun . . . but something hit him on the shoulder, a hard blow which seemed to sever the nerves between shoulder and hand and his fingers fluttered out of the jacket, twitching. "You son of a bitch," the man said, "you put us off the road." His tone was almost petulant; in just a moment, Williams thought weakly, the man might begin to whine. "You wrapped up a fucking ten thousand dollar car," the man said. He shook his head like a dog, shaking blood into his eyes and he paused, wiped them clear, then gripped Williams's wrist and pulled him through the passenger side of the Ford.

Too weak to fight him, too shocked to feel, Williams fell out of the car into the mud, slowly got arms and feet underneath him, tugged himself to a standing position. The man thrust a hand into his pocket, took out Williams's pistol. This is where it all ends, Williams thought, unceremoniously, without hope, on an interstate highway. The other man had come out of the Mark, was already working on the U-haul, struggling with the slats, trying to break down the doors but the impact had wedged them shut. The man stopped, cursing, turned, looked at Williams with hands on hips. "Have you got it?" he said.

"Got what?"

The man who had pulled him from the car slapped Williams hard on the side of the head. "Answer the question," he said, "have you got the shit?"

"I have nothing," Williams said, thinking that that was quite right, he had nothing at all. "Nothing."

"What's in there?"

Williams followed the angle of the arm to the U-haul. "I don't know anything about that," he said.

"You don't, eh? You don't know a thing."

"Nothing," Williams said, "nothing." And the man hit him again, harder, a savage blow to the temple that knocked him into the mud. He lay there in a curiously detached, peaceful position, the murmurs of the men as they started to confer with one another strangely pleasant. He was sliding out, he was moving apart from all of this, he was totally detached. It didn't matter. Dying could be pleasant after all; feeling had been disconnected. The men were talking frantically to one another, something about the Mark being totaled, something about having to try the Ford then and he felt himself lifted, carried, vaulting on air into the abscess of the sedan again. Then he was lying on the back seat, looking upwards, the others in the car already, the car beginning to move somehow, the U-haul clattering. The thought hit him: *They aren't going to kill me: they have a different plan.* This gave him comfort, somehow, for he had not wanted to die, not really, he could admit that and he drew it up around him like a sheet, swaddling himself with the knowledge that he was not going to die . . . and everything passed away from him and for a very long time Williams, twenty-five years old, heard and thought nothing at all. Leave it up to the assailants. They seemed to know exactly what they were doing.

XVIII

He was in another rooming house again, this one far out on Wilshire Boulevard, which seemed to cater less to washed-up and would-be actors than it did to unambitious homosexuals. At least that was the impression that Wulff got, although he tried to keep his public appearances in this boarding house and his circulation generally, at a very low level. He suspected that it was filled with homosexuals, however, because there were peculiar scufflings and singing in the bathrooms down the hallway and because the few people he did see looked at him in an appraising way, not the casual glance of strangers. Actually the place had more the aspect of a YMCA than it did of a rooming house: there was the same communal feeling, the same sensation of men leading public as opposed to private existences, fragmentary relationships rather than isolation, but he did not want to think about any of it too much. Los Angeles was a different state of mind than New York and it stood to reason that the YMCA mentality, if it were transplanted, would take on a somewhat different hue. Instead of cubicles there was sunshine, instead of snifflings and snufflings in the corridors there would be a lot of boisterousness and good fellowship. Better not to think about it. Homosexuality was a normal and inevitable part of life; it fit somehow into the whole failure-syndrome which you were likely to find in fringe residences of this sort, but as far as Wulff was concerned he simply did not want to think about it. He had never been on the vice squad. Narco was bad enough. Vice squad to him was the bottom of the barrel and at the bottom of *that* had been the miserable operatives who had spent their

duty-time in public toilets standing over urinals, waiting for a
proposition so that they could make an arrest of some miserable
creature. Those were the worst cops of all; even in his most
humiliating days on narco Wulff had known that he was superior to
them.

He was in another rooming house and he had not heard from
Williams in three days and he was beginning to get the feeling that he
would never hear from him again. It had been the last thing that he
had worked out with the man; Williams going back East with the
munitions, the all-clear signal coming from Williams when he had
returned to New York and unloaded on Father Justice. Why this had
been so important to Wulff was beyond proper figuring. He guessed
that it had to do with the fact that he felt responsible for everything
that had happened to Williams and needed desperately to know that
he was all right, wedged back into his life, before Wulff could proceed.
There might be another angle to it also; they couldn't eat that
ordnance or really make it disappear; he wouldn't feel safe until it
went back to the source. He had picked the name of the rooming house
out of a telephone book knowing nothing about it; it seemed as good a
place as any to stay and sweat out a contact, that was all. Also after
what had happened Wulff wasn't too hot on the idea of surfacing,
making his way directly to Chicago. Better to stay under wraps for as
long as possible; wait out an all-clear signal from Williams, along with
whatever other information the man could give, and then go onto his
next stop.

But the rooming house was a horror all right, three days here was
like spending three months back on narco: the same corruption, the
same stupidity, the same dense feeling of isolation in the midst of this
madness. He was also fairly sure that Williams wasn't going to get in
touch after all. Something had happened on the trip back East. He
didn't like it, he didn't want to face it, because it meant that he was at
the beginning of the situation rather than at the end but he had to
come to terms with it. Williams had been waylaid. Somehow,
somewhere, they had picked him up and now he was in trouble. Or
dead. It was very possible that he was dead. Williams had told him
about the crew who almost got him in Nebraska.

He didn't know how he felt about that either. Williams dead was bad
news, of course; probably the only real connection he had made since
his Odyssey had begun (because two helicopter pilots were dead and
the girl had walked out on him) and there was the feeling that he was
personally culpable. If it had not been for him, Williams would not
have taken this route. He would have been still tucked away in the

house in St. Albans: maybe he would have been a fool but he would have been a healthy, happy one, making the system work for him at least a little. What did Williams have this way? What had he been given him?

Fuck it, Wulff wanted to think, it's his life, not mine, I didn't force any damned choices on him, but as much as he wanted to take that point of view he knew that he could not. He simply could not get away with it. He was as responsible for Williams as he had been for everyone else whose lives he had touched during these months and Williams had been the best of the lot, the only one who he had been able to count on, the only one who had stood up with him when the screws had been put on. It would be nice to abandon him, and Wulff thought grimly he probably would be better off, a more efficient workman if he could . . . but he could not. He was responsible for the man. In a sense he was responsible for everything. Face it. He had to.

It was only then that slowly, reluctantly, Wulff got up from the one ruined chair in his two-room furnished and went to the door of the apartment. He had lost all perception of time; he might have been sitting in this posture for several minutes or hours trying to work out all aspects of the situation; now, having reached some point of decision without even a conscious choice he was already locked into it. He went out into the hall, over the ragged, uneven surfaces of the carpet, moving toward the end where the pay phone was. A large man in his mid-twenties intercepted him, blocked the hallway, stood in front of Wulff in a sports shirt and bathing trunks. "It's a bitch, isn't it?" he said.

"I suppose so."

"This fucking climate gets me sick. Where did they get a reputation for having a good climate? It's all public relations. Listen, you want to go back to my room and watch a little television? I got a new set, a good one, a Philco twenty-one incher. Color."

"I don't like television. I don't believe in it."

"You'd be amazed what kind of color reception you can get with an indoor antenna. That's one thing they got; great reception." The man licked his lips, put a tentative hand on Wulff's shoulder. "Why not?" he said, "we can watch a little television, put our feet up, talk a bit. I think they got some sports on now. You like sports? I don't mind them; that is, I got nothing against them."

"No," Wulff said, "I don't want to watch television. I have to make a phone call." The booth was vacant but he did not know how much longer it would be; also the pressure of the man's hand on his shoulder, still there, digging in, was unpleasant. "Please," he said, "excuse me."

"Look," the man said, tightening his grip a little more, "look, I'm not asking you to fuck or anything like that." His eyes glared. "You ask a guy in this place to be a little companionable, to be friendly, maybe share a little time together and right away they got you labelled as a pervert. That's what I hate about this fucking LA, they got you nailed as a pervert if you just try to do a normal human act. I don't like you looking at it that way. I'm a scriptwriter; I mean I got stuff all over with the major studios. They're not buying it, at least not just yet, but they aren't rejecting it either, you know what I mean? I got an agent." A little saliva peeked from the man's lips, his tongue was moving. Still he would not relinquish the shoulder grip. "Come on," he said, "I'll tell you about myself."

"Forget it," Wulff said and brought up his hand angled sidewise, broke the grip with a chop, the man's arm springing away from the shoulder, involuntarily flying upward, temporarily paralyzed.

Then the man was mashing it with a tormented expression, saliva cascading from him. "You're really crazy, you know that?" he said.

"Forget it," Wulff said again but the man was blocking his way. The only way through him was simply to push on but it would topple the man, he would probably send out a little cascade of shrieks, and what the hell good would that do him? Why was he pursued by involvement every step of the way? Having made the difficult decision about the phone call, he now seemed unable to complete it. "Come on, man," Wulff said, trying to cajole him, "just let me down the hall, let me make a phone call."

"Whole fucking town is full of crazy people," the man said, "all of them, everyone. I say watch a little television, try to have a little fun, relax, forget your troubles, establish a true human relationship between two men, one that won't be corrupted by sex and desire, filth and fucking, and what do you get? You get a send-up, a rip-off." The man's face convulsed. "I've taken too much from this fucking town," he said, "too goddamned much, I can't stand it anymore," and aimed a clumsy punch at Wulff's face.

Wulff knocked him out with a single blow, a fast cross to the jaw that sent the man reeling back into the wall then onto the frayed carpet, with a peaceful expression, the most peaceful and benign by far of all the faces he had made in front of Wulff. His eyes moved up and down, he peered out from them as if trying to evaluate the situation, and then closed them all the way, his head lolling to the side. Wulff did not even know what room he had come from. Looking up and down the hall he saw that there was no one looking out, no one, if they were around, was going to get involved at all, but nevertheless there was a problem lying on the floor and he just was not going to go away.

"Screw it," Wulff said, "screw this," and went back to his room, pulled open a valise, put the few possessions he had into them furiously, checked ordnance, stuffed two pistols into his jacket and grabbing the valise off the bed went down the hall and out of this place. He would make the call from somewhere else. The man was still lying in the hall; he had brought his hands up now, cupped them, made a little pillow for his head and was lying that way with an almost benign expression, something soothing and peaceful about his sleep, little pleased gurgles bubbling out of him. Probably in sleep he was getting what he had sought; sometimes sleep was the only way; for a large proportion of the world sleep *was* the only means by which they could get what they needed. But Wulff, thank you very much, did not want to think about that now. A tendril of purpose waved like a grass-stalk within him, became harder, became a twig. He had had it with LA. Win or lose he had had it with this fucking town; he could not take it anymore. Somewhere there were people who could adapt to it or who growing up in it never knew the difference, but he had had it. It was a gigantic lunatic asylum and even the Calabreses mostly steered clear of it; there was just no way to regulate any kind of an organization or life-style here other than the mad one of the city itself. You couldn't beat it and if you were a sane man, you couldn't quite join it either.

Wulff went downstairs and into the back lot where the Sedan de Ville, frame settling around its chassis, rested. He hadn't started it for three days. He wasn't able to start it this time either. The battery was dead, the ignition deader, not a twitch; the motor, as he lifted the hood slowly, magnificently caved in upon itself like a dismembered building, little splices of dead wire rotting amidst the filthy, oil-spattered metal that had taken him a thousand miles but would never take him anywhere again.

Fucking luck.

XIX

You waited and waited for something, Calabrese thought, and then it came through and it was so ordinary, so routine, that you wondered if it had been anticipation you were feeling or simply the act itself, already throwing back its implications so many times that by the time it came off you were bored. There was a spark of philosophy in that but he didn't want to pursue it. The phone call from the guy came in almost to the hour, when he thought it would, and the guy and he, as soon as it got through the referral network, resumed their previous relationship almost as if nothing had intervened. Why didn't I kill him? Calabrese thought. It would have been so easy; I had him where I wanted him, why didn't I kill him? No answer to that. But he knew now that there would be a second chance.

"Where is he?" the caller said. "Just tell me where he is."

No fencing around. Too late for that now. "That's none of your business," Calabrese said, "but we got him. Oh, yes, we've got him."

"How do I know that?"

"How do you know that? Do you know about a yellow U-haul? Do you know enough about what was in that U-haul, enough stuff to blow up Chicago, you prick, you fuckface? Don't start quizzing me, you son of a bitch; I'm going to have plenty of time to answer your questions when I get hold of you. I'll get hold of you."

"Did you kill him?" the voice said.

"That's for you to wonder about," Calabrese said. "Why don't you come on over and just find out?"

"Well, why don't I?"

"Why don't you come over and have a look at the situation? We'll keep him on ice for you until you come; I promise."

"Did you kill him?"

"That's for me to know and you to find out, you evil son of a bitch," Calabrese said. He held onto the edge of the desk seeing the fluttering and trembling of his hand thinking, I didn't expect to lose my temper like this, he's not worth it, I must exercise some control over myself. I cannot allow this bastard to make me lose control just when things, finally, are beginning to sort themselves out. I won't, I just won't do it. "Think about it," he said, aiming for some lightness of tone, "think it over and when you're in town give me a call. We'll always be happy to hear from you."

"You're holding him, aren't you?"

"This isn't a fucking quiz show," Calabrese screamed. The bodyguard in the room with him looked up in surprise, looked down again. They must think I'm losing my grip, Calabrese thought, that must be the word going all through the house: the old man is losing his grip, he's screaming and swearing at people. Somehow, some way that word is going to get around and someone is going to want to find out first-hand, take a shot on the fact that the old man at seventy-three was blowing it. That was about the way these things worked, he thought, there was no reason to let it anger him further; he was seventy-three years old. If he were in someone else's position he would make the same move . . . in fact, he had. "Come on you bastard," he said again, "come on out, make a house call. We'll be glad to see you."

"Let him go, Calabrese. He doesn't matter."

"I didn't even say I had him."

"Let him go. Let him out of the way. This is only between you and me."

"You and me and the world, you fucking scum," Calabrese said, and the bodyguard yanked his head up from the newspaper again. "You come on out and I'll let him go. That's a deal. I'll let him out of here in return for you."

"How do I know you have him?"

"You don't. You don't know a fucking thing. You're just scrambling around in the dark and trying to make it stick. Fifteen men. I counted, you son of a bitch; there are fifteen men gone."

"That's your fault."

"Come on!" Calabrese said a little hysterically. He had lost control and all right, he could live with that, anyone could: just let it all come screaming out of him. It was healthier that way, not bottling it up. "Come on out to Chicago. I'll give you safe conduct. I'll let them give you a nice free passage. You give me an address. I'll even send you tickets and arrange to meet you at O'Hare. A welcoming committee."

"Where is he, Calabrese?"

"You let me worry about that."

"Is he alive?"

"He's alive. He's alive and screaming a lot. I think I'll let him scream more."

"All right," the voice said, "all right, I'm coming out there. You won't kill him because you know that he's the only good hold you've got on me and you won't even push him too hard because you don't want to take any chances on killing him. I know how you operate. But don't fuck with me, Calabrese."

"We've got another hold," Calabrese said, and then, relishing it, he let the words come out smoothly, slowly, imagining how the scum's face must look at this moment. "There's a girl in San Francisco."

The response was everything that he could have hoped for. There was a long pause; it extended into ten, twenty, thirty seconds surrounded by little gasps and intakes of breath and Calabrese let him have it. There was no rush. This pig was hooked good now; he wasn't going to go anywhere. "Leave the girl out of it," the voice said faintly. "I want to make that clear, you leave her out of it."

"For the moment. Because it suits our purposes. I take it that we can get our hands on her in ten minutes, though, if I want to. Just think of that, Wulff. Think of it good, now."

"All right," the voice said after another pause, not quite as extended, this one, as the last. "All right, Calabrese. We have a date: the two of us. You and I are going to meet. But it's going to be just us."

"Don't bet on it."

"I'll bet on it," the voice said with a sudden, chilling authority. "You know who I am and how I work and what I can do and I'm telling you right now that this is *mano a mano*. I'm coming to get you, Calabrese. I'm coming to get you and after I've taken care of you you'll never be the same again."

"I'm waiting."

"You won't be waiting long," the voice said and hung up.

Calabrese, holding the phone like a dead fish, looked toward the walls, turned on the swivel chair to look out at the lake below, holding the phone for so long, locked so deeply into an abstracted state that when he finally became aware of a pressure in his hand and looked down it took him a couple of seconds to remember what he was holding and how had gotten into that position. Slowly he put it back in the cradle, shoved the receiver away from him, and looked over at the bodyguard who was ostentatiously reading the newspaper now, flipping the pages frantically, his lips moving in little purses and circles as he skimmed a finger down the racing charts.

"Get out of here," Calabrese said.

The man stood, letting the paper fall. "Are you sure?"

"I'm sure," he said. "Get out. And I want this place locked up tight."

"All right."

"I want this place buttoned up like the Vatican, you hear me? Nobody moves for any reason. No traffic in or out without my express approval."

The man shrugged. "Okay," he said. He went out quickly, closing the door, using a key on the other side to click the tumblers shut. Step one in security; lock everything. The man was showing reasonable intelligence. Good. Good: at least he had a staff that was functioning. Maybe he even had one that he had trust in. No one had ever worked harder at it; that was for sure.

But no satisfaction. I'm getting old, Calabrese thought, sitting behind the desk, I'm getting old, gray, stupid, and frightened and I don't know if it's this guy or seventy-three years that are doing it to me. Maybe a little bit of both. Maybe this guy is seventy-three years given human form; maybe he's just death that I'm dealing with. If I can beat him, then I can beat death itself. It may be a one-way ticket but you can hold on until the last stop and sometimes, some way, you could get a little control over the Master himself by taking him into your own hands. If you killed, that made you death itself, at least for the moment, and if death was your servant . . . well, you could have control over your staff, couldn't you?

Calabrese sat in the room for a long time, looking up at the ceiling, perching his feet on the desk. After a while his head lolled back. His eyes closed, he folded his hands. Little images of blood and torment danced through his mind and then he was sleeping, sleeping more comfortably perhaps than he had in a long time.

One way or the other now, it was coming near to being over.

XX

Williams sat in the hotel room, across from the other guy, looking at the green curtains, and tried to keep his mind blank. That was Wulff's trick, had to be. If you didn't think, then you didn't fear; the engines of the imagination were what conveyed horror but you could beat them by simply pulling the switch. It wasn't that bad after all, he had to remember that. It could be a hell of a lot worse. They weren't going to kill him, at least now. That was obvious. If they were going to do it they would have done it already. So you had to look at it that way; that his life was as precious to them now as it was to him because if he got killed they were going to be in a hell of a lot of trouble.

Of course, orders could change. You had to remember that things were out of his hands and essentially out of the hands of these two also. They were just doing a job the best they could; that involved listening and obeying. Orders could change, they certainly could, but to think that way was just to start up the engines once more and thank you very much he would not. He would not do it. If you didn't think, if you refused to project your mind didn't think, if you refused to project your mind even a moment ahead, living only in the present, then they couldn't get you. What got you, what created the fear, was living in the future. The present, however, was only itself; expressionless, without form. What was it they called it? Existentialism. That was a fancy name for a modern philosophy of death that most American blacks, he thought, had been living with for two hundred years. That was what had kept the slaves going and that was what had made them eventually, not-slaves. You simply weren't a slave if you refused to think.

Another man came into the room sweating lightly, dabbing a hand at the perspiration. He looked at the man observing him in the chair, then at Williams who was bound against the bed in another chair, not uncomfortably. "All right," he said, "no change."

The man guarding him said, "I figured that. There's never any fucking change."

"There are going to be a lot of changes but for the moment just go on like before. That's it. Hold steady."

"Fuck this," the first guard said. He stood, stretched, leaned against a wall. "I'm going to go downstairs and get some coffee. You want some coffee?"

"I want some coffee," Williams said, "black, heavy on the sugar, and maybe a doughnut."

"You're very funny. You're really a character, aren't you?"

"No. I just want some coffee."

"I like your cool," the man who wanted coffee said. He came over, hit Williams on the face once, hard, the cheekbones seeming to splinter a little under the blow although Williams knew that this could only be his imagination. Fuck it. Imagination was the fuel that fed the engine. So think nothing at all. "You're a sweetheart," the man said, rubbing his knuckles and walking away from Williams, "I can see why your partner would ransom his ass to get you back. Maybe he likes your ass itself for that matter. I've heard of such things."

"Lay off," the man who had been on the phone said, "lay off that shit. I don't like to hear it."

"I don't frankly give a shit what you like to hear. I want some coffee, that's all. You want some coffee?"

"I don't want nothing except for you to get out of the room. And you lead anyone back to it I'll have your ass, speaking of asses which you always are."

"Fuck you," the man who wanted coffee said and walked out. Williams braced himself against the bed, shook his head, closed his eyes. He would have liked to have gotten a hand up to rub the cheek but that was impossible. So you had to live with it, that was all. What was a little pain? He hoped that Wulff was out of it. He hoped his wife was out of it. He wondered if he had a son. He wondered if his wife had noticed, maybe, that he was nowhere around and had put out an all-points bulletin. That would be a big help in this hotel room, of course.

"Want to rub the cheek?" the man said. Williams opened his eyes and looked at him; the man extended his hands, began to work slowly on the ropes holding Williams's right hand. He did this one-handed, the other one holding the gun. "Go ahead," he said when Williams's hand was free, moving away then out of any possible grasp. "Go on, rub it, that will help a lot. You know, I don't like this anymore than you do."

Heavy and the nice guy. An old police technique but they probably had picked it up from the other side of the fence, the cops never having had an original idea in their lives. Williams rubbed the cheek slowly, getting a little fresh blood through, finding as he would have expected that it did help. He said nothing.

"We got in over our heads, that's all," the man said, "we didn't think it would be a job like this. We thought it would be fetch and carry or maybe a hit. We didn't think it would be a goddamned kidnap."

"My heart bleeds," Williams said. He extended his hand. "You want to tie me up again?"

"No," the man said, "leave it free."

"Your partner may get goddamned pissed-off if he comes back and finds that I've got a hand out."

"I don't give a shit about my partner."

"I do. I very much do."

"He's not going to do anything to you until the words comes down. He just bitches a lot." The man seemed to give Williams a nearly ingratiating smile. "Hell, we don't like this anymore than you do," he said again, "it's a goddamned pain in the ass. You think we like this? Living in a stinking hotel room, babysitting? We could be here for weeks. We didn't plan on it being weeks."

"I know," Williams said, "it's tough. It's just real tough. It's just real tough to be in that kind of a position."

"It's a lousy job. We'd just as soon be home, I know I would. I don't have anything against you. I don't even know who you are."

"I won't bother telling you."

"Except that they want you awfully bad," the man said, "oh, yes indeed, they seem to want you very bad, indeed. So I guess you must be pretty important or at least that guy you're running with is pretty important."

"Read the papers."

"I don't read shit," the man said and the other guard, holding some coffee walked back into the room, two cups in his hand.

He extended one toward Williams and said, "Untie his right hand, did you?"

"Yeah. Bother you?"

"No," the man with coffee said, "it's just as easy. Here, you can have some coffee," he said and handed the steaming cup to Williams. Williams grasped it, sipped tentatively while the man holding his own coffee looked at him with a puzzled expression. "I'm sorry I hit you," he said. "I didn't mean to do that."

"Sure, sure."

"No, I don't like the rough stuff. I don't like this job anymore than you do, you know it's—"

Williams and the first man exchanged a look; the first man, unreasonably, stifled a smile, then put a palm to his mouth. Perhaps he was giggling. Oh, they were a lot of laughs, all right: these were wonderful people. They were the kind of people you might want to dedicate your life to knowing, that is if your business was in genocide.

"I know, I know," Williams said quietly, "you don't like it anymore than I do. It's dirty, sweaty, mucky business and actually you wouldn't have been in it at all except that you never had the right opportunities and your old man left the family when you were seven years old and instead of getting the money to go to college and take a degree in the English classics you had to go to work as a hard guy for the organization. Tough. It's really tough shit, I'm weeping," Williams said and then he sat there thinking for a moment that he might blow the whole scene by doing just that: by weeping, by breaking apart. But no, his control held, pride of the black man and so on and so forth, and so for awhile in the hot, dense little room in Skokie, Illinois the three of them just sat there, whiling away the spaces of the afternoon while slowly like a blanket Williams felt circumstances closing in on him—

Or was that just the engine of the imagination again doing its wicked work?

EPILOGUE

Finally, air brakes screaming, the big oil tanker cranked to a stop thirty yards down the interstate and Wulff sprinted after it in the hitchhiker's open-legged waddle of a run, hand extended. The driver looked down at Wulff as he closed in, shook his head, and then apparently deciding that he had already stopped and it was too much trouble to get the big truck out quickly again sat there impassively while Wulff got up on the running board and then into the cab. "I'm going to Chicago," he said wearily.

"That's good," Wulff said, "that's exactly where I'm going."

The driver nodded slowly, grimly, calculating apparently the fact that he would have Wulff beside him for twenty hours or more. Little drops of sweat fell from his forehead to the steering wheel; he seemed already to have regretted the impulse to stop. "All the way in," he said, "you're riding all the way."

"That's right," Wulff said.

"Got business in Chicago?"

"Got a lot of business," Wulff said, "got a hell of a lot of business." The driver began to work on the air brakes, releasing them one by one, struggling with the transmission, unlocked that, slipped it into the first gear of ten and slowly, groaning like an animal the tanker came off the shoulder. It began to move down the interstate, achieving forty, then forty-five miles an hour as the driver played the transmission like an organist, finally settling into seventh forward speed or something like that.

"Can't get any speed out of them," he mumbled, "fifty miles an hour the son of a bitch starts to come apart. And I'm loaded with explosives, too."

"I know," Wulff said, "I know, I know, I know the feeling," feeling the solid jiggle of the guns within his clothing, feeling the dank wind of America on his face, feeling the pain and pressure of his quest as the poisons flowed throughout every vein of his body. He thought, Calabrese, I'm coming to get you, Calabrese you son of a bitch, I'm almost there, Calabrese, you better enjoy the time you've got left . . . because this is it, you old fucker, this is where it began and this is where it was going to end.

He hoped it would be that simple: that finally there would be the confrontation and an end to the quest. That was something to hope for.

Don't count on it, though.

26 August 1973: New Jersey

THE END

Afterword:
Putting It Together

By Barry N. Malzberg

Wulff had been an NYPD narco for three years... He had come back from mid-sixties Saigon in a total rage, a rage which was only partly compounded of PTSD; mostly it was the clear intimation that it was here that it had all began. Saigon was the living, breathing heart of the worlds' corruption, and it was this heart that was being used by the blood of America to test the most bizarre, exciting or simply ugliest forms of death. Here funneled the poison and from there the poison spread everywhere: through the trunk and limbs of the world and much of the poison, all of it if you regarded this in the right way was junk. Saigon was awash in drugs.
                        —Lone Wolf #8: *Los Angeles Holocaust*

But of course so was Los Angeles, Detroit, the castles of Manhattan, the sheds of the broken farmlands, the nation was sinking into drugs with a determination which looked from close range like celebration. Wulff, seeing only what he needed, was able to make that deduction in every pit stop of his odyssey and on the homogenous, the flaring roads between and the quadrilateral occasion with its multiple and equally valid solution had scored its way in every corner. By the eighth novel Wulff was really rolling and so was his author, so might have been Bolan and his acolytes, his imitators, the parasites which were attached to a series which by this time had succumbed to a single savage ambition: wipe it all off the table and start anew.

There was a certain purity to this: the Bolan ethic and its inevitable extension by Wulff or perhaps the simpler-minded Butcher had a transparent goal: *Wipe all of the evil from the face of the Earth.* That was the objective of the peerless Book of Zephaniah, stated in its first paragraph and all of the boys were chained to that simple task. In some cases it was the Mafioso or the politicians, in Wulff's it was the drug distributor, but they could all be traced to a single source as envisioned in the previous novels: the highways and byways of the

Mysterious East which had been refitted as the central rite of passage.

Wulff was crazy, even crazier than his peers. I had attached to that terrible assumption from the origin of the work, there seemed to be no other explication. But only a madman could have taken up his mission and that mission was being conducted in a nation so crazy that his job could be defended as inevitable and therefore necessary. It had no apparent end but that was the human odyssey, wasn't it? No *deus ex machina* loomed to shift the situation.

No one was going to get out of this, revealed events if anything were working to take us to the furthest reaches of implication. About a decade later a high CIA official testified in Los Angeles about that Iran-Contra deal, he denied it all, nothing to see here, move along: How could the CIA, America's finest, subtlest line of defense, be doing business with the drug trade, how could the CIA be funneling drugs into neighborhoods throughout the country using the dealers as cover and then funneling the money to overthrow the Nicaraguan government? That would obviously be illegal if not exactly sedition. Then again, if any of you residents in the audience here suspect that something like this is going on, why don't you call the police?

Well, why not call the police, turn in your neighbors' fathers, sons, cousins, partners? In the end wasn't defense of the nation your responsibility? It was with this argument that the mood of the crowds attending these meetings shifted from incredulity to fury. Not that this had anything to do with quelling the business.

In one of Philip Roth's late novels, might have been *The Human Stain*, might have been *American Pastoral*, might have been *I Married A Communist*, all of them blended in retrospect to different pitch levels of outraged Schoenberg, the protagonist embarks upon a rodomontade depicting all history as a compilation of betrayal. Betrayal began with Eve in the garden. Adam had briefly let her alone to wander, had gone on to Judas, Caesar and Brutus and then skipped a few centuries to the Holy Roman Empire, ravaged the Middle Ages, found foundation stones in the catafalque of the French Revolution, on and on to the revolution here and the exploration and seizure of the continent, further progress or devolution in the murderous Industrial Revolution after a brief pause in Ford's Theater, a sub-incident in retrospect and so on and on to the gas chambers, Hiroshima, McCarthy, the House Un-American Activities Committee and now, freshly unwrapped, Watergate and Nixon's destruction before it became his own. Watergate was a cheap anticlimax but like the Rockefeller drug laws it fit nicely, chronologically, into the dimensions of cruelty and craziness which were televised to an audience of millions. A list of betrayals, some moving continents, some as trivial as the school of violent paperbacks, the illegitimate children of Chandler and Spillane who had sired them through joyous threesomes with Patricia Highsmith. I was by then storming through these novels with the careless persistence of the determined blackmailer, I was threatening the nation with its own past and true consequence and Wulff and I were centered in the terrible conviction that at four cents a word they were opening the curtains of bombed out theater to show the truth. Just as the lovers had patrolled the atomic-ravaged sites in Hiroshima, so I was conducting a shabby guided tour of international, endless historic consequence. No less than Wulff, I had the righteousness and grandiosity of the eternal tour guides: Father, Son and the Holy Ghost.

16 January 2022: New Jersey

Barry N. Malzberg Bibliography

FICTION (as either Barry or Barry N. Malzberg)

Oracle of the Thousand Hands (1968)

Screen (1968)

Confessions of Westchester County (1970)

The Spread (1971)

In My Parents' Bedroom (1971)

The Falling Astronauts (1971)

The Masochist (1972, reprinted as Everything Happened to Susan, 1975; as Cinema, 2020)

Horizontal Woman (1972; reprinted as The Social Worker, 1973)

Beyond Apollo (1972)

Overlay (1972)

Revelations (1972)

Herovit's World (1973)

In the Enclosure (1973)

The Men Inside (1973)

Phase IV (1973; novelization based on a story & screenplay by Mayo Simon)

The Day of the Burning (1974)

The Tactics of Conquest (1974)

Underlay (1974)

The Destruction of the Temple (1974)

Guernica Night (1974)

On a Planet Alien (1974)

Out from Ganymede (1974; stories)

The Sodom and Gomorrah Business (1974)

The Best of Barry N. Malzberg (1975; stories)

The Many Worlds of Barry Malzberg (1975; stories)

Galaxies (1975)

The Gamesman (1975)

Down Here in the Dream Quarter (1976; stories)

Scop (1976)

The Last Transaction (1977)

Chorale (1978)

Malzberg at Large (1979; stories)

The Man Who Loved the Midnight Lady (1980; stories)

The Cross of Fire (1982)

The Remaking of Sigmund Freud (1985)

In the Stone House (2000; stories)

Shiva and Other Stories (2001; stories)

The Passage of the Light: The Recursive Science Fiction of Barry N. Malzberg (2004; ed. by Tony Lewis & Mike Resnick; stories)

The Very Best of Barry N. Malzberg (2013; stories)

With Bill Pronzini

The Running of the Beasts (1976)

Acts of Mercy (1977)

Night Screams (1979)

Prose Bowl (1980)

Problems Solved (2003; stories)

On Account of Darkness and Other SF Stories (2004; stories)

As Mike Barry

Lone Wolf series:

Night Raider (1973)

Bay Prowler (1973)

Boston Avenger (1973)

Desert Stalker (1974)

Havana Hit (1974)

Chicago Slaughter (1974)

Peruvian Nightmare (1974)

Los Angeles Holocaust (1974)
Miami Marauder (1974)
Harlem Showdown (1975)
Detroit Massacre (1975)
Phoenix Inferno (1975)
The Killing Run (1975)
Philadelphia Blow-Up (1975)

As Francine di Natale

The Circle (1969)

As Claudine Dumas

The Confessions of a Parisian
  Chambermaid (1969)

As Mel Johnson/M. L. Johnson

Love Doll (1967; with The Sex Pros
  by Orrie Hitt)
I, Lesbian (1968; as M. L. Johnson)
Just Ask (1968; with Playgirl by Lou
  Craig)
Instant Sex (1968)
Chained (1968; with Master of
  Women by March Hastings & Love
  Captive by Dallas Mayo)
Kiss and Run (1968; with Sex on the
  Sand by Sheldon Lord & Odd Girl
  by March Hastings)
Nympho Nurse (1969; with Young
  and Eager by Jim Conroy &
  Quickie by Gene Evans)
The Sadist (1969)
The Box (1969)
Do It To Me (1969; with Hot Blonde
  by Jim Conroy)
Born to Give (1969; with Swap Club
  by Greg Hamilton & Wild in Bed
  by Dirk Malloy)
Campus Doll (1969; with High
  School Stud by Robert Hadley)
A Way With All Maidens (1969)

As Howard Lee

Kung Fu #1: The Way of the Tiger,
  the Sign of the Dragon (1973)

As Lee W. Mason

Lady of a Thousand Sorrows (1977)

As K. M. O'Donnell

Empty People (1969)
The Final War and Other Fantasies
  (1969; stories)
Dwellers of the Deep (1970)
Gather at the Hall of the Planets
  (1971)
In the Pocket and Other S-F Stories
  (1971; stories)
Universe Day (1971; stories)

As Eliot B. Reston

The Womanizer (1972)

As Gerrold Watkins

Southern Comfort (1969)
A Bed of Money (1970)
A Satyr's Romance (1970)
Giving It Away (1970)
Art of the Fugue (1970)

NON-FICTION/ESSAYS

The Engines of the Night: Science
  Fiction in the Eighties (1982;
  essays)
Breakfast in the Ruins (2007;
  essays: expansion of Engines of the
  Night)
The Business of Science Fiction: Two
  Insiders Discuss Writing and
  Publishing (2010; with Mike
  Resnick)

The Bend at the End of the Road
(2018; essays)

EDITED ANTHOLOGIES

Final Stage (1974; with Edward L.
Ferman)
Arena (1976; with Edward L.
Ferman)
Graven Images (1977; with Edward
L. Ferman)
Dark Sins, Dark Dreams (1978; with
Bill Pronzini)
The End of Summer: SF in the
Fifties (1979; with Bill Pronzini)
Shared Tomorrows: Science Fiction
in Collaboration (1979; with Bill
Pronzini)

Neglected Visions (1979; with
Martin H. Greenberg & Joseph D.
Olander)
Bug-Eyed Monsters (1980; with Bill
Pronzini)
The Science Fiction of Mark Clifton
(1980; with Martin H. Greenberg)
The Arbor House Treasury of Horror
& the Supernatural (1981; with
Bill Pronzini & Martin H.
Greenberg)
The Science Fiction of Kris Neville
(1984; with Martin H. Greenberg)
Mystery in the Mainstream (1986;
with Bill Pronzini & Martin H.
Greenberg)

Made in the USA
Middletown, DE
18 September 2022

73443302R00121